HAPPILY
NEVER
AFTER

HAPPILY NEVER AFTER

RACHEL NORTH

CORVUS

Published in Great Britain in 2024 by Corvus,
an imprint of Atlantic Books Ltd.

1 3 5 7 9 8 6 4 2

A CIP catalogue record for this book is available from the British Library.

Paperback ISBN: 978 1 80546 055 8
E-book ISBN: 978 1 80546 056 5

Printed in Great Britain by CPI Group (UK) Ltd, Croydon CR0 4YY

Corvus
An imprint of Atlantic Books Ltd
Ormond House
26–27 Boswell Street
London
WC1N 3JZ

www.atlantic-books.co.uk

MIX
Paper | Supporting
responsible forestry
FSC® C171272

With love to Val,
my Best Girl, then and now.

The Wedding Attendees

Maddie Laughton: the bride

Alex Archer: the groom

Raymond Archer: father of the groom

Marilyn Archer: mother of the groom

Colette Archer: general manager at the Finca Encantata and the groom's sister

Bobby Fraser: the best man / Alex's best friend

Louise Haddon: the maid of honour/ Maddie's best friend

Ruby Davis: Alex's old school friend, and bridesmaid

Lily Eames: Bobby's girlfriend

Priya Cahill: friend of Alex, and bridesmaid

Tom Weeton: friend of Alex

Charlie Morgan: friend of Alex

Paul and Yvette Stainforth: Alex's 'aunt and uncle', the Archer family accountant and Letty's parents

Letty Stainforth: flower girl

Mateus and Natalia Torres: a business associate of Ray, and his wife

Teddy Largos plus one: a business associate of Ray, and his girlfriend

Luther Fleming: general aide and one of Ray's drivers

I catch my thumb on the edge of the envelope and before I know it, there's blood everywhere – enough to leave fingerprints. I suck the wound to stem the flow. My mouth fills with saliva and the metallic taste of dirty pennies. Paper cuts are bastards. They might be small and insignificant, but they hurt. They also make one hell of a mess. The blood-smeared invitation lies on the countertop. It looks more like something destined for an evidence bag than a mantelpiece.

I've been expecting it.

MR AND MRS RAYMOND ARCHER

request the pleasure of your company at the marriage of their son,

ALEXANDER GEORGE ARCHER

to

MISS MADDIE LAUGHTON

at

Finca Encantata, Sierra Norte de Mallorca on Saturday 25th May

The celebrations will take place from
Thursday 23rd to Sunday 26th May

RSVP

by 31st January

Of course I'll be there. I wouldn't miss Alex and Maddie's wedding for the world.

It will, after all, be my last chance to put a stop to it.

Prologue

There has always been a cat at the Finca Encantata. A black cat. It was there long before the fairy-tale castle, with its high tower and cobbled courtyard, was built; and it will, no doubt, still be there when the finca once again sinks back into the dark, whispering embrace of the surrounding forest.

No one has ever been foolish enough to try to get close enough to the cat to ascertain its sex, although the appearance of a litter of mewling kittens every few years would suggest that it's female. But even the cat's own offspring never seem to stay around for long. They have a habit of finding themselves stuffed into sacks along with a few carefully selected bricks, or they are eaten by their mother, or they get carried off by one of the red-eyed wolves that periodically come down from the mountaintop to scavenge for food. There are any number of fates available to a small, defenceless creature at the Finca Encantata. Either way, the mewling always stops eventually, the kittens vanish, and the cat returns to its solitary existence. What's hers is hers and she has every intention of keeping it that way.

The cat has witnessed a lot of change in her time. She has seen the finca grow, mellow stone on mellow stone, spawning ever more rooms and floors and outbuildings, exerting its solid, showy presence on the landscape, until it has become what the guidebooks apparently describe – the cat cannot, of course, read – as 'an impressive example of mid-eighteenth-century architecture'. The cat is not impressed. Shack, farmhouse, barn or castle – the type, style and number of buildings are irrelevant to her, it's the human inhabitants that provide her with rich pickings. They are stunningly lax when it comes to food. They leave windows open and dishes uncovered. Not that they are happy for her to take her share – they may be wasteful, but they are seldom generous. If they catch her feasting, they shout and lash out with whatever is at hand. And that's the other thing the humans afford her – a source of entertainment. They are, with very few exceptions, easy to provoke yet slow to react.

The current incumbents are no different.

They appeared after a blissful fallow period, when the finca had once again been humanity-free and the cat had been able to roam without observation or interference around the buildings and the extensive grounds. Indeed, it had been so peaceful, for so long, that the cat had let down her guard. As a result, she was literally caught napping, in one of the upper rooms in the tower, when this new batch of humanity arrived. It was the slam of a car door that woke her. She leapt onto the window ledge in time to see three large men and one small woman emerge from a sleek black Land Rover with tinted windows. The cat watched the new arrivals. They stood, eyeless behind their dark glasses,

6

sizing up the finca. She knew within seconds which was the king and which the underlings. She also recognised, with a sinking feeling, that these humans meant business and that the peace of the past year was about to be shattered.

She wasn't wrong.

But there again, the cat rarely is.

When the cooler air of autumn arrived, so did the workmen and the machinery. Once again, the finca was filled with noise, dust and destruction. The cat watched the frenzy of activity from the shelter of the trees. It soon became apparent that this was to be a no-expense-spared reincarnation. The cat looked on in disgust as the lake was dredged of its luscious, fertile mud – a process that resulted in the deaths of hundreds of the juicy snacks that resided there – as the innards of the buildings were ripped out and replaced and as the land around the finca was tamed.

The renovation was overseen, with steely efficiency, by the small woman with the blonde hair and the phone perpetually stuck to her cheek. It was brutal, quick and probably impressive – if you were into *luxury accommodation set in a breathtaking location in an area of outstanding natural beauty*, which the cat obviously wasn't. On the day the last workman loaded up his van and roared away the cat breathed a sigh of relief. She waited impatiently for nightfall then emerged from the forest to reclaim her home.

For all the remodelling and refurbishment, the cat was relieved to discover that enough of the original finca remained for her purposes. The gaps underneath the floorboards had largely survived intact so that it was still possible to travel around the majority of the site undetected. And they had, thankfully, left the bougainvillea on the outside walls, which meant that most of the upper rooms remained accessible, with some inelegant scrambling. Therefore, all in all, there was enough natural cover for her to go back to her old ways. Namely: spying, stealing and generally pissing on their parade.

But the cat was wrong about one thing: the nature of her adversary *had* changed. Because, as she was about to find out, the small woman with the fast walk and the firm voice was different to the other human beings that the cat had come across and bested in the past. This woman was smart, tenacious and much more observant than any of her predecessors. That spelt trouble for the cat, and, as it turned out, for everyone else associated with the Finca Encantata.

Two Days Before the Wedding

Chapter 1

ALEX

Alex woke with the sun on his face. He kept his eyes closed and let the weight of his limbs anchor him to the bed. He watched the colours and shapes dance on the inside of his eyelids. It was blissfully quiet. The sense of inoculation from normal life was profound. He luxuriated in it. Maddie lay beside him, breathing softly, utterly relaxed.

Shine here to us, and thou art everywhere; This bed thy centre is, these walls, thy sphere. Alex smiled. Bobby would be proud of him – poetry in his head and his heart, two days before his wedding. His best friend's work was done – Alex was no longer a philistine. Okay, one verse, of a short poem, learnt as an early wedding present, did not Renaissance Man make, but it was proof, surely, that he was well and truly in love.

The decision to stay at the finca rather than at his parents' place further up the mountain had been a good one. He and Maddie badly needed some time alone together after the stress of the past few months. Being tucked away in one of the basic rooms in the annex had turned out to be a blessing in disguise – the much nicer rooms in the main building were being readied for their guests. Their simple

11

box, with its low ceiling and small en suite bathroom, had afforded them the one thing they'd needed most – privacy. Alex glanced at his watch on the nightstand. Their guests would be arriving at lunchtime; they had only a few hours of freedom left. The prospect of sharing the finca with his closest friends provoked mixed emotions in Alex. It would be lovely to see everyone, and to get their wedding properly underway, but he was also aware that, along with their best wishes and their nicest outfits, the guests would be bringing with them their opinions about his and Maddie's upcoming union.

He and Maddie had been together sixteen months, which, depending on how you looked at it, was either a whirlwind romance or plenty of time to find out if they were 'meant to be'. People had been surprisingly forthright in their views on his marriage, and on his choice of bride. At work the guys had lectured him on the attributes that made a woman 'a keeper' and the red flags that he should 'run a mile from'. He'd said little in response. Where Maddie rated on their 'stupid scale' was none of their damn business. His parents had been a little more circumspect, although not much. Predictably, they'd been very interested in Maddie's background – more specifically, who 'her people' were. Whatever the hell that meant! Their first meeting had been like some sort of ghastly, extended audition. Alex didn't know how they wanted his bride to sound, act or be – they themselves having travelled quite a long way from their working-class, South London roots to a mountain in Mallorca. Maddie, to her credit, had coped admirably, but it had hardly been a warm welcome to the family. His sister's passive-aggressive silences hadn't helped either. Colette normally didn't give a stuff about what was happening in his life or who he was seeing, so he hadn't understood her reaction. As far as Alex could tell, him getting married would make zero difference to her. Staying close to the family was her thing, not his. If she wanted to be their father's right-hand man, that was fine with Alex – it meant he didn't have to be.

His friends' reaction had, thankfully, been more positive. Once Bobby had got over the shock of their engagement, he'd been happy for Alex. It had been touching to see how much time and effort he'd invested in getting to know Maddie once they'd made it official. It had mattered. Alex had wanted, no, he needed the two of them to get on. He couldn't imagine a life where his wife and his best friend disliked each other. These people were his future. Tom and Charlie had also been pleased for him but in a much more blokey way. They'd taken him out for many, many beers to celebrate. When well-pissed, both of them had, individually, expressed a touch of jealousy that he was 'sorted'. Tom chose the urinal to make his lonely-heart admission; Charlie the queue in the kebab shop. Once sober, their mutual desire for a soulmate had never been mentioned again. And Priya, lovely Priya, she had, as always, been really sweet about his news. As a diehard romantic, the thought of love triumphing across the social divide obviously appealed to her, although she was far too polite to say anything so crass to his face. Priya was, come to think of it, one of the few people he knew who could have an opinion but not feel compelled to share it. As for Ruby, his second-longest-serving friend and confidante, well, her response had been – classic Ruby. When he rang to tell her that he'd proposed to Maddie, the line had gone dead for a second or two, then she'd said, and he remembered her exact words, 'So, you are bourgeois after all, darling. It's a shame. I thought we'd have at least another few years before you threw yourself off the cliff with the rest of the lemmings.' Then she'd laughed, her signature full-throttle laugh, that made unforgivable things forgivable, congratulated him and asked when, and where, the 'evil deed' was happening.

Alex rolled onto his side in order to get a better view of his wife-to-be. It was a cheesy phrase, but he'd found himself using it a lot over the past few months. Maddie was still fast asleep, her back to him, the sheet pushed down around her waist. It was already very warm in the room. Although she'd been careful, she had caught the sun on her back. She'd not wanted to get any strap marks – that had to be a clue to the design of the dress. Maddie's paranoia wasn't simple vanity. He knew she was worried that the scars on her spine would be more noticeable if she tanned. They were visible, not that he would ever say that to her. The original wounds from her fall had been so deep that some scarring had been inevitable, despite the meticulous application of every type of cream and ointment available. The memory of how badly injured she'd been, how uncertain her recovery, how close they had come to postponing the wedding, made Alex want to reach out, hold her and keep her safe.

No one else's opinion mattered. Maddie was the woman Alex wanted to marry, have children and grow old with. He'd never been as certain of anything in his life.

Their relationship had begun, predictably enough, with a drink after work. Alex remembered worrying about where to suggest they meet. Maddie already had him marked down as a flash bastard and he hadn't wanted to confirm that impression by choosing somewhere too ostentatious. Odd as it sounded, the fact that Maddie wasn't easily impressed was partly why he'd been so keen – he'd taken her flirty mockery as a sign that she was interested in who he was beneath his Armani suit and his six-figure salary. Also, the weird circumstances of their introduction had set them off on a different trajectory to any of his previous liaisons. Getting mugged outside of her place of work and needing her first-aid skills might not shout 'ideal boyfriend material', but at least it had made him memorable. His challenge was to turn that flash of intrigue into something more.

In the end he plumped for one of the traditional old boozers on Fleet Street. It was Friday evening, so it was busy, but having pushed their way through to the back bar, they miraculously managed to nab a table. As the City talk swilled around them, they chatted. Initially it was friendly banter, a continuation of their exchange in the coffee shop as he'd sat bleeding on the floor, but by the second drink they started to relax and began to talk properly, taking it in turns to reveal glimpses of their real selves. So absorbed were they in their voyage of mutual discovery that they didn't notice the crowd around them start to thin. It was only when Alex went to buy another round that he registered the pub was virtually empty. The barman declined to serve him, pointing out that they were shutting early due to the adverse weather conditions. This came as news to both Alex and Maddie, but as they stepped outside, they saw the reason for the mass exodus.

Winter had arrived, and not the usual cold, grey, non-entity January weather that usually prevailed in central London – this was winter wonderland stuff. For the first time in either of their adult experience, snow was falling thick and fast on the city. In the glow of the street lights the flakes looked like a child's drawing of snow – lacy, intricate, beautiful. They were both delighted.

He doesn't remember which of them suggested going for a walk, but he can clearly recall her slipping her arm through his as they headed for St Bride's. Walking along the largely deserted streets was magical. By the time they reached Middle Temple Garden the snow was a good few centimetres thick – unheard of in the centrally heated, glare-lit Square Mile. It transformed everything – even the bins looked pretty iced in white. The whole city was muted, the normally incessant traffic noise muffled, the presence of humanity dialled down. It was perhaps a bit of a stretch of the imagination, but it had felt like they were the last two people on earth. When the cold finally got the better of them, they made their way to the Tube station, and that's where fate intervened. The entrance at Holborn was dark and shuttered. The handwritten sign inside the grille explained that services had been suspended 'due to the inclement weather'. Maddie checked on her phone. The whole network was shutting down. The snow swirled around them.

'Come to mine,' he suggested, hastily adding, 'I've got a spare bedroom.' She raised an eyebrow. 'We can try and get a cab.' They both looked – the road was empty. 'Or we can walk. It's not far.' He can't remember her saying yes.

When they reached his block, the shock of stepping into

the brightly lit lobby was disorientating. They travelled up to the twenty-first floor in the lift silently. The heat in his apartment was tangible, welcome. He took her damp coat and hung it up to dry. Then he switched on a few lamps, trying to create a relaxed mood. To help, he fetched them both a brandy. They took their drinks and stood at the huge picture window that Alex rarely looked out of. This high up, the snowstorm was dramatic. The flakes swirled down in erratic gusts onto a London that was cloaked in white. They watched the weather, saying nothing, for a long time. They eventually parted with a taut hesitation, but no kiss. She slept in the guest bedroom. He lay awake in his own bed long after the light in her room clicked off, glad she was there.

In the morning he was up before her, by design. He made coffee. Ground the beans. Did it properly. He wanted the opportunity to make a joke – the customer serving the barista – and to impress her, even if it was only in this small way. He had it all worked out. He carried his offering carefully down the corridor to find that her bedroom door, which had been pulled closed the previous night, was wide open. The sun streaming through the window was bright, amplified by the snow. It fell on her like a spotlight. He felt he should look away. She was asleep and vulnerable, in his home.

He couldn't.

She lay on her side, her knees pulled up to her chest under the covers, her dark hair spread out like an unfurled flag on the pillow. One arm lay across her chest, her hand cupped around her cheek. A sleeping beauty. The sentimentality of the thought took him by surprise. He knocked on the doorframe to break the spell.

She stirred, yawned, sat up and tucked the covers into her armpits. Barriers restored. 'Is that for me?' She gestured at the cup.

He smiled 'Yep', any attempts at humour forgotten, but what did linger – what grew and had continued to grow ever since – was the desire to keep her safe, even if, as she professes, often, she has no need of his protection.

Stirred by the memory of their first date, Alex reached out and traced his fingertips down Maddie's spine, neither lingering on nor avoiding the scars. He loved who she was. Her wounds were proof of their love for one another. Battle scars. She stirred and stretched. Alex was fully aware that his family and many of his friends thought Maddie was the lucky one in their relationship, but after everything that had happened, Alex knew it was he who should be grateful. Maddie had stuck with him when the going had got tough. That loyalty and determination were exactly what he wanted and needed in his wife-to-be.

She was awake now.

He whispered into her hair, 'So what do you want to do with our last few hours of freedom?'

She rolled over to face him and silently gave him her answer.

Chapter 2

LUTHER

Another sodding run to the airport. There were times when Luther felt he was little more than a bloody taxi driver, but at least the job meant he could get away from the finca for a few hours. It was surprising how quickly paradise could become a prison. Their location, high up in the mountains far away from civilisation, or even a crappy bar with flat beer, certainly added to the sense of being cut off from real life. The only people who came to the finca were being paid, badly, to work there, or paying through the nose to stay there. Upmarket came at a price, all ways round.

With typical over-efficiency Colette had already email-ed him this weekend's guest list, complete with the flight numbers, arrival times and confirmation of which gates they were due to come into – twice. Colette didn't trust anyone to do even the simplest of jobs without checking up on them. Or maybe it was more that she didn't trust him. That in itself wasn't too much of a problem, because Ray, Colette's father, still had faith in Luther, despite the incident in Dover.

Still, her attitude grated, as did the isolation and the sense that he was on the wrong stage, missing all the action. The nature of the work he was given to do at the finca was also doing his head in. It was so menial and mundane – a total waste of his very specific talents. Added to these injustices was the uncertainty. The length of Luther's sentence on the island was unclear, but he wasn't fool enough to ask for clarification. He would be allowed back to London when Ray said so – not a minute sooner. So for now he must hold his tongue, and his fists, and endure.

He was sitting on the footplate of the minibus, having a smoke, when Colette appeared. Without so much as a 'hi' or a smile, she thrust a printout at him. He didn't look at it. He simply took it and tossed it onto the passenger seat. Such micro-aggressions were pathetic, beneath him, but they at least made his feelings clear. And despite his reputation, Luther did have feelings. Quite a lot of them, actually.

'A late cancellation?' he asked. If there was anything that pissed off the efficient *Ms Archer* (as she insisted on being called by the staff) more than Luther himself, it was changes to arrangements, especially at short notice. Although she'd be prepared, because, as she repeated ad nauseum in their endless staff briefings, *failing to prepare was tantamount to preparing to fail*. Christ, she was such a tight-arse.

'No,' she snapped.

He got why she was even more stressed than usual. Falling short was not an option at Finca Encantata – not with the prices they charged. Everything had to be the best, the finest, the most tasteful, the most Instagrammable. That's what they sold – photogenic perfection, on the most important day of your life. And this particular wedding had more riding on it than any they'd hosted before, so it was

20

imperative everything went to plan. If it didn't, there would be consequences for little Miss – sorry, Ms – Perfect. The thought made Luther feel slightly better. 'So, it's just you thinking I can't count to seven.'

His attempt at humour went down like a two-finger salute, as he'd intended. Colette's expression hardened, if that was possible. 'You need to get going. You're going to be late.'

He wasn't, but he climbed into the van and put the key in the ignition. If nothing else, the noise of the engine drowned out her further instructions.

An hour and a half later Luther reversed the minibus into one of the pick-up bays at the front of the Arrivals hall. He left the A/C running. It wasn't his money he was burning. As for saving the environment, oh come on, he was parked at an airport, in a diesel-guzzling people carrier, watching an endless stream of well-off bastards, who didn't give a toss about climate change, but spent their time jetting around the world to their much-needed 'few days in the sun' or to stay in their lovely second homes 'just down the coast' or, come to think of it, to attend yet another over-the-top, no-expense-spared wedding that could just as easily have taken place in the UK, where nearly all of the guests came from.

Bored, Luther sat watching the travellers dragging their heavy suitcases along the baked pavement and bumping them precariously up and down the kerbs. He noticed it was often the smallest women who had the largest luggage. Many of the suitcases were big enough to accommodate a body. He amused himself for a while imagining who these ferocious little women had offed, how they'd done it and the configuration of the corpse inside their bags. A foetal curl? A tidy arrangement of neatly severed body parts? Or a modern-art mess of limbs? Human flesh presumably didn't show up on the X-ray machines, but bones surely would. It was surprising that so many murderous women got through security. Although Spanish border officials were, or so he'd been told by Ray, famously open to inducements to look the other way. There were lots of reasons why so many Brits lived in Spain, and they weren't all to do with the weather. Luther moved on to thinking about the opportunities for a new business venture – a brand of luggage specifically designed for the easier and more secure transfer of corpses. The stability and quality of the wheels would be a key feature to emphasise, especially for female customers, along with the latest hi-tech anti-theft and anti-leakage features. And his teachers used to say he had no imagination.

Late! Fat chance. He still had half an hour to kill before the first plane touched down. He'd checked – both flights were on schedule, thank Christ. Late arrivals pissed him off. Hanging about for another bunch of whining guests was like waiting for a punch to land. The list of complaints that Luther had been forced to listen to over the past eight months beggared belief. There was the heat – as if that was a surprise, on an island in the Med; the length of the transfer from the airport to the finca – its selling point was its isolation; the angle of the extremely bright light through the shutters in their bedrooms in the morning – they came for to Mallorca for the sun, for God's sake; the temperature of the water in the lake – an unheated pond; the thickness of the mattresses on the sun loungers, the shape of the ice in their negronis, the noise made by the geckos on the roof of the outdoor bar, the wobble of chair legs on the original eighteenth-century flags in the central courtyard. His response nine times out of ten was to pretend to do something to remedy their complaint and in reality do nothing. The real bastards were the ones who then moaned to Colette. That usually resulted in a bollocking and actual work to do, normally in full view of the fuckers, as they sat on their arses on the dreadfully uncomfortable sun loungers and dangerously unsteady chairs sipping their inadequately chilled cocktails.

Luther knew that this lot wouldn't be much different. He'd met a number of them before. He'd been part of Ray's crew – first on a freelance basis, then as a full-time employee – for years, indeed since Alex had been in short trousers. The thought depressed Luther. He was getting old. Even more worryingly, Ray's need for Luther's brand of service seemed to lessen with each passing season. The Archers were, largely, legit now, if you didn't look too closely or in certain directions. Maybe it really was time for him to start looking for another way to pay his bills.

He checked the flight arrivals again on his phone. The Heathrow plane had landed. They'd be clearing passport control soon, depending on the queues. The Rome flight was due in at 12.08. Luther picked the list up off the passenger seat and scanned it.

Mr Robert Fraser: the best man / Alex's best friend
Miss Louise Haddon: the maid of honour / Maddie's
    best friend
Ms Ruby Davis: Alex's old school friend

Miss Lily Eames: Bobby's girlfriend
Miss Priya Cahill: friend of Alex
Mr Tom Weeton: friend of Alex
Mr Charlie Morgan: friend of Alex

The amount of formality and redundant detail was classic Colette. 'Friend of': it was like something off *Downton* sodding *Abbey*. There was one guest in particular that Luther was interested in seeing again, and that was the lovely Miss Davis. Having first spotted her as a fresh-faced sixteen-year-old at the Archers' house in Kent, Luther had watched Miss Ruby Davis develop over the past decade into an absolute stunner. Alex's old school friend? Yeah right, and pigs were aerodynamic! Even as a teenager Miss Davis … *'Call me Ruby. Miss Davis sounds like a maths teacher'* … had been way out of Luther's league – pure class – but perhaps there was a glimmer of a chance now she was older and still, evidently, unattached. Luther gave his fantasies free rein for a minute or two. Miss Davis – he still preferred to think of her by her formal title; that was possibly something to do with Luther's repertoire of schoolteacher fantasies – might get drunk on the wedding booze. The measures were larger in Spain, she wouldn't be the first to be caught out. She might be laid low by a touch of sunstroke and have to retire to the shade of her room where he could tend to her needs. Or she might, and this was his best hope, fancy a bit of rough as a holiday treat – she had always been close to Ray. A man could dream. There was no law against it, although it often felt like there was.

Then there was Bobby. Despite his stupid name – it made him sound like a toddler – Bobby Fraser was okay in Luther's book. Alex Archer and Bobby had been friends since school. Luther remembered him as a quiet kid who'd grown into a quiet man, never demanding, always polite – even to Luther, and that was a rarity. Bobby had been a frequent visitor to the house in Deal. The fact that the Archers tolerated his presence was interesting. Mrs A. was normally as welcoming as a slap in the face, but Bobby had been allowed on the reservation. Over the years he'd become part of the fixtures and fittings, staying for long periods over the summer and rocking up for the big New Year parties that the Archers used to throw. And there you had another reason why the anal Ms Archer was such a total bitch – sibling rivalry. In the Archer household there'd always been one set of rules for Alex and quite another for Colette. And not much appeared to have changed now that they were adults. Sure, Ray relied on Colette, but Luther had never observed what you'd call love or even much affection between the two of them. Families – they were more trouble than they were worth.

Luther looked through the other names.

Judging by the guest list, Bobby had finally snared himself some skirt in the form of one Miss Lily Eames. Good on him! There were two other women on the list. Miss Priya Cahill, another 'friend of' Alex, and Miss Louise Haddon, maid of honour. Luther hadn't come across either of them before. They were both attending alone. They might be worth a look.

Luther had had the misfortune of meeting Tom Weeton and Charlie Morgan before – when he was based in London, driving for Ray, and by extension for Alex. He vaguely remembered them as chinless wonders, the types

25

that made his fists itch. He'd had to run them to restaurants and bars, listening to them braying like donkeys in the back of the Merc. More irritating still had been the requests to pick them up in the early hours of the morning and take them wherever they wanted to go, stopping off, on occasion, to let them vomit in the gutter. Pointless fuckers, the pair of them.

Luther indulged in another ten minutes of ruminating on what irritations and opportunities might present themselves over the next few days – when the Archer clan gathered there were always tensions – then he accepted the inevitable. He switched off the A/C, climbed out of the minibus, donned his jacket, grabbed the laminated *Archer Wedding* sign that made him look like a complete dick, and headed into the terminal.

It was time to get this expensive show on the road.

Chapter 3

LOU

Lou's experience of her best friend's wedding so far had been little more than a series of stark changes in temperature. The arctic chill of the air-con on the plane had been followed by the slam dunk of heat on the top of her head as they'd disembarked, which had been swapped for the draughty coolness of the arrivals hall that had now been replaced by the choking fumes and heat outside the airport building. Maddie and Alex's wedding was not ticking any luxury boxes yet.

For some reason the surly-looking driver – who had greeted Bobby like his best buddy, but hadn't even looked at her when he took her bag – refused to put the air-con on in the minibus, turning it into a furnace. Consequently, to avoid getting on and broiling to death, they were milling around on the concrete, risking sunstroke. Sweat pooled in Lou's armpits and coursed down her back. So much for glamour. The reason for the delay? Ruby, of course. Lou wasn't surprised. Ruby Davis was the type for whom being late was a matter of principle.

Lou had met Ruby three times. Briefly at the very awkward get-to-know-each-other's-friends drinks do the previous summer, up close on the weird wedding-dress shopping trip and, at uncomfortable length, at the disastrous Valentine's party. Lou had disliked Ruby on first, second and third sight. She'd tried to subdue her instinctive distrust of Alex's best girl mate, aware that it reflected badly on her sisterhood credentials – hating the good-looking girl was so clichéd – but after a grand total of twelve hours in Ruby's company it had been impossible to ignore the many and varied signs that this was a woman who was accustomed to the world bending to her will simply by virtue of the distribution of her body fat and her excellent bone structure. It wasn't Ruby's self-confidence that bothered Lou – she was a supporter of kick-ass women – it was the assumption of being liked.

Because Ruby evidently believed that everyone who came into her orbit – and this was a woman who had an orbit – loved her. Bar staff, waiters, the general population – male and female, but especially the former – Uber drivers, probably even dogs, cats and wild animals; they were all expected to fall under her spell. The fucking frustrating thing was that they did. At the painful drinks do, Lou had watched the waiter linger at Ruby's bronzed shoulder far longer than at anyone else's, and at the Valentine's party it had been like the parting of the Red Sea when Ruby, finally, went to the bar to buy a round. That was the danger of physical beauty; it blinded people to the faults and flaws of the person in possession of it. If Lou had been late to the pick-up point, she was fairly confident that they wouldn't have waited for her. They would have been out of there quicker than you can say, 'Fuck her. Her loss.' Hence her suggestion that they set off and leave Ruby to make her own way to the villa.

Well, that didn't go down well. Not one bit. All it served to do was to cast Lou as a selfish cow who was happy to sacrifice another guest for her own comfort. No, the general consensus was that they should wait for Ruby – which they did, standing around in the suffocating heat, for another half-hour.

They were only freed from Ruby's long-distance thrall when Bobby eventually managed to get a response to one of his many text messages. 'Something's come up. She's had to stay on at work. She's going to catch a later flight.' So Ruby wasn't just late, she hadn't even set off for the airport. Had she sent a profuse apology for keeping them waiting? Of course she hadn't. People with the lives and looks of Ruby didn't say sorry – ever. But at least now they were finally able to get going. It was a blessed relief and, very possibly, a piece of orchestrated theatre, that the climate control in the minibus kicked in just as they struggled free of the urban sprawl of modern Palma and began their voyage into the Mallorcan countryside.

As they sped smoothly and coolly along, Lou put in her earbuds and slipped into the comfortable, familiar surroundings of her own head. Her soundtrack of choice for this trip to the fairy-tale wedding of the year – the Arctic Monkeys and Fontaines D.C. Lou preferred some light and shade in her life. She had thought her best friend was the same, which just went to show how wrong you could be about a person you thought you knew, inside and out. They'd 'got' each other from the moment they met – waitressing at some boring-as-sin awards dinner at Olympia.

They'd gone out afterwards, got pissed, danced, laughed, talked for hours, liked each other more than was normal, and that had been it – friends for life. Lou had loved Maddie's energy and been impressed by her. She had a knack of maxing out whatever opportunities came her way. Through Maddie Lou had got onto the books of the same temp agency and as a result she'd picked up work at some seriously upmarket dos, where the tips, and the food, were much better. It had been great working together, good fun, even when the clients were dicks. Lou also discovered that Mads was a skilled blagger. She'd managed to get them into bars and clubs that Lou wouldn't even have attempted on her own, and once in, scoring free drinks had never been a problem. Together they'd made a great team. Or so Lou had thought, until Alex had appeared on the scene. As Grian Chatten sang about his broken heart Lou revisited her jealousy and found it justified. Maddie might be entitled to fall in love, but Lou still couldn't wrap her head around why she'd gone for someone as shallow and shiny as Alex Archer. Her old best friend would have dated him, taken him for what she could, and dumped him – not married him. Maddie claimed that it was simply a sign that she'd grown up and that she wanted a more stable, mature relationship. Lou called bullshit. But her coherent and well-argued objections had made no difference. Which was why Lou was now on her way to watch her best friend, or the person who used to be her best friend, throw away her identity, her freedom and her principles – for a cushy life.

Just look at how OTT the wedding was.

This was not going to be some package deal wedding in the sun. No, this weekend would be a good few notches up from that. Lou had gone straight onto Google as soon as Maddie told her where they were getting married. According to the website, the Finca Encantata was a triumph of style *and* substance, from the luxury rooms in the eighteenth-century finca itself to the bridal suite at the top of a fourteenth-century tower. No kidding, the place was the witch in *Rapunzel*'s ideal venue. There was also a freshwater lake, which apparently was perfect for a cooling dip, and an olive grove. The surrounding holm oak and pine forest was supposed to contain all manner of wildlife, including snakes, mountain goats, wolves and falcons. Then there were the nearby caverns that were a worthwhile and fascinating half-day excursion for anyone interested in the rich history of the region. And the food! Lou had spent a couple of hours browsing the sample menus. What had been noticeable by its absence was a price list. But this was the land of bespoke wedding services, the implication being that if you had to ask, you couldn't afford it. Yes, there was no doubt that whatever horrors lay in wait over the coming weekend, they were in for a treat.

The company on this five-star, once-in-a-lifetime holiday – at least, in Lou's lifetime – might, however, present more of a challenge. Lou knew that she struggled to 'play nice' with people she didn't like, and this wedding was going to be attended by quite a few candidates who fell into that category. But if that was the price she was required to pay to spend some time with the one person she used to love more than any other, then she was prepared to pay it. There was no way that she was ever not going to come.

The minibus slowed, drawing Lou's wandering attention back to her surroundings. Caution was needed; the road had narrowed. They were climbing now, away from civilisation, up into a pure blue sky, past rocky, sloping fields and a scatter of buildings. It looked like they'd time-travelled into a different century. Lou removed her earbuds and joined the rest of the guests in gazing out of the window.

Eventually the morose driver indicated and they turned right. After about ten minutes there was another sharp turn and they found themselves in a different realm. The change from stark bright light to deep bottle green was like plunging underwater – cooling, refreshing. A transition from one world into another. The flicker of sunlight through the branches added a strobey, trippy element to the last few miles of their journey. Everyone on the bus fell silent. Lou watched the forest oscillating by through the window, half expecting to see a troll peeking out from behind a tree or a unicorn standing in a sunlit clearing. It felt like they were travelling towards some sort of promise, which Lou supposed they were.

Then, just as suddenly, they emerged back into the sunlight. The sky was huge and blue, the mountains looked like a painted backdrop, and in the midst of it all sat the Finca Encantata. It appeared both substantial and ethereal, the classic setting of a thousand storybooks and films and, for the next four days, the exclusive venue of Alex and Maddie's wedding. The minibus shuddered to a stop and the air-con died with a whisper. For a moment or two, no one moved.

The driver broke the spell. 'Well, this is it, folks!'

So, this is it. The setting for Alex and Maddie's wedding. A castle, high up in the mountains, in a land far away from everything and everyone.

It's perfect.

For their purposes, and mine.

Chapter 4

MADDIE

A crunch of gravel and a spray of dust announced the arrival of their wedding guests. Colette, with her usual efficiency, had been keeping Alex apprised of their ETA by text for the past hour. There must have been some sort of tracker on the minibus. Maddie had struggled to see Colette's regular updates as anything other than a countdown. The cocktail of excitement and nerves in her stomach was making her feel jittery.

Bobby was the first off the bus. He and Alex embraced. Maddie liked Bobby, liked what Alex's choice of him as a best friend said about her husband-to-be's judgement. They were close. She took that closeness as a good sign. It demonstrated emotional maturity – something she'd not expected in two products of a highly selective boarding school in deepest, darkest Dorset. Maddie watched the rest of their guests disembark. Lou was near the back. She was the last off the minibus. There was no sign of Ruby. For a moment Maddie's heart lifted. She immediately felt ashamed. She'd promised Alex, and herself, that she'd dealt with her jealousy, laid it to rest, like a ghost. But it was the nature of ghosts to linger, and Ruby's anticipated arrival, and unexplained absence, was enough to blow the dust off the grave. What Ruby was – or had been – to Alex still haunted Maddie. How could it not? Ruby looked like something out of the pages of *Vogue*, she had brains as well as beauty and she'd known Alex for years. They had history. The question was – what kind?

But any complicated feelings that Maddie might harbour about her fiancé's 'other best friend' were literally knocked out of her by Lou. She ran across the car park, dropped her bag in the dust and hurled herself at Maddie with the exuberance of an excited puppy. Her sweaty hug felt good. Alex had Bobby. She had Lou. It was a perfectly squared circle. As long as they held their shape everything would be fine. Lou whispered in her ear. 'So, no one's locked you up in the tower for being insane, yet?'

'No.'

'Good, because even your hair isn't long enough to fashion an escape ladder.' Lou released Maddie from her grasp and grinned. Her eyes swung around the finca taking in the courtyard, the high walls, the tower and the elegant landscaping and, no surprise, landed on the waitress who was standing in the full glare of the sun, holding a tray of cava. Lou moved towards the drinks at speed. She took a glass, downed it and took another – Lou shared a close and enthusiastic relationship with alcohol. The other guests moved towards the waitress, possibly concerned that if they weren't quick enough, there wouldn't be enough to go round. The wedding party had started. There was no stopping it now.

Maddie held back as everyone else gravitated towards the refreshments. Not so long ago it would have been her standing there, in a stiff white shirt and a tight black skirt, with a straight back and a firmly held tray. Server to served – her promotion up the ranks had been remarkably swift. She was acutely aware that she wasn't the only one finding the transition difficult to acclimatise to. Maddie's attention shifted, instinctively, to Colette. Now there was a person who seemed finely attuned to the pecking order. Colette was most definitely not in party mode. She was supervising the unloading of the bags from the back of the minibus. Even from a distance Maddie could sense the tension between her future sister-in-law and the driver. Words were obviously being had. Lecture delivered, Colette tugged her skirt straight, turned to face the guests and fixed on a welcoming smile. In doing so she caught Maddie's eye. They stared at each other, both frozen in an unguarded moment. Despite the heat of the day there was no warmth in Colette's eyes, but she recovered first. She raised her hand, gave the slightest of waves and went on with her work. Behind her Maddie saw the driver take a last drag on his cigarette, before flicking it on the ground. It was a small but very pointed act of defiance.

Maddie looked for Alex. He was in his element, greeting his friends, directing people to take a glass of cava and guiding them into the shade where a light lunch had been laid out on a long trestle table in the lee of the castle walls. These were his people, his friends. Alex laughed at something Tom, or was it Charlie, said – she never knew which was which. Her husband-to-be looked happy and relaxed.

Maddie followed the group into the shade. She poured herself a glass of iced tea and took a seat at the far end of the table. Not that she was much in demand after the first effusive greetings and hugs were over. Even Lou was distracted – by the glamour of the setting, by the dazzle of the sun high up in the pure blue sky, by the mountains, by the heady scent of pine and bougainvillea and by the baked-in heat that told you you weren't in England any more. And, of course, by the lavish lunch.

When the guests had all loaded their plates with cheese, sobrasada, coca de trampo, fresh figs and vine-ripened tomatoes and found a seat, Colette began her spiel. 'Welcome to the Finca Encantata. This place holds a very special place in our hearts and we hope, over the next few days, to share that magic with you.' The guests, already well on their way to being seduced by the heat and the chilled cava, murmured their agreement.

Colette went on, 'The finca began life in the early 1400s, when a patch of forest was cleared to make way for a humble farmhouse. The magnificent buildings you see before you came later. A wealthy Portuguese trader called Alvaro Braga was passing through the area in 1754 and fell in love, not with a woman, but with this plot of land. So began a love affair that was to last fifty years and which resulted in many of the beautiful buildings, the landscaped lake and the olive groves that you're about to spend some time exploring and enjoying. But, like so many love stories, this tale is a turbulent one. Over the intervening years the finca has seen its fair share of high and lows. When my father and myself arrived in the spring of 2018 it had fallen into a sorry state of neglect and disrepair. But, like Alvaro Braga before him, my father was smitten, and so began the restoration of the buildings and the surrounding gardens. A labour of love . . . and considerable cost . . . the result of which is the beautiful hotel you see before you today.'

The end of Colette's speech was marked with a polite smattering of applause.

'Now, given that the heat is rising and many of you seem to have eaten your fill, can I suggest that I show you to your rooms? Give you a chance to freshen up. Once you have, please feel free to explore the finca and the grounds. If you're looking for something to invigorate you after your long trip, I can thoroughly recommend a dip in the lake. That will definitely blow away any travel fatigue. The only thing I would advise against, strongly, is walking out beyond the boundaries of the finca onto the hillside itself. We'd hate to lose any of you. And . . .' she paused for effect, 'here there be wolves.' Again everyone laughed politely. 'So . . . if you'd like to follow me.' And, like blind mice, they rose and followed her. All of them, except Maddie and Lou. They stayed behind in the shade, reflecting on how a twist of fate had resulted in one of them ending up halfway up a mountain on a Mediterranean island about to marry the son of a man so wealthy that he owned his own castle and olive grove.

But for a random act of violence Maddie and Alex would never have been more than barista and paying customer.

Maddie had been working at The Shed on Throgmorton Street, round the corner from the Stock Exchange, for a couple of months on the day they met. She'd been there long enough to be trusted to churn out hundreds of flat whites and espressos every day, clean the machine – 'properly' – and to open up on her own. The awarding of the latter task was no compliment. No one wanted to start work at 6.00 a.m. in the middle of winter, but the City boys and girls were at their desks early and where there was footfall there were sales, especially when you were the only place open.

Despite the inhumanely early start – Maddie was living in a room in a shared house in Alperton at the time and the commute into the City was long, tedious and eye-wateringly expensive – the location of The Shed had one major advantage. Its proximity to wealth. Being near money always opened up opportunities, no matter how small and seemingly insignificant. Maddie's mother had taught her the value of serendipity from an early age and Maddie's share of it would surely be increased by working in the richest square mile of London. She needed it to. At that point in her life, as she had been many times before, she was skint.

She'd already clocked Alex before the incident. He stood out among the waves of Jermyn Street suits and Hermès ties who crashed in and out of The Shed, having their booming phone conversations that were far too important to interrupt to add a 'please' to their coffee orders. Sure, he wore the same uniform, spoke with the same confidence, moved with the same instantly recognisable pace of a titan of commerce, so he was, essentially, one of them, but for two small but very noticeable differences. Firstly, he had genuine kerb appeal. He was irrefutably good-looking. He had a rugged jaw covered in soft, smooth, no doubt expensively moisturised skin, cerulean-blue eyes, kissable lips, white teeth, broad shoulders, slim hips, and – something she always looked out for – strong hands. So on a very basic level he was noticeable. And secondly, and this was as important, especially for her needs, he seemed nice. He was polite and he had a genuine smile, qualities that he extended to the staff. In other words, he wasn't a rude prick like the rest of them.

The name of the coffee shop was a nod to its bijouxness, but that was where any shed-like attributes ended. Their tiny slice of retail space was not cosy and reassuring. It was minimal to the point of clinical, designed, as Jo, the owner, proudly confessed, to deter lingering. 'In. Buy. Out' was the business model. Consequently, staff fraternisation with the clientele, e.g. chatting, was actively discouraged. Hence the first drop of serendipity. The timing of the incident. Namely, when neither Jo, the other staff members or any other customers were around.

Maddie turned on the lights to push the darkness away and fired up the machine, ground the first batch of beans and put the advertising board out on the pavement. Despite the cold, she propped open the door hoping that the chill would wake her up. There was something hypnotic about moving slowly and quietly, serving the first, monosyllabic customers of the day. It was into this calm that her future husband crashed.

It started with shouting. Maddie only semi-registered it – braying seemed to be a standard form of greeting in the City. She wiped the steam nozzle absent-mindedly and studied a burn on the inside of her wrist – an occupational hazard. The next thing she knew there was a loud bang. She looked at the window. A man, a classic City type, judging by his rather nice dark wool overcoat, was being pressed up against the glass by an older man who was most definitely not a banker or a broker. His tracksuit and the thick gold chain around his neck indicated that he was more a delivery driver or perhaps he owned a small backstreet boxing gym where the suits went, fancying themselves in *Fight Club*. Tracksuit Man was yelling – threats, by the sound of it. He had one huge, inked hand clamped around the smart man's neck; with the other he was pummelling him in the face, chest and stomach, basically anywhere that his meaty fist could reach. With each punch the back of City Guy's head thudded against the glass so hard that Maddie was worried the window would shatter.

Then, as quickly as it had begun, it stopped.

The dude administering the beating took a step back. He was blowing with the effort. He drew a deep breath and said, 'When you see your old man tell him that *he* might have forgotten, but we haven't. And make sure you tell him that we never will.' He let fly one last punch, then spat, copiously, at the suit guy. Having delivered his message, he wiped his mouth and walked off.

For a second neither Maddie nor the beaten bloke moved.

Then time started up again. The City guy peeled himself off the glass, leaving a mark that Maddie would have to clean later. He turned around and their eyes met. It was Alex. Name known because of his coffee order – *an almond-milk, double-shot flat white*. He of the manly jaw, piercing blue eyes and nice smile. Oddly, he smiled at her now, but instead of pearly white teeth his mouth was full of blood. It made him look vulpine. There was more blood oozing out of his nostrils. The gore galvanised Maddie. She grabbed the roll of kitchen paper and ran outside. 'Are you okay?'

41

'Yeah, I think so.'

He didn't look it. 'Come inside.' She took his arm and guided him into The Shed. His face was paper white. Or perhaps it was simply the contrast with the blood. She passed him a wad of kitchen roll and he held it to his nose and mouth. There was a definite sway in his stance. 'I think you should sit down for a minute.' They both looked around. Damn Jo, there wasn't anywhere to sit. The sway was pronounced now. There was no option. She pressed his shoulder and he slid down onto the floor. Bizarrely, her first thought was, what a way to treat such an expensive coat. Blood, another man's spit, then a dusty floor. 'Tip your head forward.'

'Forward?'

She understood his hesitation, but that was what she'd been taught. 'Yep. Forward. It stops the blood going down your throat. I'll get some ice, to stop the swelling.' She couldn't imagine his bosses would be happy with him walking around looking like he'd come off worst in a brawl. The fighting might be accepted, but the losing wouldn't go down well. He swapped the paper for the bag of ice, winced as he pressed it to his face. It would be a shame if his nose was broken, but Maddie guessed that such an imperfection probably wouldn't spoil the overall effect too much. 'Do you want me to call the police?'

His response was swift. 'No. There's no need. Besides, he'll be long gone by now.'

Maddie felt awkward leaning over him, so she slid down the wall and sat on the floor next to him. 'But he assaulted you.'

Alex nodded. His nose seemed to have stopped bleeding.

He lowered the bag of ice. Grinned at her. 'Have I still got all my teeth?'

It wasn't a pretty sight, but there were no gaps. 'Yeah, you're good.'

'Thank Christ for that.'

'Keep the ice on.' Calm in a crisis. She did have skills other than making coffee.

'Yes, Miss.' He was well-spoken, but not crackers posh, not like some of his breed.

'What was that about?'

'Not a clue. I'm not sure blokes like him need a reason.'

So Alex wasn't averse to half-truths or perhaps even flat lies himself. The attack had not been random. In Maddie's experience, albeit limited, muggers tended not to ask victims to pass on messages to wider family. Alex's lie piqued her interest even further. She pushed, but only gently. 'I heard him say something about your dad.'

Alex attempted a laugh. It sounded odd through the blood. 'Obviously a case of mistaken identity.' He held the makeshift ice pack up to his face again.

Something possessed her – a desire to make him see her as more than a first-aid-trained, coffee-making floor mopper. 'Maybe he has an aversion to men in Armani suits who earn more in a month than he takes home in a year.'

'Ouch. Talk about kicking a man when he's down.' But he said it with a smile in his voice. 'And, I'll have you know, it's more like in a week, if I'm on a roll.' Arrogance, self-mockery and a hint of an interesting backstory. It was a winning combination for Maddie. The following silence was comfortable. He broke it by getting to his feet. She stood up as well. He passed her the ice and, after a polite

43

hesitation, the wad of bloody paper. 'Well, thank you for coming to my rescue.'

'My pleasure.' They walked the five steps to the door together. 'Are you sure you're all right? I assume you're going into work?'

'Of course. It's just round the corner. Stonehaven Trading.'

'That means nothing to me.'

'As it shouldn't. I promise to cause less trouble next time I come in for my flat white.'

She smiled. 'No worries. Your little altercation brightened up a very dull early shift.'

He started to mock-bow, but thought better of it given the pressure in his battered face. 'No, really, thank you. And I'm sorry about the mess. See ya soon.' With that he walked out.

Maddie watched him cross the street and disappear around the corner. It was as she turned to head back inside that she spotted the wallet lying on the ground, underneath the sign. She picked it up, checked the street. He was definitely gone. Feeling justified and excited, she slipped the wallet into the pocket of her apron. She stepped back inside the shop, went behind the counter and dumped the wad of bloody paper into the bin. As she did a power-dressed older woman, one of their regulars, came in and ordered a double espresso. Maddie washed her hands and went back to work.

When Cherelle arrived at 10.00 a.m. Maddie asked if she could take a break. She claimed that she needed to make some calls ASAP, and that if she didn't, she might get kicked out of her digs. Cherelle shrugged, not bothered.

Cherelle wasn't bothered about most things. But instead of going into the side alley where the staff normally took their breaks – there was no space anywhere inside The Shed apart from a tiny toilet and Jo's cubby-hole of an office, and that was most definitely out of bounds to the staff – Maddie walked along the street to the statue. She never did find out who the jowly, ringleted guy in the frock coat was who looked out over the square. The City was full of such monuments to rich, fat bastards. Maddie sat down on one of the benches, trying her best to avoid the worst of the pigeon crap. Jo would get pissy if she came back with bird poo on her trousers, not that the customers saw the staff from the waist down.

The weight of the wallet nestling against Maddie's stomach inside her apron had felt good all morning. Now she took it out and looked at it. It was a Mont Blanc. Who knew they did wallets as well as pens. It was a simple, classic design. As she held it on her lap and ran her index finger across the soft leather, she noticed a smear of blood on the pad of her thumb. She rubbed at it, but the stain was stubborn. The blood had dried in the whorls of her skin. Surely that was some sort of omen. With her heart rate dancing, she flipped open the wallet.

It *was* his. She hadn't really thought that it belonged to the knucklehead, but stranger things had happened when she'd lifted wallets in the past. You could never really tell what people had on them until you excavated your 'find'. Alex's wallet contained: eighty quid in twenties, no coins – of course there weren't, he didn't look like the type to waste his time with small change – a platinum Chase card and a black Amex card, both in the name of Alexander

Archer, and an office pass. There was no address on the security pass for obvious reasons, but that didn't matter; she already knew where he worked – because he'd made a point of telling her. Surprisingly, in this digital day and age, there were also two photos, both very battered, as if they'd been carried in this and previous wallets for years. The first was a shot of three people, two guys and a girl, who looked to be in their late teens. They had their arms around each other; the girl was in the middle. The boy on the left was obviously Alex, a younger, slimmer, less polished version, but still undoubtedly him. The other lad was nondescript: slim, dark, shaggy hair, trendy glasses, a kind face. And the girl? Well, she was simply gorgeous. Maddie noted her reaction, a mild sense of dismay, and stored it away for later consideration. The good thing was it was a photo of a threesome, not a solo shot of the girl on her own. Not his childhood sweetheart, then? A group of friends, who had got together at university or maybe even further back, in their school days? Maddie slid the picture back into the wallet. The second photograph was of an older, very glamorous woman. Her age was hard to determine. She could have been anywhere between an elegant, if old-fashioned, thirty-five and a very well-preserved sixty. The photo was stylish: the lighting was great, the woman's skin flawless, her hair beautifully styled and the cream silk shirt she was wearing had obviously been carefully chosen to show off her tan. It looked like a professional headshot. Was she a relative? It was hard to tell. There wasn't any obvious likeness, although she was so polished that any quirks or natural flaws that might indicate a familial link to Alex had been ironed out. Could she be his lover? It was possible. They looked well matched in terms of wealth and confidence.

One of the pigeons that had been scratting around at Maddie's feet must have been emboldened by her stillness because it suddenly fluttered up and landed on the bench beside her, its scaly claws scrabbling against the wooden slats. She flapped it away. She didn't want company, even of the non-verbal, feathered variety.

What did the contents of the wallet represent? Some ready cash – small change to Alex, no doubt, but enough for a fortnight's groceries for Maddie. Two bank cards – the loss of which would be a minor inconvenience. They could have had some street value to her, especially the black Amex, but, by virtue of her being trapped at work, that window had probably already closed. Hot cards only had a street value in the first few hours of being lifted before they were flagged or cancelled and Maddie imagined that the service provided to the customers of Chase and Amex would be impeccable. Then there were the photos. They had no monetary worth, but the loss of them might upset Alex, and, more importantly, they could be of value to her. It all depended on what she did with the serendipity that the wallet represented. Should she see it as nothing more than a welcome, if modest, cash windfall? Should she keep it as a memento of a nice moment with a handsome stranger? Or could she use it as a potential route to Alex and everything he represented?

The pigeon cocked its head and stared up at her with its beady black eyes. It was probably wondering why she'd been sitting in the freezing cold in her work togs and thin jacket for so long. Maddie looked up at the huge gilt clock on the front of the Barclays building. Time was getting on.

But Cherelle wouldn't be bothered if Maddie was late back because Cherelle wasn't bothered about anything.

He emerged from the lift and spotted her.

She crossed the marble expanse of the lobby. 'Hey.'

'Hey to you.' They both grinned.

Maddie could feel the receptionist's interest. She didn't care. 'You're bruising up nicely.' She indicated his battered face.

He bowed.

'You dropped something.'

'Apart from my dignity and any hope of convincing you that I'm a hard man?' He was flirting atrociously with her. She held out his wallet. He nodded. 'I was going to swing by at lunchtime to see if you'd found it. Do I need to check the contents?'

'Charming!'

He took her response as mock offence. 'Thank you. I appear to be even more in your debt now. Emergency first aid and wallet retrieval. You really do go the extra mile for your customers, don't you?'

'Only for a select few.' He smiled some more. The receptionist continued her close observation. Maddie shoved her hands into the pockets of her trousers. 'Well, I'd best be getting back to work.' She made to leave, playing it cool, praying the distance across the shiny lobby floor was enough.

It was.

'What time are you working till today?'

'Two p.m.'

'Over lunchtime, then?'

'Yep.'

'Okay.'

'Bye, then.'

'Bye.'

She was at the sliding doors.

'Catch you later,' he shouted.

She didn't look round. 'Yeah, whatever.' But she hoped could hear the smile in her voice.

Alex walked into The Shed two hours later, at the height of the lunchtime rush. The flowers he'd bought took up as much space as a person. There was a visible frisson of irritation amongst the other customers. He didn't queue. Maddie was in the middle of making her one-hundredth oat-milk flat white of the day. She saw him, clocked the bouquet then channelled cool by carrying on as if he wasn't there. He seemed to like that. He stood his ground, causing an OTT floral obstruction. One of the blokes in the queue brayed, 'Do you want something or not, mate?'

He responded calmly and loudly. 'Yes. I'd like to speak to that young lady, there, if her colleagues can spare her for five minutes?'

And so it began.

Chapter 5

COLETTE

Colette hoped to God that Luther had put the luggage in the correct rooms. She had her doubts. It wouldn't surprise her if he mixed up the bags deliberately simply to irritate her. She really could do without his passive-aggressive defiance this weekend. Most of the guests were staying in the main building, on the second and third floors. Those were the rooms with the best views. You could even catch a glimpse of the sea in the far distance from Rooms 2 and 6. She'd put Paul, his wife, Yvette, and their daughter, Letty, in the ground-floor apartment. It would give them more space and it meant that they had their own kitchen. It was much less indulgent than the other rooms and had no real view, but that's what having kids got you.

It felt good offloading the guests. Colette did it politely but rapidly, leaving them to their *ooh*s and *aah*s as they spotted the wine fridges and the integrated sound, light and air-conditioning system – the fitting of which had been a total ball-ache. Old buildings and new tech were not a marriage made in heaven. Colette herself was immune to the loveliness of the finca. When she passed through it, at speed, all she saw was the huge amount of effort and

50

investment that had gone into it. For her it was a place of work, and there was nothing magical about that. The luxury and indolence were reserved for the paying guests. Not that this bunch were putting their hands in their own pockets. No, her mother and father were footing the bill for this weekend: flights, rooms, food, booze, the lot. It was a bill – Colette knew because she ran the books – that would easily exceed £150,000. The fact that the costs would be largely covered by whatever Russian or South American client needed their considerable revenue legitimatised was an irrelevance. The excess still stung. Colette would never be the one picking out which grade of linen she wanted in the bridal suite nor how many specially flown-in, alabaster hot house roses she thought were enough for the wedding bower – from experience it was a minimum of three hundred; five hundred if you really wanted to nail 'abundance'. No, Colette was at the finca to work, not to indulge.

She put Bobby and Lily into Room 2. Alex was going to be moving next door into Room 4, at his request. The tradition of separating the bride and groom before the wedding was being observed, God knows why. Both of them would have had to be able to time-travel at least a decade to regain their virginity. Colette found Bobby and Alex's friendship puzzling. She'd expected it to wane once they left university, but it hadn't. They still seemed weirdly joined at the hip. But who was she to judge? She'd never really had a close friendship with anyone, at school or since. She wondered whether that was because of the peculiar demands of her job, but in her more honest moments she suspected it was her nature. A loner, with trust issues, who had a short temper and whose father was a well-known hard man, hardly shouted 'fun times'. But people could change, couldn't they, especially if someone gave them a chance? She sincerely hoped so.

Colette chided herself for letting her mind wander. She got back to the task in hand – depositing the guests.

Room 3 had been set aside for Ruby. It was the best room, with a huge bathroom and a balcony that looked out over the lake. It was almost on par with the bridal suite at the top of the tower, but without the same sense of solitude. Ruby had put in a request for Room 3 when she'd RSVPed. She'd stayed in it before. It had seemed easier to comply with her demand than refuse – failure to accommodate Ruby's wishes would, no doubt, have provoked complaints, either from Ruby herself, when she finally arrived, or from Colette's father. Ray had a soft spot for Miss Davis. He would have been livid if he'd found out that Colette had done anything to make her stay anything other than marvellous. It was small consolation, but the fact that Ruby was not taking up the offer of a plus-one gave Colette some satisfaction. It was interesting and pettily reassuring that, stunning as she was, Ruby had no 'significant other' to bring to an all-expenses-paid wedding in a five-star hotel.

Colette had reserved Room 5 for Mateus Torres and his wife. Mr Torres was a long-standing business associate of her parents, one of the very small number of contacts who had survived from the early days. He still travelled extensively – a requirement, in his line of work, which was, on the face of it, exporting sherry and port barrels from Europe to the US and Japan. Using his contacts and network, Mateus Torres could also be relied upon to transport whatever you wanted to whoever and wherever you wished, no questions asked – as long as the price was right.

Mr Torres had confirmed that he and his wife would only be coming for the day and evening of the wedding itself. He was a busy man. Likewise, Room 6 was reserved for another of Ray's business contacts, Teddy Largos, and whichever new girlfriend he was currently trialling. Teddy was relatively new on the scene. Colette knew very little about him other than what she'd gleaned when they'd hosted his sixtieth birthday at the finca a couple of months back. That had been another bells-and-whistles affair, all costs absorbed by Archer Inc. Her father had been especially keen for Teddy to come to Alex's small, select wedding. Why, Colette didn't know, but when did she ever get briefed on Ray's many machinations? Her role was not to ask questions, but to execute wishes – be that as his daughter, as the manager of the finca or as general dogsbody in her parents' many business dealings. The thought of making sure that these subtext guests were supremely well looked after, as well as running the wedding itself, made Colette feel tired and pissed off. Nothing was ever what it appeared to be at the Finca Encantata. Pleasure always had to yield a profit.

Mateus and Teddy requiring the bigger, better rooms meant that Colette had had to put Priya, Tom and Charlie up on the third floor. Priya in 7, Tom in 8 and Charlie in 9. On seeing Priya's expression as the four of them climbed up the stairs to the top floor Colette wondered whether her room allocations had been wise, but she swiftly dismissed her concerns. Needs must, business came first. And she had given Priya the room with the four-poster bed – she could at least play princess in style and comfort, on her own, or with company, as she saw fit.

Guests dropped, Colette retraced her steps. She needed to get Maddie and Lou settled in the tower, then she could go back to the kitchens to see how preparations for the big set-piece evening meal were going. As she made her way down the stairs, her thoughts turned to Maddie. She was not what Colette had been expecting of Alex's choice of bride. Why? Well, because when it came to her little brother the stereotypes applied. Up until Maddie, Alex had chosen exactly the sort of women that his private education, his degree from UCL, his City job and his expensive lifestyle dictated. To be precise: polished, posh, educated and nakedly relentless in their pursuit of a certain standard of living – namely, high; and of a certain breed of man – namely, successful. It still shocked Colette to see how little of her and Alex's shared history had survived their childhood. It had been eradicated – no, it would be more accurate to say, it had been obliterated by their different paths through life. It wasn't just the accent, there was no hint of their South London heritage in Alex's voice; or his manner, which was now so smooth as to be slippery; it was his essence. Her little brother genuinely seemed to have forgotten just how much muck-shovelling was necessary to ensure that the family's fortunes continued to flourish.

But that, of course, had always been the point. That is, for one of the Archers, and it was always going to be Alex, to come up smelling of roses rather than of shit. He was the chosen one from birth. The considerable investment that had been ploughed into her brother's refinement had paid off. He was living proof that at least one of the next generation of Archers had not only moved up in the world, but on. He had broken out of the cage of their family's class and criminality and become a clean skin. Why her parents had poured so much money and effort into Alex's transformation, and what price they would ultimately extract for it, had yet to be revealed, but revealed it would be – eventually. Because her father and her mother only ever invested in anybody or anything if there was a return to be had. It was all about the money – even when it came to the golden child.

And that was the key difference between her and Alex. Colette was under no illusion about her place and her purpose within the family. She might be the eldest, but she knew she was, and always would be, second best. Useful, oh yes; Colette definitely had her uses. She'd been raised to be valuable, but only in terms of the grubby practicalities of the business. She'd been taught every aspect of the Archers' varied and various enterprises and subsidiaries, criminal and legit, while Alex had been kept well away from it all. Her education had not taken place in a cosy private school in the rolling Dorset countryside; no, her schooling had been in the back rooms of pubs and on windy docksides with her father, often at the crack of dawn or in the dead of night. It had, ironically, been good practice for her current role at the finca: namely, coping with tricky, often unpredictable customers. Had her education at her father's knee, or more accurately, watching her father's back, made them close? Well, yes, after a fashion, if you classed shared street smarts as a solid basis for a relationship, but Colette often wondered whether either of her parents ever saw her as their daughter. She was more an asset.

Look at this weekend. She was the sister of the groom. By rights, she should have been a guest. It was Colette who should have been shown into a luxury room, with a sea view and wine chilling in the fridge, the air-con set at a comfortable 21°C, with nothing to do but waft around eating and drinking and socialising for the next four days. Instead, here she was clumping around in the heat catering for everyone else's whims and desires. When she reached the bottom of the stairs she paused in the shadow of the archway. The cold stone on her back through her shirt provided some balm to her agitated soul. Maddie and Lou were sitting at the table on the other side of the courtyard. The housekeeper in Colette was pleased to see that the debris from lunch had already been cleared – one less job for her to supervise. They too were in the shade, but Lou's lime-green, swirly-patterned top still popped, bright and garish, against the mellow stone of the courtyard walls. Maddie was laughing at something Lou had just said. Her head was thrown back, her long dark hair loose and messy on her shoulders. She looked properly relaxed. A rare sight. Colette experienced a stab of jealousy as they sat fooling around, shooting the breeze. It disturbed her how much some people changed when in close proximity to the people they loved – whether for the better or the worse. Hot on the heels of Colette's envy came a wave of uncharacteristic self-pity. The problem was that she was never *with* anyone other than her parents, the guests or the staff. And when she was with them, she was always, and only, a fixer, a doer, a facilitator and occasionally, if required, an enforcer. Did that mean that that was the sum total of what or who Colette was? If no one was looking for the other sides of you did that mean they no longer existed? The thought terrified her. Colette wanted to *be* someone, for and *with* someone else, but she knew that was never going to happen unless she stepped out of the shadows.

Chapter 6

BOBBY

Bobby left Lily exploring their room. He was pleased she was so thrilled with everything; her desire to try out the rainfall shower, the crisp cotton robes, the luxe toiletries and the bean-to-cup coffee machine meant that he had a free hour or two. He'd missed Alex. What with the wedding build-up and their work commitments they'd had very little time together over the past few months – over the past year, if truth be told. It was what happened when your best friend met 'the one'. He got it, but that didn't mean he hadn't felt sidelined. He also knew that over the next few days there would be a lot of demands on Alex's time – it was his wedding, after all. So, while there was a gap in the schedule, Bobby was determined to grab some time with his best friend. Clutching his swim shorts and a towel he set off for the lake.

It was quiet around the finca; it felt as if everyone and everything was taking a siesta, even the geckos. In the courtyard all evidence of their arrival lunch had been whisked away – shoemaker and elf-like. Bobby wasn't surprised. The Archers had 'had people' to do their bidding as long as he'd known them, and that was a very long time.

Man and boy. It was such a cliché, but it was true when it came to his connection with Alex and his family.

Initially, Bobby hadn't been interested when a thirteen-year-old Alex had rocked up at King Henry's in the middle of the summer term. He appeared to be just another cocky, sporty, one-dimensional boy – the type who would slot seamlessly into the brutal but efficient pecking order at the school.

But that wasn't what happened.

King Henry's was a £15,000-a-term establishment where the standard of education that the boys received, despite what the glossy prospectus claimed, was middling to poor. The head, Mr Bowker's, oft-repeated boast was that the school specialised in turning out *gentlemen, not geniuses*. The one thing that they did take seriously at King Henry's was tradition, or more accurately traditions. Part and parcel of that adherence to outdated practices and beliefs was a high tolerance of bullying – which at King Henry's took the form of 'plays'. 'Plays' was the code word for pranks perpetrated by the popular boys – the perps – on the unpopular boys – the prey. It was a surprisingly well-organised system, with a league table and points awarded by a committee of the self-appointed ringleaders. There was even a cup that was presented at a secret ceremony at the end of every term to the top perp. Bobby himself had been caught up in the 'plays' for a short while before he wised up and managed to extricate himself. But had it not been for the Laycock 'play' Bobby and Alex might never have been more than two boys who happened to attend the same stuffy, small-minded boarding school.

Laycock was the type of kid who was destined to have

a rough time. His 'crimes' included his general weediness, his propensity for snotty colds, his habit – that he stead- fastly refused to grow out of – of coming top in most of his classes and, of course, his name. (Many years later Bobby discovered that Laycock went on to become a prosecution barrister – one of the genuine King Henry's success stories – so the joke was on the perps after all.) But at thirteen life must have been fairly relentless for Laycock. There was the daily low-level stuff – tripping him up at any opportunity, making wanking gestures behind his back, sniffing in uni- son whenever he answered a question in class; then there was his popularity as prey.

The incident that brought Bobby and Alex together took place on Founders' Day at the end of Alex's first term at King Henry's.

Founders' Day was the largest, most prestigious gath- ering of the school year. There was a prize-giving in the mock-Gothic hall, attended by the gowned masters and a few random local dignitaries, followed by a garden party in the school grounds with professional catering and some glasses of rather good wine. It was billed as a celebration of the boys' achievements, but in reality it was a tightly choreographed performance designed to reassure parents that the hefty fees King Henry's charged were worth it. As the assembled parents watched a parade of sombre-suited boys go up to receive their cups and certificates they felt confident that, at the very least, King Henry's was some- how managing to shape their amoebic teenage sons into the type of men who would one day rule the world.

Bobby had a good spot from which to watch events

unfold that day. As a member of the school council he had a seat on the left-hand side of the hall, on a raised dais, alongside the masters and the prefects. Hence he was in a good position to witness Alex peel away from his form and join the line next to Laycock. Alex breaking ranks was an obvious red flag that something was afoot, but none of the masters seemed to notice. They were probably too busy dreaming of their long summer break. The other thing the staff failed to notice was that Alex obviously had something concealed inside his jacket.

As at every Founders' Day, the ceremony was interminable. The more offspring that got awards, the higher the number of satisfied parents. Laycock, by virtue of being bright and by working hard, was in line for three subject prizes and a special Civics Prize for community service. All the more reason that he was due some comeuppance in the minds of the perps. In a brief pause during the seemingly never-ending list of names and prizes, Laycock cried out. It was a classically Laycock high-pitched squeal. One of the prefects hissed 'hush'. On droned the headmaster. In the sea of somnolent, drooping bodies Bobby could see that Laycock was in some sort of distress. He was tense, squirming in his seat, his shoulders a pinch of misery. Alex, sitting perfectly still and upright next to him, appeared the model student, but Bobby knew better.

'And now we move on to the Whitworth Prize for Chemistry and this year it goes, once again, to Jonathan Laycock.' There was smattering of, by now, tired applause as the audience anticipated yet another boy with short hair and an ill-fitting grey suit walking up to the stage to receive an awkward handshake and a few encouraging words. But nothing happened. This was all they needed. Outside the sky was blue. Not so far away, chilled wine was being uncorked and poured, or so the staff and a good number of the parents fervently hoped. 'Jonathan Laycock?' The head raised his voice, expecting an immediate response. None came. Feet shuffled, chairs creaked, heads turned and the direction of their gaze was four rows from the back.

Okoro, the boy to the left of Laycock, nudged him. Laycock didn't move. Indeed, he seemed frozen, his head lowered. The whispering began. Then, in a move that was really quite slick, they all saw, and heard, Alex lean in and stage-whisper: 'Jonathan. That's you, mate.' Now the whole school, staff, pupils, prefects and parents were staring at the boy with the bowed head. Why on earth hadn't he stood up? Mr Jacks, PE – he of the wall-penetrating voice and stare intervened. 'Laycock!' he yelled. The whole hall jumped, their heart rates shooting up. Slowly Laycock rose to his feet and started to make his way along the row to the aisle. As he did so the sniggering began.

Bobby was fascinated. So Laycock wanted the prize badly enough to tolerate the humiliation? Or was it that he was too weak to resist the collective expectation of the school and his parents? Whatever the reason, he was choosing to let the 'play' play out. Because as he mounted the stairs to the stage the reason for the mockery became clear – Laycock had a huge wet patch on his groin. Alex must have emptied a full bottle of water into his lap. Even the head, consummate performer that he was, hesitated when he saw the state of Laycock's trousers. But, after a couple of excruciating seconds of very pointed staring, the head recovered. He shook Laycock's hand, muttered the obligatory *well done*, then started the applause. Slowly the audience joined in, which resulted in Laycock having to leave the stage and walk back to his seat to the sound of a slow handclap. How Alex kept a straight face through it all Bobby didn't know.

But there was worse to come – a problem that the collective 'intelligence' of the supposedly eminent teaching faculty of King Henry's didn't seem to register. Laycock had been awarded *four* prizes. Hence three more times Laycock's name was called. Three more times he rose and made his way slowly to the stage. Three more times the boys sneered and tittered. Three more times the head kept his gaze high and his praise brief. And three more times Laycock returned to his seat to the sound of ironic applause. But on his fourth return he didn't lower himself meekly and wretchedly into his seat – instead he paused. He passed his latest award to Okoro, then, without warning, launched himself at Alex. The noise of chairs clattering to the floor and boys colliding with each other in the rush to get out of the way was loud, but not as loud as Laycock. Everyone in the hall heard him scream, 'You fucking arsehole, Alex Archer!' There followed an ungainly wrestle. The grunting, puffing, piglike noises echoed around the vaulted hall, punctuated by urgent instructions from a number of the staff to *cease, this instant* and by a number of the parents tutting. The kerfuffle seemed to go on forever, and yet also to be over in seconds. It was, of course, Mr Jacks who put a stop to it. He waded in, pulled them apart and frogmarched them both out of the hall. Amidst embarrassed coughing and chair-scraping, the head concluded his speech with a speed and brevity that was appreciated by all.

The garden party went ahead as planned, but without the head in attendance for the first half-hour, the correct assumption being that he was needed elsewhere, to tear a few strips off the two boys who had not only disgraced themselves, but also, far more importantly, disgraced the school. When he did finally appear, as smiling and urbane as ever, the incident was not spoken of – at least not within his vicinity – but as soon as he moved on to chat about the school's grand plans for the coming year with another group of bored parents, it *was* discussed, at length, and with varying degrees of glee, disgust and, very occasionally, sympathy. Of Jonathan Laycock and Alex Archer there was no sign. Nor did the parents of either boy put in an appearance. Bobby only managed to slip away from his own mother after a very tedious hour by claiming that he hadn't finishing packing – about which she chided him.

Bobby headed up to the dorms. He was looking for Alex, not Laycock.

Alex's stuff was in his room, so he must still be on school premises, somewhere. Tempting as it was, Bobby didn't look through Alex's trunk. Instead he thought about the hiding places around the school that a person might seek out after a roasting from the head. One such place was the supplies cupboard in the art room. And sure enough, that was where Bobby found Alex, sitting on the floor, his knees drawn up to his chest, his arms resting on them, his head down, the pale nape of his neck visible. He was a compact square of what – anger or shame? His pose certainly didn't shout triumph.

'You okay?'

Alex lifted his chin. 'Yeah. Why wouldn't I be?'

Bobby noted the aggression, but didn't respond to it. 'No reason.'

But Alex didn't get up off the floor, which undercut his claim to being fine. They eyed each other, both trying to suss out the next move. Bobby noticed the livid red mark on Alex's cheek and his split lip. Bobby doubted that the damage was weedy Laycock's doing. Their coming together had been more of a scuffle than an actual fight. Physical punishment then, meted out swiftly and sharply. But by who? Bowker's MO was verbal batterings rather than physical ones; whether this was down to personal preference or the fear of prosecution was unclear. Neither of the boys said anything, nor did either of them leave. Bobby hoisted himself up onto the counter and sat, swinging his legs. The cupboard smelt strongly of white spirit. 'Did Bowker tear you a new one?'

Alex picked up a tube of glue and started stripping lumps of residue off the nozzle. 'Nah. He just banged on about the importance of knowing the right time and place for *high jinks*.'

It made sense. The head knew all about the 'plays', but he never made any attempt to put a stop to them, never mind bring the ringleaders to heel. But if Bowker had been his usual ineffectual self, who had thumped Alex? 'So what are you doing hiding up here on your own?'

Something dark flashed across Alex's eyes. 'I'm not hiding.'

'Okay. Whatever.' But Bobby refused to take the hint and leave. He watched Alex flick globs of glue around the cupboard. The mark on his cheek showed no sign of fading.

From experience, Bobby knew that it would bruise. 'Was it your mum or your dad?' he asked.

Alex stilled. 'What?'

'Who smacked you in the gob?'

Alex lobbed the tube of glue at the shelves. It skittled over some cans of spray paint. The silence that followed the crash was loaded. Bobby didn't rush him. There was no need. They'd crossed a line, into the scary, exposed no-man's-land of home truths. 'It's the humiliation that's the worst, isn't it?' Alex didn't respond. Bobby kept his tone conversational. 'My father wears a signet ring on the pinkie finger of his left hand. He's right-handed, but if he's extra pissed off with me, he'll swap it over.' Bobby raised his hand to his brow. His eyebrow still didn't grow normally because of the scar tissue.

Alex met Bobby's gaze at last. Recognition. Bobby bided his time. Finally the dam broke. Alex's indignation came out in a gush. 'My mum and dad just sat there, in total silence, while Bowker waffled on. Then my mum apologised for my behaviour and my dad offered to sponsor a prize next year. It was all very polite. They waited until Bowker left, then my dad said, and I quote, *We sent you here to learn how to behave like a gentleman, not a fucking five-year-old.* Then he backhanded me.'

Bobby contemplated his response. Risked it. 'Well, I hate to say it, but he has got a point.'

Alex did a double-take. Then, to Bobby's relief, he laughed. A short, sharp bark of shock and release. The tension dropped out of their exchange. 'Yeah. Maybe.' He raised his hand and touched his swollen lip, finally acknowledging the blow. 'It's the last time I'm going to do anything that bloody Gus Harwood suggests.'

Bobby jumped down off his perch and extended his hand to Alex. 'Lesson learnt, then.'

Alex took Bobby's hand and allowed himself to be hauled up off the floor. 'Cheers.'

They walked back to the dorms together. At the stairwell they parted.

'See you next term,' Bobby said.

Alex smiled. 'Yeah – if the bastards don't kill us both first.'

Most of the boys gave Bobby a wide berth when he returned to King Henry's in the September. News of his father's death had got round. It made most of the boys uneasy. Any emotion, especially a big, uncomfortable one like grief, scared them. Not Alex. They opted for the supplies cupboard again – something about that narrow, confined space seemed to allow confidences to be shared. Alex went straight to the point. 'So what happened?' His directness was a welcome change after all the feet-shuffling and eye-avoidance.

Bobby kept it simple. 'He had a stroke.'

'Shit.'

'Yeah.'

'Out of the blue?'

'Yeah. Although I suppose there were warning signs. The perpetual rage, for example.'

'Did he . . . ?' Alex didn't go on.

'It's okay. I don't mind you asking. Apart from my mum, no one else seems to want to talk about it. You should have heard Bowker's little pastoral care speech. It was embarrassing.'

'I bet it was. The guy's a twat.'

Alex wasn't wrong. 'So, what were you going to ask?'

'Did he die straightaway?'

'No. Well, yes, in that he was dead by the time the ambulance arrived.'

'You were with him?'

'Yeah.'

'Shit. Sorry, that must have been tough.'

'Actually, I'm glad I was there. Better than him dying on his own.' They were both silent for a minute. 'It was sort of good, in a weird kinda way. We had a chance to say goodbye. He said he was sorry for riding me so hard. Said it was the way he'd been brought up.' Bobby paused. 'He must have known he was in trouble because he told me he loved me. I don't remember him ever saying that before. It's a bit shit it took a stroke to force it out of him, like, but what are you gonna do?'

Alex dipped his head in acknowledgement. 'How do you feel?'

It was *so* not a King Henry's question – which was why Bobby appreciated Alex asking it. He paused, thought. He remembered the coffin being lowered into the ground, his mother and a bunch of his father's work colleagues standing in the rain, everyone with mud on their freshly shone shoes; he could hear the drip of rain on the umbrellas and the drone of the priest; he could remember the wet handle of the trowel with the earth piled on it that he'd flung into the hole, the hollow thud as it hit the coffin; but he couldn't conjure up any emotion. 'If I'm honest, I feel okay.'

For a split second Alex had looked shocked, but Bobby wasn't going to lie. 'I know he was my dad, but he was a nasty bastard. Life's going to be a lot easier now he's gone.'

Alex blinked, absorbed Bobby's confession, then put his arm around Bobby's shoulders and pulled him in for a hug. 'I get it. If my old man went, I think I'd feel the same.'

The sight of Alex waiting for him by the lake all these years later made Bobby smile. Seventeen years on, and their friendship was as valuable to Bobby now as it had been then. More so, probably.

They greeted each other with a bear hug. Alex stripped off his shirt and Bobby quickly changed into his swimming trunks. Ready, they walked out along the jetty. The water was glassy, black. It looked deep. 'How cold is it?' Bobby asked.

Alex grinned and took off running. 'Fucking freezing,' he yelled as he jumped.

Bobby had no option, as he so often hadn't in the past, but to leap in after him.

Chapter 7

LOU

Colette led Maddie and Lou around the side of the main building and along a path flanked by palms in huge terracotta pots. The tower rose up in front of them, part imposing guardian, part lookout post. The fairy story overtones intensified. At the foot of the tower Colette produced a huge bunch of keys. Lou resisted the urge to make a gaoler joke. Colette selected the biggest key and slid it into the keyhole. To enhance the Disney impression, the big wooden door made a satisfying creak as it swung inwards.

Lou and Maddie stepped inside and the sense of being transported onto a film set was further strengthened. They found themselves standing in what looked like a man-made cave. A stone staircase rose up from the flagged floor. There were two doors, but Colette ignored them and started to climb. They followed her. Weirdly, the stairwell seemed to widen as they rose. After two turns they came to a halt. On this level there was a single door. Colette opened it. They stepped into a large darkened room. Colette crossed the floor and started unhooking the shutters. She pushed them open with a bang, one after another, letting in the shafts of sunlight.

'Wow.' It slipped out before Lou could stop herself.

Colette barely paused. 'There's a sitting room, two bedrooms,' she indicated the layout of the suite like an air stewardess, 'and two bathrooms. I thought you'd like to be together.' She didn't add, 'for your last two nights of freedom', but the implication was there. Lou looked at Colette, but she refused to meet her eye. She'd noticed that Colette did that a lot, avoided direct eye contact. It was an effective habit if your aim was to protect whatever thoughts lay behind your calm, implacable exterior. Lou found Colette interesting and provoking, precisely because she appeared to be neither.

'Thank you,' Maddie murmured.

They walked Colette to the door. She handed them each a keycard. 'For the suite. I suggest we leave the bottom door open, if that's okay with you.' She didn't wait for an answer. 'We only have one master key for the tower, because of the age of the lock, and I'm loath to let it out of my sight. Besides, you're perfectly safe at the finca. I'll leave you to get settled.'

It was then that Lou noticed someone had strung a satin ribbon across the stairwell leading to the upper floors of the tower. 'Is the bridal suite out of bounds, then?' she asked, hoping to provoke a reaction.

Colette turned. 'Yes. We've set aside the apartment on the floor above as your dressing space for the wedding, Maddie. It'll be perfect for the hairdresser and the stylist. Plenty of natural light. And your dress has already been installed, out of the sun, of course. The actual bridal suite is another two flights up, at the very top of the tower . . . to make the most of the views.'

'And to guarantee some privacy.' Lou didn't know why she winked, like an old comedian telling a nudge-nudge joke. Yes, she did, it was discomfort, with the whole set-up and at being with Colette.

But Colette didn't so much as blink. 'Well, I'll see you at dinner. If not before.' Without waiting for a response, she disappeared down the stairs.

Instinctively, Maddie and Lou waited until the staccato hammer of her heels had faded away before either of them spoke.

'Fucking hell, girl, we're not in Kansas any more.'

Maddie grinned. 'No shit, Sherlock.'

Lou's heart lifted. Oh, it was so good to hear Maddie swear. They fell back into their palatial suite, giggling like idiots.

Chapter 8

COLETTE

Colette only went as far as the turn in the stairs. She heard the laughter the minute she was out of sight, and the sound of the door slamming. She gave it another few minutes before she retraced her steps back up to their landing. Through the door she heard the thump of music, what sounded like the pop of a cork, then another burst of laughter – this time from Maddie. Lou seemed to be the only person who could make Maddie loosen up. Well, becoming Mrs Archer would likely put a stop to that easy friendship. Lou and the Archers? Now there was a combination that was never going to work; Colette couldn't envisage Lou being invited back to share in any future family gatherings. As Colette stood like a spy listening to Lou and Maddie having a good time on the other side of the door, she felt a queasy mix of shame and jealousy. This was another reason why Alex's wedding was a nightmare for her – at every turn there were reminders of the contrast between the narrowness of her life and the breadth and richness of other people's.

Given that she was already in the tower, Colette decided that she might as well check that everything was in order upstairs. She didn't trust Luther to have stocked the drinks fridge correctly. When he was around alcohol, especially the good stuff, bottles, indeed on occasion whole crates, had been known to go walkabout. Besides, Colette reasoned, if she checked the dressing room now it would save her a job the following day. She ducked under the ribbon and took off her shoes before climbing up the staircase, not wanting to be heard by Maddie and Lou. She unlocked the suite on the upper floor and slipped inside, leaving her shoes by the door. Again the shutters were closed, but even in the half-light the room looked lovely. Colette had been surprised by how much she'd enjoyed choosing the decor for the interiors at the finca. The irony that, at thirty-three, she'd never so much as rented, never mind owned, her own home, and therefore hadn't ever been able to decorate her own place, wasn't lost on her. She'd always lived in rooms in her parents' houses, or 'above the shop', and she'd never cared about those spaces. But at the Finca Encantata her imagination and her talents had been given free rein. True, it was within a very strict brief, namely 'romantic luxury', but a good designer could always fulfil the client's vision, even if it was a million miles away from their own tastes. She scanned the room. The fridge was correctly stocked and the stemware was all spotlessly clean, which was a nice surprise. It appeared that Luther could, occasionally, be trusted to do things as instructed. She checked the bathroom. It all looked in order. The flower arrangements for the rooms were ready and waiting in the separate cold room that they'd had specially built for the wedding flowers. It was one of the most important pieces of kit at the finca. Importing thousands of hothouse flowers and keeping them looking their best in the heat was one of the biggest challenges. This weekend, aside from the bouquets for the bride, bridesmaids, flower girl and the mother of the groom – there was no mother of the bride – there were the hundreds of separate blooms and the swathes of greenery that would be needed to dress the courtyard for the ceremony itself, plus all the centrepieces for tables at the wedding feast, oh, and the arrangements for this room and the bridal suite. Attacked by a sudden stab of tiredness, Colette pulled out the chair from beneath the dressing table and sat in the bridal hot seat, her back to the mirror – correction – mirrors; there were four of them in total, all the better to enable a 360° view. She gazed at Maddie's dress. It was, objectively, exquisite.

Despite it being way beyond her remit, it had fallen to Colette to organise the wedding-dress shopping trip. 'It just makes sense, darling, given you already have everyone's contact details. And, besides, you know how hopeless I am when it comes to texting and emailing people.' Her mother's fake incompetence infuriated Colette. Marilyn was perfectly capable, as she demonstrated within the business, often to devasting effect; it was simply that she deemed certain tasks beneath her. And doing anything for anyone, including her future daughter-in-law, definitely fell into that category. After all, what was the point of having staff if you didn't use them?

And it had, in essence, been a simple enough task. A shopping expedition followed by a nice, late lunch in central London for the bride, her maid of honour, her two bridesmaids, Ruby and Priya, and the mother-in-law-to-be. As with any trip to London for the Archers, there would be business done while they were over, so there were those meetings to coordinate as well. But it would all have been relatively straightforward for Colette to organise, if the bride hadn't seemed so reluctant to commit. Colette had her suspicions, at the time, that Maddie's hesitancy was less reticence about picking a dress and more pushback at the wedding being so thoroughly managed by Alex's family. Well, good luck with that! Once she was an Archer she would discover that personal choice was something of an illusion. Whatever the real cause of Maddie's hesitation, it had made things tricky for Colette. First Maddie struggled to provide any midweek dates due to *work commitments* – at a job in a coffee shack that she was leaving in a matter of months! This was followed by weeks of indecision about which shops she wanted to visit. She emailed Colette to apologise and explain that she was hoping to find something 'a bit less traditional' and was, therefore, nervous of going to 'a classic boutique' – or some such bollocks. Colette had skim-read her messages, bored to the bone and frustrated. Did Maddie think the world revolved around her? Probably. In Colette's experience, most brides did.

In the end Colette did what she did best; she went ahead with arrangements as she saw fit. She booked appointments at three bridal boutiques for the first Friday in December and included, as a gesture to Maddie, a more alternative shop in Shoreditch. The plan was for them to meet for coffee at 9.30 a.m., get the 'Maddie-placatory' Shoreditch option out of the way first, then head to Mirror, Mirror in Islington. The last appointment was at Cala, in Fulham, Marilyn's preferred boutique, by which point any remnants of Maddie's resistance would be in tatters. A late lunch at The Doyen, around the corner from Cala, would complete the day's mission. Success being that a hand-made gown from Cala would be in the bag, or rather on order, charged to her mother's Amex.

On the day Colette tried to duck out of attending, but a look from her mother and a noise from her father from behind his newspaper had put an end to that hope.

The place in Shoreditch was actually quite nice, but it was not where Maddie's dress was going to be bought. Still, they went through the motions with their glasses of pro-secco and their positive comments. Colette noticed that both her mother and Ruby only pretended to drink their heavily chilled fizz. Maddie was clueless about what she wanted, even with some good advice from the owner, and as a result tried on lots of dresses in wildly varying styles: vestal virgin, milkmaid, vamp, extra in a BBC costume drama. It slightly shocked Colette to realise that she had an opinion, but then, she had seen enough wedding gowns in her time to know what she liked and what she detested – despite having no intention of ever wearing one herself. The shop had a nice enough range, but there was noth-ing that stood out. There again, there wouldn't be with mass-produced, off-the-peg dresses. Ruby declined to try on any of the bridesmaid dresses in the Shoreditch shop, which was rude, but as expected. Maddie eventually picked out a shortlist of two, both wrong. Much to Marilyn's and Ruby's relief, the cars were summoned to whisk them off to Islington.

Mirror Mirror was far more high-end and the dresses were all beautiful, but still Maddie seemed at a loss. Onwards they progressed to Cala, their last hope. There a softly spoken, elegant Frenchwoman saved the day. She took Maddie away saying she'd selected just two dresses that she hoped would be *parfait*.

By some alchemy she was right. The first dress was 'the one'. It was obvious to everyone, including a by then achingly bored Colette, the minute Maddie stepped out of the dressing room. She looked simply stunning in it. It was a long-sleeved, plunge-front, backless lace gown that the owner of the shop had paired with a gossamer-thin veil and delicate oyster silk slippers. The overall effect was a cross between a fairy-tale bride and a siren.

Colette remembered looking at the other women rather than at Maddie as she twirled slowly, like a ballerina in a child's jewellery box, showing off her loveliness to her assembled entourage. Colette sought out her mother first. People sometimes commented that she and Marilyn were similar, not in terms of their physical appearance, but their expressions. Looking at her mother now, Colette saw what they meant. Marilyn's face subtly, but unmistakably, radiated simultaneous approval and disdain. It was hard to say how she managed it. The smile on her lips indicated assent, the incline of the head expressed a degree of interest and the adjectives she was using to describe the dress were all positive, but somehow the overall effect was unnervingly judgemental. Colette glanced at herself in one of the many mirrors, trying to catch herself out. But, of course, that was impossible. What she saw on her own face was indifference rather than disapproval; fatigue, not criticism. Staying with the reflections in the glass, rather than the reality – it was easier to observe the others that way – she looked at Priya next, her brother's innocuous, very pretty single friend. Unlike Colette and her mother, Priya had succumbed to the romance of lace and satin. She was leaning forward, her eyes shining, her lips parted. She was drinking in the gown almost as if she wanted to ingest it, her expression one of yearning. Poor Priya, a no doubt lovely, but suitably understated bridesmaid dress awaited her. Always the bridesmaid, never the bride? Colette wondered. Then there was Lou, Maddie's spiky best friend, who, despite her current surliness, had been no hassle in terms of arrangements for the day. In fact, she'd been the most responsive and accommodating of them all. When she'd said, 'Whatever works for Maddie', she'd meant it. Her reaction was perhaps the most interesting. Because, despite her loud, crude protestations that weddings were *a total waste of time and money* and marriage was *an anachronistic and sexist institution*, the minute Maddie emerged from the dressing room Lou had fallen silent. She'd sat up very straight as if she was about to be tested. Her expression, which had been unrelentingly scornful all morning, had softened. It was like seeing a totally different person emerge, as if seeing Maddie as the classic, beautiful bride had cast some sort of spell on her. It wasn't too much of a leap to read her expression as a confession – of love and pain. In that moment it was obvious to Colette that Lou wasn't simply Maddie's best friend.

There was a loud thud. It sounded like a sofa being shunted backwards. Lou flopping down on it, jumping on it, larking about? They'd better not be marking the floors. Yes, a lot had happened since the elegant Frenchwoman had plucked Maddie's wedding dress from the ranks of other beautiful gowns and decreed it 'the one'. Spend enough and you really could buy the perfect fit – but the world of haute couture was simpler than life.

Colette got to her feet. She walked over to the man- nequin. Tentatively at first, she stroked the bodice of Maddie's dress, felt the intricate whorls of the handmade lace beneath her fingertips. It truly was a labour of love. The hand-stitching was so fine that it was impossible to see any of the seams – it was as if the dress was one organic whole. The cut was exquisite. It hugged the stand-in bride perfectly. The veil was even more delicate. It seemed to float rather than fall into a pool on the floor. Colette lifted a section of it, let the tulle slip and slide through her fin- gers. The tension in her body built up. Her hands curled into fists. She yanked at the fragile fabric. It would be so easy to tear the whole fucking thing to pieces. The urge to dismember the dress was overwhelming. A mad rush of destruction. It would be such a glorious release of all the pent-up emotions that she carried within her.

But, of course, Colette did no such thing.

She let the veil fall back into position, returned Maddie's dress to its pristine loveliness. Then she retraced her steps out of the suite and down the stairs, her shoes in her hands and her secrets in her heart.

It doesn't take me long to shower and change, but I have more incentive than the rest to arrive early to the party. I want to assess the 'lie of the land'. It's an odd phrase. I like it. It conjures up an image of the ground as a living thing, with a will of its own, something capable of working with you, or against you, laying down a smooth path to ease your progress or deliberately bunching up to create trip hazards for the unwary. And I am wary. I have no intention of stumbling and revealing myself.

There's no denying it, I'm as easily seduced by romance as the next person and the setting for this evening's event is, without question, bewitching. Tables and chairs have been 'planted' in amongst the olive trees. Each table is covered with a crisp white cloth and anchored by a cluster of waxy cream roses and glossy greenery. The flowers look sumptuous and rich, but still natural, as if they've grown up through the tables. The cutlery and crockery shine. Someone has gone to the considerable effort of threading thousands upon thousands of tiny white lights through the branches of the trees, creating a canopy of stars. It's an oasis of warmth and light, which is all the more appealing given that it's encircled by almost total darkness. To add a Bacchanalian touch there's a large table in the middle laden with food and

81

drink. Too much, surely. But I suppose that's the point of a feast – excess. There are platters of charcuterie and cheeses, wooden boards piled high with crusty loaves and savoury tarts topped with asparagus and slices of blood-red vine tomatoes. There are two cooked whole chickens, a leg of ham suspended on a special stand into which someone has plunged a huge knife, and there are numerous cut-glass salvers filled with figs, cherries, peaches, lychees and raspberries. On a separate table under one of the trees sits the booze – a jostle of ice buckets and wine bottles, that shine by the light of the trees and the candles. It's perfect. It almost seems a shame to spoil it by adding guests.

I'm about to return to my room – it's important that I appear with everyone else, like everyone else – when my attention snags on something. There's a shadow, moving along the ground. No, it's not a shadow. It's a cat. It is tar black. Scrawny. Feral? The cat slides past the banquet table as if uninterested. It goes a few paces, heading back into the darkness, then stops. It looks around. It's in no hurry, but it is alert. It hasn't seen me. I stand completely still, go to the place inside me that's quiet and calm and closed off. I wait. Patience is one of my virtues. Satisfied it's safe, the cat turns and springs, like a splash of ink, from the ground onto the food-laden table. I expect it to grab some morsel and flee, but I'm wrong. It takes a moment to look round then delicately places its front paws, one followed by the other, into a space on the pristine tablecloth, like a ballet dancer taking up their position. I know I should shoo it away from the food. I don't. It stretches – head low, tail high. A precursor to action? I pray that no one arrives and disturbs it. I want to see how this plays out.

Stretch complete, the cat begins its journey through the feast, stepping its paws carefully in between the cheeses and the salads, sniffing as it goes. It is selecting its dinner. After a few seconds it pauses and I see its small, precise, whiskered jaws open. There's a flash of a salmon-pink tongue, then it sinks its yellow teeth into the tart. It bites off a lump and lifts its head to swallow. The delicacy is not to the cat's liking because I hear a wet cough. An eggy gobbet is returned to the tart. The cat moves on. It sniffs, considers, rejects, accepts, dips its head, chews on some cheese, lowers its paw into one of the salads. Thinks better of it. The regular flash of its teeth and tongue and its failure to linger are a sure sign that nothing, as yet, meets its needs. I try to guess where next . . . surely the chicken or the jamon serrano. I'm pleased to be proved right. At the ham the cat settles on its bony haunches and proceeds to tuck in, ripping with its sharp teeth, tearing off lumps of meat, swallowing without chewing. I watch appalled and fascinated as it slakes its hunger.

'Vete! Vete! Pequeno bastardo!' It's one of the waiters, waving his arms around.

We both jump. Me, backwards into the darkness. The cat, off the table, its now full belly flapping, scrotum-like, beneath its spine.

The waiter's furious indignation is the cue for us both to scram.

Chapter 9

ALEX

After some thought Alex opted for linen trousers and a slim-fit shirt, no jacket – casual, but still smart. Unlike his earlier rendezvous with Bobby, the purpose of this meeting by the lake was not pleasure. In his father's world there was always business to be done – a wedding was no exception. But this evening was different because this time Alex wasn't simply there as set dressing, a prop to demonstrate how far the Archers had come. This evening he had a vested interest in the scheming.

As Alex checked himself in the mirror, he felt a pang of guilt. There were benefits to having a room to himself. Freedom to sneak off for a while being one of them. If Maddie had been with him she would, understandably, have wanted to know where he was going and who he was meeting up with. And he would have had to lie. Their future was riding on how things went over the next twenty-four hours, but he wasn't ready to tell her about his plans just yet – not until everything was agreed. He smoothed his hair, set his shoulders and slipped out of his room. It was time for Alex to prove that he had something that his father did not.

The rumble of male voices and the glow of Paul's cigar set the tone on the terrace. It was no longer a place for sunbathing. His father and his contacts had transformed it into an open-air gentleman's club, complete with the pungent notes of tobacco, expensive aftershave and greed. Some people carried their universes with them wherever they went. Mateus Torres Alex knew, he'd been around since the early days. Teddy Largos he did not, but he knew of him. Both men were big fish, not as big as Ray, obviously, but landing them mattered if they were going to be able to proceed at the scale they wanted to. Alex understood that it was imperative that he made a good impression. These soft-looking men with hard eyes had the power to change his fortune and his future. In a clear demonstration of the pecking order, Ray had opted to sit on one of the fancy stone benches that were dotted along the terrace, the king on his throne. Mateus and Teddy had pulled up a couple of sun loungers on which they hunkered, somewhat awkwardly, and Paul was pacing with the impatience of a go-between with skin in the game – which was exactly what he was. Paul was always on the lookout for a juicy percentage. When Alex joined them there was a general grasping and shaking of hands. Teddy was the bone-crusher in the group. There was always one. Alex chose to perch on the low wall that ran behind the stone benches. This positioned him next to, but slightly lower than his father – lineage claimed and deference paid in the simple act of sitting down. In some ways their little gathering was no different to the meetings he had at Stonehaven – it was still all egos and money. These were the levers that made the world go round, wherever you were and whoever was 'in the room'. For a moment they all looked out across the glassy surface of the lake, taking in the beauty of the setting, or least silenced by it.

Then Ray set the ball rolling.

It was time for Alex to make his pitch.

Chapter 10

MADDIE

The party in the olive grove was in full swing, but Maddie was outside the flow. She'd suffered from these social outages for most of her life. Her mother had tried to convince her that they were her superpower. Kath had said that being an observer gave you an advantage. Maddie wondered whether her mother had sensed that her daughter's wiring was different from other people's and had – out of love – decided to frame what was really a handicap as an advantage.

It was an affliction that she was trying hard to break.

Being with Alex had changed things dramatically for Maddie. For the first time in her life, Maddie felt safe. She was loved, she was about to become part of Alex's family, they might have children of their own before too long and she was financially secure – to an extent she'd never dreamed possible. This security meant that her approach to relationships, to life itself, had shifted. She no longer needed to see people as a resource from which she could extract cash or favours. Now they could be friends and relatives. Alex was good for her. His full-throttle 'here and now'ness had a magnetic quality that pulled her in and along with him. He lived his life expecting good stuff to happen, and it often did. This confident optimism was one of the many reasons she was marrying him. She didn't want to be an outsider any more; she didn't want to scheme and hustle; she wanted to live, to feel, to go with the flow – like he did.

But after everything that had happened in the run-up to the wedding, Maddie found that, even in paradise, she couldn't fully relax. Not unless Alex was physically close by. And currently he was on the far side of the party sitting with Bobby. They were laughing and joking like teenagers, revelling in being back together, no doubt riffing on each other's faults. Piss-take as affection, the default setting of so many men. Instinctively, Maddie turned and looked for her own lodestone, Lou. But she was – surprisingly, given the quality and quantity of alcohol on offer – nowhere to be seen. She'd said she needed to make a call, but that had been ages ago. Maddie and Lou's relationship was like an inverse mirror image of Alex and Bobby's. Lou was the light to Maddie's shade, whereas with the boys the roles were reversed. Which was why it was so frustrating that Lou and Alex didn't get on – a case of being so similar that neither of them could see it? Maddie worried that the distrust between her best friend and her husband-to-be or, more honestly, their dislike of each other, was going to make holding the two halves of her life together after the wedding hard. But surely those differences didn't have to turn into a rift? She would have a husband, but that didn't mean she didn't still need her friend.

Suddenly there was a shift in the mood of the party. A slow quietening. People's voices faded. The clatter of

cutlery fell silent. Single sounds stood out. The fizz of bubbles in a glass. Something winged flapping through the
branches of the trees. Faces lifted and searched beyond
their immediate social circle. Maddie followed their gaze
and saw the object of interest.

It was Ruby. Arriving late, and in style.

She sashayed down the path through the trees, an
undulation of femaleness. Under the lights her hair looked
raven black, her skin glowing. Her dress was virginal white,
loose, deceptively simple. As she walked it rippled, creating
a clear silhouette of the body beneath. Full breasts, nipples
visible, curving waist, slim hips. The overall effect, com-
plemented by the repeated flash of her long, tanned legs,
was hypnotic. Maddie watched, waiting to see who would
rise and go to meet her. It was Alex, closely followed by
Bobby. No surprise there – they were the Three Musketeers,
after all – but seeing them embrace, arms wrapped around
each other, a self-contained knot, gave Maddie's treasured
sense of security a severe jolt. Which was both ridiculous,
and understandable. Ruby provoked many reactions, but
nervousness was definitely on the list. Maddie couldn't
hear what was being said, but their greeting surely went on
far longer than was necessary. She looked away, sought out
Lou, remembered that she wasn't there and felt, briefly and
pathetically, abandoned.

'Ruby!' Maddie jumped, shaken out of her reverie by
Ray's booming voice. 'Late, as ever. Come here, and let
me have a proper look at you. I want to see how our very
own Olympic goddess is faring.' Ray's bantering summons
broke up the love-in. Alex's father had risen to his feet and
was holding out his hands, beckoning Ruby to him. Ruby

laughed, tossed a glossy hank of hair over her bronzed shoulder, for all the world like a shampoo ad, and made her way over. There was another embrace, this one observed, at close quarters, by an impassive Marilyn. It struck Maddie that neither of Alex's parents had ever embraced her with such affection or enthusiasm. Maddie didn't expect it of Marilyn; she was not a hugger of anyone, not even of Alex, who was plainly the apple of her eye, but Ray usually couldn't keep his hands to himself. He was the type of man who was forever grasping people by the hand, clapping them on the back, throwing fake punches. It was the way he made his presence felt, literally. A place-setting was laid and Ruby settled herself in between Ray and Marilyn. Alex and Bobby dragged their chairs over and joined in the party. The old gang was back together again.

The rest of the guests returned to their champagne and their conversations, but Maddie continued to watch the dynamic at the table with a growing sense of unease. Seemingly out of nowhere, Lou appeared. At a glance Maddie could tell that she was already quite drunk. In a stage-whisper that drew a glance from Priya, she hissed, 'Only the delectable Miss Ruby Davis would wear white to someone else's wedding.'

'Shush.' Maddie appreciated Lou's presence by her side, but she wished she would keep the volume down. 'It's not the wedding tonight.'

'Oh, come on. I'm only saying what you're thinking.'

Maddie didn't deny it, but she didn't encourage Lou either. The sensation of being snagged on the barbed wire between her past and future lives and loyalties was painful.

'They're very tight, aren't they?' Lou said, observing the

buzz of conversation between Ruby, Bobby, Alex and his parents. She didn't wait to be served by one of the staff, but sloshed some wine into her glass and waggled the bottle at Maddie, offering a top-up.

Maddie put her hand over her own glass. 'Yes. They've known each other a long time.'

'Hmm.' A lot could be communicated by a very small word.

They were all laughing, even Marilyn. Or at least, she appeared to be smiling. It was hard to tell what her true feelings were, given the tightness of her skin and her sphinxlike expression. It hurt that Alex hadn't beckoned Maddie over to join them. Maddie watched Ruby's hands dance, emphasising a point, bringing one then another of them into the conversation, recreating connections, orchestrating everything and everyone. It was fascinating to watch. They looked good together. Relaxed. Right. And most right of all were Alex and Ruby.

Maddie knew the backstory of their friendship. Alex had told her it, with a little prompting, a few months into their own relationship, his manner shouting 'nothing to see here'.

They met when they were sixteen. Ruby was in the first cohort of girls to join the sixth form at King Henry's when the school finally conceded that it was the twenty-first century and went co-ed. The three of them apparently clicked immediately. When Alex talked about their time together at school he smiled. Initially Maddie had been charmed by the pleasure he obviously derived from their friendship and reassured by how important it still was to him after all these years. She wanted her future husband to be capable of making and maintaining meaningful relationships – with women, as well as men. The problem was that Ruby wasn't just another girl, she was gorgeous. Not pretty, not beautiful, but gorgeous, a full-on assault on your senses, and Maddie simply did not believe that friendship snuffed out sexual attraction. They'd argued. It had been their first real fight, but Alex had remained adamant that he'd never thought of Ruby as anything other than a good mate.

Maddie had challenged him. 'But how is that possible? Even I think she's hot.'

She remembered that he'd paused, then said, 'You know how difficult I find it to trust people? Well, Bobby was the first person I ever properly trusted and Ruby was the second. They matter more to me than my family. We chose each other.' He paused, realising his omission, and added, 'And you are the third.' He'd taken her hand. 'It's a very small, exclusive club that you've joined.'

She'd wanted to take him at his word, hadn't wanted to be 'that sort' of girlfriend.

It hadn't been too much of an issue, initially, because Ruby wasn't around. She was away a lot with work, and when she was back in London, she always seemed to be busy. And so, although Alex continued to carry Ruby's photo in his wallet and he was obviously in touch with her, he saw her infrequently and, importantly, he seemed perfectly happy with that. And then Maddie met Ruby at the drinks do that Alex insisted on organising. Maddie tried to talk him out of it, but he said he wanted to introduce her to his friends. They'd been together for six months by this point, not yet living together, but he had mentioned it, more than once. Of course, Alex being Alex, the drinks do turned into a big deal. Instead of simply meeting up in a pub, he went and hired the rooftop bar at the Trafalgar, booked a DJ, laid on food. It was totally OTT.

The first hour was a blur of faces and names, none of which Maddie remembered. She smiled so much her cheeks hurt. When Lou and her other friends arrived that helped. The booze flowed, the tunes kicked in and Maddie started to enjoy herself. She was on the dance floor when Ruby finally rocked up, fashionably late and on her own. Maddie wasn't the only one who noticed. Ruby was like a magnet, drawing everyone's attention. Maddie stopped dancing. In the flesh, Ruby was even more stunning than in her photos. She was tall, glamorous and, most telling of all, totally in possession of herself. The moment held, then it was broken by Alex emerging from the scrum by the bar, crossing the floor. He greeted Ruby with a kiss. Maddie looked away. Her gaze snagged on Bobby. He smiled. She stepped off the dance floor and made her way over to him, turning her back on Ruby and Alex.

'Great moves!' He raised his glass in salute.

'Thanks.' Maddie thumped down into the empty seat next to him. 'You not dancing?'

'Hell, no. No one needs to see that.' There was a beat. They really didn't know each other that well. They'd had the occasional meal out together and Bobby had been round to the apartment a few times when Maddie had been there, but that was it.

'Alex is in his element, isn't he?' Bobby said. They both glanced at the bar. Alex and Ruby had been absorbed into the group.

93

'Has he always been this sociable?' Maddie asked.

Bobby scratched his ear. 'You mean so much more popular than me?'

'Sorry, that wasn't what I meant . . .' Maddie stuttered.

But Bobby laughed. 'No need to apologise. I am sitting in a dark corner, at a party, on my own – quite happily. What can I say? Opposites attract.' He took a sip of his beer. 'He puts himself out more than me, wants people to have a good time. It's his way of feeling part of things. Me, I think other people's happiness is their own responsibility.' Alex and Ruby definitely looked happy in that moment. Bobby must have followed the direction of her gaze. 'Is this your first exposure to Ruby up close and personal?'

Maddie blushed. It was like he could read her mind. 'Yes.' She shifted her attention to him.

Bobby had sat back in his chair and raised an eyebrow. 'And?'

'What?'

He smiled again. He had a nice smile. He was mocking her, but gently. 'I'm not daft. I've seen the Ruby Effect in action for years.' Maddie held her tongue. 'You're worried that there's history between Ruby and Alex.' She flushed even redder. 'I get it. People look at Ruby and see sex, specifically her having sex with *anyone* she wants to.' Maddie said nothing. She couldn't deny that was exactly what she'd been imagining. He went on, saving her from having to deny it. 'Therefore, it would be unnatural if those mental images didn't, on occasion, feature Alex. Am I right?' She nodded and waited, praying he would tell her that her concerns were baseless. He didn't. 'They are both ridiculously good-looking – in that they are, patently, well matched.

94

People always assume they're a couple. Have done ever since our King Henry days. They were prom king and queen, you know, two years running, and that's just greedy, isn't it?' He smiled again, then seemed to realise that this new snippet of information was hardly reassuring, given certain prom traditions. 'It will come as no surprise to you that no one, and I mean literally no one, has ever thought that me and Ruby were an item.' Maddie was going to say something nice, but Bobby held up his hand, signalling not to bother. 'But, as far as I know, they've never . . .' she leant forward, 'done the deed. They love each other. *We* love each other. We're best friends. End of.' It was a surprisingly direct admission. He wasn't finished. 'I think what makes us close is that we all have what could politely be described as problematic relationships with our families. We understand the damage that bad parenting wreaks. It's a bond. An important one.' He reached for his drink. 'Does that put your mind at rest?'

Maddie nodded, and some of the heat left her face and her heart. The feeling that lingered was embarrassment.

Bobby must have sensed it. 'Maddie, listen, if it helps, I've seen his other relationships at close quarters, and none of them have come close to his connection with you.'

Maddie had a sudden, very uncharacteristic urge – which was to hug this man that she barely knew. So she did, much to the surprise of both of them.

It was at that point that Maddie and Bobby's relationship shifted up a gear. He was no longer just Alex's friend, he was hers as well.

And so he had proved to be, through the good and the bad times, ever since.

Maddie looked at Bobby now, sitting surrounded by Alex, his parents and Ruby. She was glad she had at least one ally within the Archer camp.

After what felt like an age, but was probably no more than a quarter of an hour, Alex remembered that he had a wife-to-be. He came and ushered Maddie over to his family. It was Bobby who gave up his seat for her. Once she was ensconced at the table, Ray got to his feet and tapped a knife against a wine glass, demanding quiet and attention.

'Thank you. Thank you.' His audience settled. 'First of all, I want to welcome you all to the Finca Encantata. *Mi casa es su casa.*' There was a murmur of appreciation for his generosity. 'We are gathered here . . .' it was odd to hear Ray channelling his inner vicar, 'to celebrate the union of Alex and Maddie.' Someone whooped, probably Tom or Charlie. Ray continued. 'And to celebrate family. Those of you who know me, and I like to think that's all of you, know how important family is to me. It's the bedrock of everything we do. And extending that family is a good thing. A very good thing.' He paused and smiled at Maddie. She smiled back. 'To that end, there's something I'd like to announce, before we move on to the real business of the weekend, and by that, I do mean the wedding.' He chuckled, signalling self-deprecation. It didn't quite wash. 'It's something that I have every hope will strengthen and sustain Alex and Maddie as they set out on the exciting journey of creating a family of their own.' There was another whoop. Tom or Charlie really did need to learn to read the room, or in this case olive grove, better. Ray was unfazed. 'As you all know, Alex has been making his way in the shark-infested waters of the financial markets for a good few years now, learning how the real money-makers operate. He's done well, built an impressive portfolio of blue-chip and tech companies and, as a result, he was made an associate partner at Stonehaven Trading last year. We,' a nod to Marilyn, 'are very proud of him.' There was a smattering of applause. 'But Alex feels that the time has come for him to spread his wings.' This was news to Maddie. 'And we want to help him do that. To this end *we*, as in Greenwich Holdings, namely myself and a couple of my oldest business partners,' here he gestured at the fat man with the thin, much younger girlfriend and the quiet Spanish man with the elegant, age-appropriate wife, 'are going to be the first, but we sincerely hope not the only clients, of . . . drumroll please . . . Archer Asset Management.' Ray picked up his glass. 'So, can I ask you to raise your glasses.' The guests followed suit, including Maddie, because what else could she do without looking clueless? 'To new ventures . . . of the heart and the pocket . . . or should I say, the offshore account!'

Chapter 11

LOU

Later, in the dark, sobering hours of the sleepless night that was to come, Lou would blame her outburst on her brief encounter in the courtyard; on the smothering loveliness of the party in the olive grove; on the sight of her best friend, tucked in amongst that bunch of smug tossers; and on the second bottle of wine that she'd finished off with the meal, all by herself, on top of the champagne she'd drunk back at the tower – oh, and on the cava at lunchtime.

Hence, when Alex's father's speech finally came to an end, Lou reached for one of the discarded napkins, wiped the sweat off her forehead, pulled her rumpled top straight and rose unsteadily to her feet. All eyes turned to her. Giving the other guests another reason to hate her couldn't do any harm. She knew they didn't really want her there. She was the messy blot on this sanitised, perfectly scripted performance. But she had a role to play in this charade, whether she, or they, wanted her to or not. So why shouldn't she take this opportunity to perform her maid of honour duties ... by reminding them that this fucking lovely wedding, in their fucking amazing castle, paid for by their obscene piles of fucking wealth wasn't all about their fucking son. Other people mattered!

Everyone waited, their less-than-friendly attention on her.

Fuck it! Lou swayed as she got to her feet, but she wasn't going be deterred by a little dizziness. She saw Maddie signal for her to sit down, but she ignored her. This was a modern wedding, after all; surely that meant that the women should be *allowed* to speak as well. She held onto the back of a chair, raised her empty glass and added, with real feeling, 'And . . . to true love!' It was only as the words came out of her mouth that Lou remembered the last time such a toast had been made and the nightmare that had followed. Judging by the horrified look on the other guests' faces, she wasn't the only one.

The Valentine's party had been Alex's idea and, as with all her fiancé's OTT ideas, a painfully loved-up Maddie had gone along with it. Her desperation to fit in with Alex's crowd was hard for Lou to witness, but she accepted the invitation nonetheless. As strained as their friendship was by this point, Lou still wanted to be part of Maddie's life.

A private room at a club called Blink in Kensington had been hired, catering was being laid on and they were to have their own DJ. Alex had even commissioned the bar staff to create a bespoke cocktail for the evening. He went for blood-orange Valentini with 24-carat gold flecks.

Ruby surprised everyone by offering to host the pre-drinks for 'the girls'. Getting ready at Ruby's place was a last-minute addition to the plan. Lou never did get to the bottom of who suggested it. Maddie said it was nice of her to offer to host, but Lou could tell that she wasn't really keen on the idea. You need to feel comfortable with a person to wander around in your bra and knickers without your slap on, and none of the girls were comfortable with Ruby. It was like expecting a flock of sheep to be happy grazing with a wolf. But at least they would get to see what the salary of an engagement strategist for the International Olympic Committee could buy in central London.

The answer was – a lot.

Sherlock Mews, Marylebone, NW8, was seriously fucking classy. It had a tasteful and deeply deceptive Georgian facade behind which expanded acres of seriously prime central London accommodation. Ruby lived in a two-bedroom, three-bathroom duplex at the front of the building. Her sitting room looked like something out of a Bond movie. True, she had a small kitchen, but Lou guessed that she did little more in it than breakfast, stylishly, on slivers of fresh mango, and pour shots of Grey Goose for her invited guests. And for one night only Lou, Maddie, Colette, Lily and Priya were her guests.

Despite Ruby's effusive welcome, the tray of chilled mimosas on arrival and the generic disco music being piped through hidden speakers, the evening started awkwardly – with a toast to *true love*. Sarcastic and sincere, their combined voices hardly seemed enough to fill the echoing space and, as a result, the dynamic from the get-go was forced. Lily was, as Lily could be when she was excited, embarrassing. Anyone observing them could have been forgiven for thinking that she was the bride-to-be. But at least her giddy twittering about every tiny little thing filled what would otherwise have been some very uncomfortable gaps in the conversation. After the generic, and deeply boring, how-things-were-going-with-the-wedding-arrangements chat, they took their drinks up the floating staircase to the master bedroom. It was so streamlined that, aside from the huge bed with its luxe bedding, the room appeared to be empty. But looks can be deceptive. At the stroke of Ruby's fingertips, a section of the wall slid soundlessly aside. Lou had never, in her life, seen a wardrobe like it. It was multi-tiered, with an array of slide-out racks and drawers all of which were filled – and this is what really got her – with a colour-coordinated collection of immaculately folded and hung clothing. There wasn't a top slipping off a hanger, a pair of jeans shoved in the bottom of the wardrobe, a pair of leggings balled up in a corner. Basically, no sign whatsoever of human use. Ruby started running her pearl-tipped fingers along the rails, making her choice for the evening. They all watched; envious of her lovely home, her tasteful furnishings, her gorgeous clothes, her perfect figure, her inbred confidence, even of her matching wooden hangers. She seemed oblivious, or perhaps that was all part of the act, a feigned indifference to any other woman's opinion. The spike of dislike that stabbed through Lou galvanised her. She grabbed another drink from the tray and headed off to one of the other bathrooms to get ready. Lou expected Maddie to follow her.

She didn't.

In the bathroom, which was obviously designed for guests, given the thoughtful provision of all sorts of lotions and gels, Lou deliberately made a mess, leaving tops off bottles and smearing foundation on the pristine towels. It was petty and pointless. It wouldn't be Ruby who would have to clean it up. It took Lou all of ten minutes to put on her 'face' and get changed, but when she was ready she found she was in no mood to rejoin the party. Instead, she sat on the loo and scrolled through her phone. Colette had still not shown. Lou wondered where she was and whether she was late through necessity or choice. Even with the door shut and the music being piped into the bathroom, Lou could still hear Lily prattling away somewhere in the apartment. Lou guessed she was in the third bathroom, probably with poor Priya. Priya was way too polite for her own good. Lou had never met anyone so prone to keeping her opinions to herself.

Another ten minutes passed and Lou's glass was empty. She went downstairs. In the kitchen she poured herself a proper drink. Vodka, a big one, on the rocks. She left the bottle on the side, to warm up. Armed with her Grey Goose and ice, she followed the sound of laughter, back upstairs to Ruby's room. Ruby herself was lounging on the bed, looking resplendent in a midnight-blue sheath dress, but it was Maddie who took Lou's breath away. The outfit that Lou and Maddie had picked out together back at Alex's apartment had obviously been rejected in favour of a short, tight, fitted blood-red dress teamed with a pair of killer heels. And Maddie's face, when it turned to Lou for approval, was different. It was made-up with a professional touch – Ruby's? She looked stunning, but she didn't look like Maddie, at least not to Lou – her best friend and the keeper of her secrets.

Maddie twirled unsteadily in her borrowed high heels. Lou saluted her with her vodka; what else could she do?

but she didn't say anything. Thankfully, at that moment the buzzer went and, to Ruby's evident surprise, Lou offered to go and see who it was, hoping more than ever that it was Colette.

Chapter 12

COLETTE

Much to her surprise, Colette found that she was enjoying the party. She had a drink in her hand and a good vantage point at the bar from which to watch everyone – which suited her just fine. The Blink staff were 'on it'. No one had asked her to do, sort, arrange, fetch or rectify anything, all evening. She sat back and sipped her Valentini, held the blend of bitterness and sweetness in her mouth, felt it coat her tongue and teeth, then she swallowed. The warmth slid down her throat into her stomach. Tonight she was off the clock. Tonight she was free. Tonight she was excited. Anticipation. It was a powerful emotion and it had been a long time since Colette had felt it this strongly. The spice of secrecy only served to up the ante. Tonight things could change for her, if she was brave enough. All she had to do was wait for the right moment to make her move.

Maddie is, unsurprisingly, drunk, but surely not so drunk that she doesn't realise that wandering around unsteadily in her tippy-tappy high heels isn't a very smart idea, even in this respectable neck of the woods. Seemingly not. She crosses the street and goes into the sparsely lit and heavily tree-edged square. In her fake fur and siren red dress she is literally signalling to any and every passing weirdo that she's alone and vulnerable. Except, of course, she isn't on her own, because I'm with her.

I'm not worried about her spotting me. If she does I can always say I came outside to look for her. That sort of consideration would be wholly in keeping with the type of person she believes I am. But she doesn't glance behind her, not once. She totters along, as if in pain, past the first bench, the second, the third. At the fourth she falters. She stops, sways slightly, then flops inelegantly down on her backside and lunges forward. For a moment I think she's being sick, but the problem isn't her stomach, it's her feet. She yanks off one of her shoes and lobs it. It's a surprisingly strong throw. The shoe arcs high through the air then impales itself in the grass. The second shoe follows. It's a less impressive trajectory – half the distance and a side-on landing.

Free of her footwear, Maddie tilts her head back and stares up at the urine-yellow glow of the London sky.

The question is – why has she fled her own party? Fresh air to clear a muzzy head? It's a reasonable explanation, but not the correct one. Perhaps the sheer upscaleness of it all has simply got too much for her. But that doesn't make sense either. It's obvious to anyone who bothers to pay attention that Maddie is enjoying her access-all-areas pass to the finer things in life – a pass she's acquired courtesy of Alex. She now has the lifestyle and the spending power that she's coveted for so long. But getting what you want doesn't always make you happy and I have my suspicions that Maddie is having moments, more and more frequently of late as the wedding draws nearer, when she's acutely aware that something doesn't quite fit. And on that, we agree. Perhaps that's why she feels safer out here, on her own, in the dark, rather than in there, with everyone else, in the light.

The truth is – Maddie is a fake. I know because I'm one too. I understand the effort it takes to present a consistent version of yourself to a world that would reject you if they knew the real you. 'Be true to yourself', that's the mantra that everyone spouts, but it's ridiculous advice. Imagine what would happen if we all gave in to our impulses and desires and revealed our true selves. It would be carnage. Maddie's fakery is, of course, quite simplistic compared to mine. She's compensating for the failings and gaps she experienced growing up – those lean years when she learnt to steal and cheat and deceive to get on. I can see how hard she has to work to sublimate the character traits that have helped her survive. In her shiny new life, with her new set of friends, she dials up her vulnerability, presents to the world, and especially to Alex, an old-fashioned femininity that offers

106

no threat, encourages no suspicion, but demands protection. She plays weak well. Why else am I out here keeping watch over her in the freezing fucking cold, when I could be back at the party pretending to be having fun? Why else, indeed?

Tired of staring at the sodium-soaked sky, she shifts position. She places her hands on her knees, readying herself for the push to standing. Poor Maddie, it must be tiring having a lovely time at someone else's expense. As she gets to her feet, I step back into the bushes. This is what she's reduced me to – lurking in the dark, like the worst sort of predator. She goes to retrieve her shoes. She picks them up and holds them, by the heels, in front of her. From a distance they look like a peculiarly spiky wedding bouquet. She walks across the grass in her stocking feet. I watch her exit the square. Follow. She crosses the empty street and makes her way back towards the bar.

It's only then that I grasp why the bar is called Blink. It's housed discreetly beneath a block of stylish new town houses. There's no indication that the basement is anything other than a flat or an office. There's no sign, no come-hither lights, no leakage of laughter and music, nothing, except for a tiny brass plaque of a winking eye that's attached to the railings at the head of a set of steep concrete stairs. Blink – as in, blink and you'd miss it. At the top of the steps, Maddie stops. She bends down and lines up the shoes ready for her feet. For a second the image of Dorothy's ruby slippers flashes across my mind. Oh, if only wishing and clicking your heels made things so. She gets her right foot in at the first attempt, but in doing so she knocks over the left shoe. That's what being pissed on gold-flecked martinis can do to a girl not accustomed to a 24-carat lifestyle. She sighs and leans down to set it upright. It's so obviously dangerous. Her stance is all wrong – her weight too far forward, her balance off

107

kilter, and she's way too close to the top of the steps. She's already wobbling before I step up behind her.

It's an accident waiting to happen.

The lightest of touches guarantees that it does.

Chapter 13

MADDIE

The walk in the cold February air had cleared Maddie's head and recharged her social battery; now it was simply a matter of cramming her feet back into Ruby's chronically uncomfortable heels and rejoining the party. She got the right shoe on – fuck they pinched – but the left one toppled over before she had a chance to put it on. She bent down to stand it back up.

The next thing she knew she was plummeting. Her cheek, hip, side, spine hit concrete. Each blow punched the breath out of her. Then, as suddenly as it had started, it was over. She came to an absolute hard stop. It felt like she'd been stomped on, her ribs burst, her head split, her back broken. Shock flooded her system. She threw up where she lay. The retching hurt. She was in the bottom of the stairwell. It was quiet as a grave. That was, until she moved. The pain set free her screams. Raised up on her elbows – the only movement she could manage – she surveyed the damage. There was a lot of blood. Her stomach heaved again. Bile filled her mouth. There was a jagged piece of bone sticking out of her right leg.

It was the last thing she saw before she passed out.

One minute she's there and the next she isn't. The noise her body makes as it hits the steps on the way down is horrible. It makes me nauseous. I peer down into the stairwell. She looks like a flung doll. I stare at her. What the hell did I do that for? I'm shocked. Acting on impulse – it's so stupid. So reckless.

After a second or two she stirs. I'm relieved, and horrified.

I step back when the screaming starts. I step forward when it stops, which is, thankfully, almost immediately. I wait. Count to ten. It helps me think. No one comes. Nothing happens. I reason with myself, cut myself some slack. Frustration drove me to it – understandable frustration. She has tested my patience to its limit. It occurs to me that, although clumsy and dangerous, that little nudge might very well achieve what my concerted but less direct campaign to date has failed to do; namely, stop the wedding.

I look around. Luck appears to be on my side. The street is deserted. There are no witnesses to what could be seen as a terrible accident or an act of pure malice. Shit, there'll probably be security cameras. I scan the stairwell. I can't see any. I'm deeply relieved. I walk down the steps, in no hurry. Panic is the enemy. I step over her. For a second I have an irrational fear that she might reach up and grab my leg. But this isn't the movies. She doesn't move or make a sound. She's obviously unconscious and badly injured. I catch sight of pulpy flesh and shattered bone. The bone is startlingly white. The gore doesn't provoke any reaction within me – which is interesting. The only emotion I feel is a small but growing sense of satisfaction. This will take some coming back from, and the wedding is supposed to be in a little over three months' time. Well, that has to be in doubt now, surely? It's easy enough to open the door without touching her – there's ample clearance. Thankfully, there's no bouncer on duty. Blink's exclusive clientele are obviously not expected to cause trouble. I close the door behind me gently, leaving her where she lies.

The corridor that leads to the bar is dimly lit by Moroccan-style wall lights. The toilets are off to the right. I contemplate paying them a visit to check my face, see if there are any tells, but I decide against it. Being back in the room is more important.

I slide back into the party. No one seems to notice my return; they're too busy having a good time. I make my way to the bar and pick up my drink. It's exactly where I left it, although the bartender has, thoughtfully, added another lump of ice. I sip. The smoothness of the Cointreau is soothing. Everyone is having a great time, downing cocktails, chatting shit, busting moves on the small dance floor, laughing, flirting, taking photos. I exchange smiles and pass comments with a few people, pop up in the background of some of the shots. I make sure my presence is felt and recorded. Ten minutes pass. Maddie has been missing from the party for at least half an hour by this point, and not a single one of them has noticed. Friends can be so shockingly fickle. I order another drink.

We were, after all, supposed to be celebrating.

Chapter 14

MADDIE

His voice dragged her back to consciousness.

The pain was so bad that she couldn't cry; instead she whimpered. She sounded like a kicked dog. Something soft had been draped over her – for comfort or to cover up the horror show? Her right leg felt like it had been doused with petrol and set alight. Not that everywhere else didn't hurt like a bitch as well. That's when the shaking started – the shock kicking in. She didn't have the bandwidth for anything other than agony. She kept her eyes shut, willed herself to pass out again, but she couldn't – the pain wouldn't let her.

His voice was close. 'Jesus, Mad. Jesus Christ! It's going to be okay. I promise. There's an ambulance on its way.' She opened her eyes. Saw Bobby. His face was a mask of horror, but the second he registered that she was conscious his expression switched to compassion. He was kneeling on the cold, unforgiving ground leaning over her as if trying to shield her. Sadly, it was too late for that. He kept repeating, 'It's going to be okay.' He was obviously trying to reassure himself as much as her, but having him there helped. She wasn't alone any more. Someone cared, she had to hold on to that. Soon an ambulance would arrive and the paramedics would take the pain away. Or so she prayed. The thought of being moved without massive doses of morphine, or whatever it was they used for situations like this, was inconceivable, but she couldn't stay at the bottom of a flight of stone steps for the rest of her life. Bobby didn't seem to know what to do with his hands. In the end he settled on gently stroking her cheek. 'What the hell happened?'

'I fell.'

'Jesus, Mad. How long have you been here? Like this?'

She was finding it difficult to form coherent sentences, but she tried – for his sake. 'I don't know.' She must have moved ever so slightly because another ripcord of agony was pulled. She clenched her teeth and breathed fast, trying to outrun it.

Sensing her increased distress Bobby stopped stroking her cheek and instead pressed his palm flat against her forehead like a compress. His hand was cool. 'Thank you,' she murmured.

'Maddie?'

'What?'

'I think I should go and get Alex. He's never going to forgive me for not fetching him.'

'No!' The panic in her voice was loud. In her desperation she reached up and grabbed his hand. A different pain shot through her; this one ran down her spine and wound itself around her hips like barbed wire. An image of herself in her wedding dress, in a wheelchair, accompanied it. Regardless, she held on. 'No. Don't leave me, Bobby. You can't leave me on my own. Stay. Talk to me.'

'About what?'

'Anything.' She took a gulp of cold air. 'Tell me about your job.'

Bless him, it was an ask – making small talk as she lay shattered on a cold concrete floor in a dimly lit stairwell while the party carried on a stone's throw away – but to his credit he gave it a go.

Which was why Maddie was listening to Bobby explain what made for a great plot twist in a thriller when the paramedics arrived. Then Maddie's small cocoon of pain exploded into a world of light, noise and, finally – after all this time – other people. A distraught, angry, appalled, shouty-with-stress Alex, a silent, pale Lou, a weeping Lily, a shivering Priya, a granite-faced Colette and, as beautiful as ever, even in the harsh, intermittent blue light of the ambulance, Ruby.

Chapter 15

MADDIE

Lou came to see Maddie a lot after the accident. Maddie knew that her visits were largely motivated by friendship, but there was some guilt mixed in there as well. Lou had finally stopped apologising for not noticing that Maddie had gone AWOL from the party, but Maddie could tell that she still felt responsible for the accident. Lou was supposed to be her wingman and she'd been MIA. Whatever Lou's motivation for visiting so frequently, Maddie appreciated it. She was feeling deeply claustrophobic and very stressed being laid up in the apartment.

Maddie's accident had certainly put a serious crimp in their wedding plans. Their trip to Mallorca to finalise everything with Colette had had to be cancelled, likewise the stag and hen weekends. Maddie had encouraged Alex to go ahead with his trip to Zermatt, but he'd said no, he wouldn't dream of leaving her to go off skiing. Then there was all the hassle of having to reschedule the dress fittings. In truth, there were times, often in the dead of night when Maddie couldn't sleep, that she wondered whether they were going to make it to the altar.

In this context Lou's visits were a welcome distraction. They also allowed Alex to take a break. Working all day and spending every evening and most of every weekend running around after Maddie was taking its toll. He didn't complain, but she could sense his growing restlessness. Alex was used to a busy social life: meals out, weekends away, activity, impulses immediately acted on and satisfied. What he was not used to was night after night in front of the TV with an invalid.

True to form, the minute Lou heard the door shut behind Alex she grinned. 'A beer?'

'I shouldn't. I'm still on quite strong painkillers.'

Lou pulled a face. 'I reckon they work better in conjunction with alcohol.' She disappeared, returned with two bottles and thumped down on the sofa next to Maddie. They clinked beer bottles and Lou made the toast: 'To the cage coming off on the twenty-ninth.'

'That's not for another three weeks.'

Maddie was only four weeks into her recovery – on crutches, her leg in a cage – and the pain was still bad, but for everyone else the shock of her fall had faded and life had moved on. Maddie must have looked depressed because Lou retorted, 'Which is less time than it takes a wombat to conceive and give birth.'

Maddie snorted. It was typical Lou – weird, but well meant. 'You made that up!'

Lou looked affronted and immediately went onto Google. She passed Maddie her phone. And there it was in black and white, the gestation period of a wombat – 26–28 days. The list revealed that hamsters had the shortest pregnancies. It was typical of Lou to have remembered the date that the cage finally came off and to have pre-looked-up a joke to lighten the mood.

'How mobile will you be when you get rid of that monstrosity?' Lou asked.

'Fuck knows.' Being able to swear more freely was another upside of Lou's visits. Maddie still regretted setting such a low profanity bar at the outset of her relationship with Alex. 'They'll fit me with a boot and a brace to start with.'

'Like a Premier League footballer?'

'Hardly.'

They chatted about something and nothing for a while. Lou fetched another beer. Maddie declined. She couldn't risk putting on any more weight. Her sedentary life had been as bad for her waistline as it had for her mental health and she had a dress fitting coming up at Cala two weeks after the cage came off. That was going to be fun, with a brace and crutches.

Lou glanced at her phone, with desultory interest this time. Suddenly she sat up. 'You've got to be fucking kidding me!'

'What?'

'You're not going to believe this.'

'What?'

'Look at the Wedding WhatsApp group.'

Maddie found herself looking at a series of photos, taken on the night of the Valentine's party, posted by Lily a few minutes ago. She went back to the beginning of the thread and started with the first picture. It was accompanied by a message. *Hi all. Was looking through my phone and found these from our lovely evening together in February – before Maddie's*

AWFUL accident. Thought I would share them to remind us all of happy times past . . . and to come. Roll on May, Mallorca and Maddie and Alex's wedding. We're SO looking forward to it. L and B x There followed loads of photos, some from Ruby's apartment, but far more from Blink, some of which must have been taken while Maddie lay bleeding and in agony in the stairwell.

Lou was flicking through the same gallery of shots. Without looking up she said, 'What a silly bitch that girl is.'

Maddie kept scrolling. It was a compulsive action; the pictures were bringing back some very sharp memories and stirring up some completely new ones.

Lou plucked Maddie's phone out of her hand. 'No. Don't look at them. I'll message and tell her to delete them.' She was already on it.

But Maddie didn't want the photos deleted. As poor taste as it was for Lily to have posted them without checking with her first, she wanted to look through them. More specifically, she wanted to be in the room, at least vicariously, for the forty minutes when not a single one of her closest friends had noticed that she was missing. And, much as she didn't want to think this way, Maddie wondered if Lou knew that was why she was so keen to see them and that was the reason she was so eager to get them taken down. Was she being paranoid? Very possibly. But she'd had plenty of time to dwell on her fall and something about it didn't add up. 'Lou! Leave it.' Lou's thumbs stopped typing, but they still hovered over her keypad ready to resume her angry salvo. Maddie needed to say something to convince her. She opted for a disingenuous reason. 'It was such a bad end to a good night that I want to be reminded of the happy parts.' Lou still looked doubtful. 'I mean it. I want you to delete whatever gratuitously offensive text you just typed.'

Lou squinted at her phone. 'Yeah, perhaps the language is a bit . . . rich. I do make reference to female genitalia and I suppose that could be construed as offensive by someone with a delicate constitution.' She held down the delete button for a considerable time, then she threw her phone aside. After that they discussed Lily for a while, or rather Lou bitched about her and Maddie didn't contradict her. It was good fun. Lily was an easy target because she was so bloody upbeat about everything and they both agreed that indiscriminate enthusiasm was one of the most irritating traits a human being could possess. Having dissected Lily's laugh – grating, her politics – non-existent, her listening skills – likewise, Lou moved on to Lily's relationship with Bobby. 'Why do you think he's with her? I can't believe it's the sex.'

'Who knows why anyone loves anyone else?' Maddie said.

'Well, I get why you're with Alex,' Lou countered. The mood in the room changed.

'Do you?' It irritated Maddie how Lou still assumed that she knew what Maddie was feeling and about who.

'Yes.' Lou didn't look away from Maddie's querying stare. It was a challenge. Lou smiled, but it was a smile with a steel edge. 'It's because he's just . . . perfect.'

The mockery hurt. Maddie felt tired. She missed the old ease that she and Lou used to share. Ever since she'd started dating Alex their friendship had felt under pressure. It was as if his presence in her life had squeezed the air out of their relationship. Quietly, she pushed back. 'Not perfect, no, but he is the right man – for me.' Lou was about to snap back, but seemed to think better of it. Maddie shifted the conversation back onto safer territory. 'Well, in terms of Bobby and Lily's relationship, he's a nice guy so I suppose they're well matched. You can't say that Lily isn't nice.'

'Yeah, but who wants to go through life being nice? And Bobby's not bland like she is and he's not bloody ecstatic about EVERYTHING.'

'Maybe it's good to live life like that?' Maddie ventured.

'Like what? With your head up your own arse, oblivious to the real world?'

It was pointless talking to Lou when she was in one of her moods. 'You are tough on people.'

Lou's acidic, 'Yeah, well some people deserve it' put paid to the evening. Maddie yawned. She made no attempt to hide it. Thankfully Lou took the hint without any further snarky comebacks. She started gathering her things together. 'See ya, wouldn't want to be ya!' It was their old sign-off, but Maddie was growing sick of it. She was pleased to hear the front door bang shut. The minute Lou was gone, Maddie retrieved her phone. There'd been quite a number of comments added to the group chat. She skim-read them, noting who had posted and, of more interest to her, who hadn't. There was nothing from Alex or Ruby. The messages were all a version of: it had been a great night, regret that it had ended so badly, good wishes for her continued recovery and excitement about the wedding. Maddie returned to the photos. She started with the ones taken in Ruby's flat. They focused as much on the furnishings and fittings as on the girls. Maddie had to concede that some of them were really quite good. The one of the mimosas on the mirrored tray with their blurred silhouettes in the background looked like something out of a fashion spread. Maddie lingered on the couple of photographs of herself in Ruby's bedroom, all dressed up with somewhere to go. Once again Lily had thought carefully about the composition, not just fired off a shot. They showed Maddie, photographed from the back, looking at herself in the mirror. In her borrowed dress, heels and make-up she looked different, but good different – more polished and glossy. Definitely more sexy, more the type of woman you'd expect Alex to be with, and want. It was hard to accept the contrast between the woman in these photos and the broken mess she was now. And all because she'd tried to walk in someone else's shoes.

She scrolled forward to the photos taken in Blink. By this point in the evening Lily seemed to have forsaken style for random snaps. There were pictures of everyone arriving, including some of Maddie herself, posing for cheesy group pictures interspersed with shots of the cocktails and the food. She'd forgotten how good the catering had been, although she did clearly remember the bitter taste of the caviar-topped crab tart coming back up her throat when she threw up in the stairwell. There were a couple of close-up shots of Bobby smiling, having fun, and a cute one of Lily and Bobby kissing, presumably taken by someone else at Lily's request? It was hard not to see how happy they looked, how much in love. Like she'd said, who was she, or Lou, to judge other people's relationships ... unless, of course, that relationship was a threat to your own?

Maddie slowed down, paid more attention to the next shots. Five pictures in particular stirred a silty, uneasy feeling in the pit of her stomach. Had these pictures been taken while she was in the park catching her breath or when she was lying broken at the bottom of the stairwell? They were generic shots of people on the dance floor – Lily trying to capture the mood of the party. But it was what was visible beyond the dancers in two of the photos that interested Maddie. The shots captured Lou sitting on one of the big leather sofas, with a genuine smile on her face, deep in conversation with a woman she'd described as a 'total tight-arse'. But Colette obviously couldn't be that much of an arse or why would Lou have found her fascinating enough to distract her from noticing the absence of her alleged best friend? Then Maddie focused in on the three other photos. They hurt even more. Because Alex had been equally unaware of, or indifferent to, her disappearance. Why? Because he'd been preoccupied too. With Ruby.

Maddie's leg started pulsing. Could psychological turmoil cause pain? Or was it just the wound reminding her that she was far from healed? Lily had caught Alex and Ruby together on the dance floor. Sure, they were surrounded by other people, in with the crowd, doing what people were supposed to do at parties, but they looked, somehow, in their own bubble. Ruby's bare arms were clasped behind Alex's head, an elegant lasso. She appeared to be pulling him towards her. He was not resisting. His hands were on her hips. The word 'clinch' came to mind. Even without the soundtrack, the synchronicity between their bodies was obvious. But as unsettling as their physical closeness was, it was their expressions that really stung. Their faces were level. Ruby was as tall as Alex, perhaps taller in her heels, but that night she'd opted for flat ballet pumps, confident enough in her glory not to rely on the go-to shorthand for desirability. They looked good together. Equal footing. Maddie's mind raced. She didn't restrain it.

After a minute or two she saw that Bobby was messaging her – direct, not via the group. The ripple of dots at least provided a sense that someone was thinking about her. And once again, that person was Bobby. She watched the pulse of the dots – it was better than looking at her fiancé getting down on the dance floor with his gorgeous best friend, while her own best friend chatted away quite happily to a woman she allegedly disliked.

When it arrived, it was a long message. *Hi Mad. Just seen Lily's post. Sorry, I didn't know she was going to do that. If I had, I would have advised against it. She didn't mean any harm. She genuinely thought that the photos might cheer you up. But I appreciate that they'll bring back some very distressing memories. They did for me, and I was just a bystander.* He'd been far more than that. *Do you want me to ask her to delete them? Let me know. I'm here on the phone or I could always call round, if you want to talk. Alex says you've been a real trouper. I hope the pain is easing and that you're coping. It must be SO constricting. One thing Lil did get right is how much we're looking forward to Mallorca. It's really not long now. Keep your chin up, M, and, as I say, you know where I am.*

It was classic Bobby, kind, thoughtful and, as you'd expect from someone who worked in publishing, well-punctuated. She messaged him back with thanks, reassurance that she was fine and confirmation that it was okay for the pictures to stay in the group chat. He responded straightaway with another well-crafted message – Bobby was not an emoji kind of bloke – with the repeated offer of

123

a listening ear, if she ever needed one. It was tempting, but uneasy as she was about the true nature of Alex and Ruby's relationship, Maddie knew that she needed to keep her anxieties to herself. She had absolutely no concrete evidence that there was anything going on between the two of them. Alex had been attentive, loving and patient with her since the accident and he was as worried as she was about how little time she had to get back on her feet before the wedding. She was simply feeling depressed from being trapped in the apartment on her own so much over the past few weeks, and the painkillers weren't helping. They were making her thinking fuzzy. As she hauled herself off the sofa and headed to bed, she made a promise to herself that she would start cutting them down – tomorrow.

Chapter 16

ALEX

'To true love!'

It wasn't a genuine toast, it was Lou picking a fight – with the wedding, with him, with his parents, with the other guests, with the world. She might be Maddie's oldest friend, but she was a total pain in the arse. Having interrupted proceedings she seemed to lose momentum. She plopped down, nearly missed her chair and had to grab the edge of the table to stop herself from falling. A couple of wine glasses wobbled, went over and smashed. What the fuck was wrong with her? It was embarrassing. She was embarrassing. A waitress appeared and started mopping up the mess. As Alex watched Lou's clumsy attempts to help with the clear-up, he reflected on the difference between Lou's reaction to him and Maddie getting married and Bobby's. They were a million miles apart. Bobby had been happy for them. Okay, he'd been a bit shocked at how quickly Alex had proposed, but that was Bobby for you – cautious to a fault. Lou, in stark contrast, had done nothing but snipe. And that was because she was a bitter, man-and-money-hating cow.

Alex took a deep breath and tried to dredge up some patience, for Maddie's sake. All they had to do was get through the next three days, then they would be married and there wouldn't be a damn thing that Lou could do about it – other than sulk. And they wouldn't be around to witness that because they would be on their way to Mauritius. And things were going to be different when they got back from their honeymoon; they would be busy. Maddie would need to focus on finding them a house and there would be business dinners with potential clients and their partners to host. Archer Asset Management was going to require a lot of investment in terms of time and effort, from both of them. The life he envisaged for them would be a world away from Maddie's old life and, hopefully, from her old friends.

Thinking about the future drew Alex back to the woman he intended to spend the rest of his life with. Maddie had been quiet all evening. Alex turned his chair and his attention where it should be, back to his bride.

Chapter 17

COLETTE

Colette stood and surveyed the ruined feast. There were napkins lying in the dust and piles of dirty crockery and glassware on every table. The large blood-red stain from the wine that Lou had spilt caught her eye. And it had all looked so pretty before they'd got their sticky mitts on it. No one paid her the slightest bit of attention. The king had crowned his successor. The Archer dynasty was secure. She was surplus to requirements.

'*Family . . . the bedrock of everything we do*.' What a lying bastard her father was! But at least now she knew for certain, and that certainty clarified her next move – made it inevitable. He was such a hypocrite. All this time, stringing her along, pretending she was his right-hand man, 'or woman', as he liked to joke – often in front of men like Mateus Torres and Teddy bloody Largos. But Colette wasn't blind or stupid. She'd noticed the more frequent trips to London over the past year. How could she not; she'd arranged most of them. The wedding preparations had been a convenient excuse, but not a very good one. Had they forgotten that she had access to their schedules? She'd also clocked the increased number of closed-door conversations with Paul, the requests for seemingly random financial summaries, the sudden drive to get outstanding debts settled. She'd known for months that something was going on, something different to their normal illegal and legal activities, something that was above her pay grade. It wasn't the first time she'd been shut out, but it was going to be the last.

Once she'd set her mind to it, it hadn't been that difficult to find out what her father – correction – her parents, were planning. They expected her to do as she was told and nothing more. Well, that was the perfect cover for doing a lot more. Like keeping up with her father's diary so that she could be certain when he would be away from the villa and she would be free to investigate. Like taking note of his passwords when they were going through the bank reconciliations. Like memorising the safe code. Like having the balls to use her carefully accrued information to search Ray's emails, bank transfers and the screeds of boring legal correspondence that he suddenly seemed to be receiving, in order to piece together a picture of what he was really up to. Which turned out to be consolidating a large proportion of their wealth into one financial wrapper. It was a huge chunk of change. Colette estimated it to be somewhere in the region of twelve million. The outstanding question, up until tonight, had been why? What was Ray's next big play?

Now she had her answer. Archer Asset Management. A family venture that had nothing whatsoever to do with her.

Colette watched them drinking, laughing and slapping her brother on his linen-clad back, so smug and self-satisfied. She hated them all. Let them stuff their faces and inflate each other's egos in the idyllic setting of the finca while they could – by the time the weekend was over they would know, in no uncertain terms, that she was far more than a mere bystander.

Chapter 18

MADDIE

After Ray's revelatory toast and Lou's embarrassing, drunken, sarcastic footnote, Maddie made her excuses, pleading the need for as much beauty sleep as possible. Even as she said it, she realised she sounded like a character out of a TV sitcom. Perhaps Lou was right, perhaps she was turning into a cake topper. Alex fussed – suddenly attentive after a night of neglect. He offered to walk her back to her room, but as he rose to his feet Paul appeared at the table, bearing an open box of cigars. The smell was intense – the pungent essence of men. 'To seal the deal! Brandy! We need brandy!' Paul gesticulated at one of the waiters.

Maddie smiled, signalling her willingness to see herself back to her room. 'I'll be fine. See you all in the morning. Ray. Marilyn. Thank you for a wonderful evening.' She didn't go in for the hug. It didn't seem wanted. As she threaded her way down through the trees to the path that led back to the finca she heard the boom of male laughter. Cigars and brandy. Ray's world. Alex's world as well? She and Alex would need to have a conversation in the morning about why he'd said nothing to her about this sudden move to being a sole trader, or, more importantly, about his father and his 'associates' investing in his start-up. When she'd first got together with Alex Maddie hadn't been that interested in the Archers, but as their fling had turned into something more serious, she had started to wonder if and how the dubious nature of their business empire might impact their lives. Alex had mainly talked about how relieved he was to have escaped. He'd expressed pity for his sister, seeing her as trapped within the family firm. Then she'd met them all and the difference between Alex and his family had been so stark that it had been hard to believe they were related. Maddie had been reassured that although Alex had obviously benefited from his parents' wealth, he was nothing like them.

So why take Ray's money to set up in business? And, on top of that, why accept men like Mr Torres and Teddy Largos as his first investors? It was hardly a good example of starting as you mean to go on. And, even more importantly, why leave her to find out like that, in front of everyone else, two days before their wedding? It had been presented as a fait accompli, which smacked of manipulation.

Maddie was far enough away from the party now to finally feel alone. It was a relief.

She knew she should have convinced Lou to come back to the tower with her, if nothing else to get her away from the booze, but the bald truth was that Maddie didn't have the energy to deal with Lou's histrionics – she had too much to cope with herself. Out of nowhere Maddie felt a sudden wave of longing for her mum. Her mother should be here with her, by her side, on her side. But she wasn't, as she hadn't been for years. Maddie was well and truly on her own.

At the foot of the tower she stopped and looked up. Instant vertigo. She dropped her gaze. She reached out and rested her hands against the cool stone. The walls that looked so solid felt crumbly beneath her fingertips. She pressed her palms against the tower, trying to make an impression. She felt the tension in her arms, the roughness against her palms and the resistance. It was a push-of-war she was doomed to lose. She conceded defeat, stepped back and this time slowly raised her gaze, floor by floor, up the height of the tower. There were lights on the ground, first and second floors. Had she left the lamps on in their suite? She couldn't remember. The remainder of the upper floors were in darkness. The view from the bridal suite at the top was supposed to be breathtaking. That treat lay in store. As her eyes adjusted to the darkness, she thought she saw movement at the very top of the tower. She concentrated. She heard the light shush of the breeze through the pines, but she could also make out a weird rustling, clicking noise high above her. She craned her neck back and stared up into the dark sky. Before her eyes the roof of the tower began to shift and flicker, becoming something alive and restless. Maddie closed then reopened her eyes, thinking that she must be imagining things. But no, the roof was definitely moving. Horrified but fascinated, she watched and waited. For what, she couldn't be sure. For her sanity to return and the seething to subside back into static black slates? Or, mad as it sounded, for the whole roof to lift, flap and fly away?

Christ. There were bats. Hundreds of them.

The realisation uprooted her. She stumbled to the door, yanked it open and stepped inside. The slam reverberated

132

around the downstairs hallway. Would the sound reach the bats and dislodge them? Maddie hoped so. She would never sleep knowing there was a seething, stirring mass above her head. She hurried up the stairwell heading to the safety of the suite, and unlocked the door with shaking hands.

The suite was an oasis of calm. No bats, no darkness, no queasy, shifting shapes and clicking wings. But she still hurried across the room to check that the windows were all shut tight. They were. She pulled the huge floor-to-ceiling curtain across, sealing herself inside. Someone had obviously been in the room in her absence. The turn-down service. Having gone out with Alex for over a year, and having stayed in some very nice, very expensive hotels in their time together, Maddie now knew what that was. Still feeling unsettled, she drifted around the suite touching the gleaming surfaces and drawing much-needed calm from the order and loveliness of the fixtures and fittings. She wandered into the bathroom, ran a bath, added a few drops of essential oil. It floated on the top of the water forming rainbows, fragrancing the steam. She took some deep breaths. Lavender was calming, wasn't it? The candles in the sconces on the bathroom wall had been lit. Recently, by the look of it. The light danced around the walls. It was almost as if the maid had known she would need soothing. Yes, a long soak would be good.

Half an hour later, Maddie emerged from the bathroom feeling much better. Relaxed, soft-limbed, more rational, once more the bride she was determined to be. She and Alex would talk in the morning. They would work things out. It was what proper couples did. Dealt with rather than ignored their problems. The dressing gown they'd left out for her was soft and yielding, far better quality than the usual towelling wraps on offer. The thought made her smile, both at the indulgence and at her newly acquired pickiness. She'd grown accustomed to luxury. And, sod anyone else, including her best friend, she refused to be ashamed of enjoying the finer things in life. Money had to be made somehow if you wanted to live like this.

It was only when Maddie had finished drying her hair and was sitting at the dressing table brushing it the obligatory twenty strokes to make it shine, that she noticed the shape in the bed.

Chapter 19

COLETTE

Paul called for a second bottle of brandy. Colette wanted to refuse, but a glance at her father guaranteed that his wish was her command. The other guests had departed long ago; even her mother had made her excuses and headed back to the villa. Now it was just the men. Ray, Paul, Alex, Mateus and Teddy. Tom and Charlie, despite their usual insensitivity, must have sensed that this was major-league stuff because they too had slunk off to bed. Colette watched the five of them lounging around under the canopy telling tales – it was the usual dick-measuring contest – and the one thought that ran through her head was, 'I need these fuckers to go to bed.' Given that they obviously had no intention of obliging, Colette took matters into her own hands. Unobserved – because who noticed her presence, unless they wanted something – she reached down to the junction box hidden in the wall and pulled the plug. She slipped away to their cries of protest. Let them break their necks in the dark. She'd had enough, and she had a rendez-vous to keep.

Chapter 20

MADDIE

The thing in the bed was the size of a small animal or child. Maddie stood perfectly still. The shape didn't move. But why would it? She was being hysterical. The logical explanation was that it must be a gift left for her by the staff that she hadn't noticed in her panic to get away from the bats. Yes, definitely a wedding gift. What else could it be?

Barefoot, she crossed over to the bed and yanked back the covers, proving to herself that she wasn't losing her marbles, or her nerve. And there, lying in the middle of the mattress, was the most exquisite bouquet Maddie had ever seen. It was made up of her favourite flowers – deep magenta and crimson anemones and delicate blush-pink peonies, offset by dark glossy strands of ivy and fronds of something delicate that she didn't recognise. She lifted the bouquet to her face and inhaled. The fragrance was subtle, more forest floor than florist shop. The flowers were obviously not native to Spain. They must have cost a fortune to air-freight over. Were they from Alex? He was in the habit of such gestures – he liked to spend money on her. Or were they from her in-laws-to-be? A welcome-to-the-family gift? Perhaps they were a gesture of, if not affection, then at least acceptance from Colette. Had she been too harsh about the Archers? After all, they had been nothing but generous. Maddie looked for a card or note. There was none. They must be from Alex. No one else knew that she loved anemones. Her love for him breathed out again. She needed to get the bouquet into water, and quickly – the anemones were already beginning to wilt. Maddie scanned the suite. Of course, the ice bucket. She lifted out the empty bottle and brought the bucket to her bedside. She untied the twine – it was fiddly, the stems were bound tight – and put the flowers in the melted ice water. Their scent would fragrance her dreams.

After everyone has finally gone to bed, I linger. I like the darkness. I head for the terrace, away from the understandably miserable-looking waiter, who has had to stay behind to clear up after Ray and his pals.

The lake is an expanse of coldness at the heart of the finca. It's strange to be near a body of water that's so silent. There are no waves or ripples, not even the soft slap of water against the jetty. I lie down on one of the sun loungers and stare up at the sky. I'm not star-gazing, what I'm doing is recentring myself after the buffeting of being with them all for so long. I need to detox and recharge. There's a faint taint of tobacco lingering on the air. Men are filthy beasts. After a little while I notice another smell, this one strong and gamey. It alerts me to the cat's approach. I don't move, communicating, I hope, my willingness to engage on its terms. This is its territory, its choice what happens next. It can launch itself at me, claws unsheathed, scratch my face to ribbons. Or it can pass on by without a glance, reaffirm its indifference to our invasion of its domain. It does neither. It stops, somewhere close by. I hold my breath. There's a soft, barely audible thud. Slowly, I raise myself up onto my elbows. I glance to my left. The cat is sitting on the sun lounger next to me, staring out at

138

the lake. In silhouette it looks like a cut-out – too catlike to be an actual flesh, blood and sinew animal. I sit up fully. The cat seems unconcerned by my presence. I resettle. Still it doesn't deign to look round. I don't know how long we sit, side by side, watching the reflection of the waxy moon floating on the oily surface of the lake. I hold myself still, playing by the cat's rules, keen to see what comes out of our silent exchange. Eventually the cat yawns. It's a very human sound. I hear a small crack as its jaws open.

The cat is staring at me. Its eyes are unnerving, yellow and black, unblinking.

It's looking straight at me. I like the sensation. Being seen. I so rarely am. I wonder what the cat sees when it looks at me. Does it recognise a kindred spirit?

Assessment complete, the cat gets slowly to its feet. The sound of its paws digging into the cushions on the sun lounger reminds me that it is armed and I am not. I refrain from holding out my hand or making any patronising 'come to me' sounds. I've no desire to befriend the cat, but I do want to connect with it. There's another beat, then the cat arches its back. Its tail quivers and it sprays – all over the sunbed. A 'fuck you' gesture if ever I saw one. So we do have things in common. As it pads away I notice that despite its thinness there's a bulge in its stomach. Some sort of swelling or growth? The lump swings from side to side as the cat walks.

Finally there's a sound from the lake. A small splash, made by some creature surfacing or diving back down to the muddy depths. It distracts me. When I look back the cat is gone.

Chapter 21

COLETTE

The narrow alleyway that ran up the side of the laundry certainly wasn't the most romantic place to meet someone, but needs must when privacy was your priority. Whether they would still come given how late it was, Colette didn't know, but she was prepared to wait, and hope. The alley was where the stuff that needed taking to the refuse centre collected. In the moonlight Colette spotted the most recent 'casualties' – a couple of the chairs they used for the wedding ceremonies. They were elegant, with slender legs and backs carved into the shape of hearts, but they weren't what you'd call robust. The wedding of the Texan couple a few weeks back had resulted in quite a few breakages. The groomsmen had all been lantern-jawed giants who looked like they'd been fed on raw steak from the age of two. They were no more drunken or rowdy than usual, but they had been considerably heavier. One of the beds had ended up broken as well, an occurrence that was rarer than you might think given the primary nature of the business at the finca. The splintered bed slats were probably some-where in the pile of cast-offs as well.

Aside from rubbish, the alley was also choked with rosemary. It thrived, somehow, without water or much light. Perhaps it lived off the steam from the laundry vents. But at least the rosemary meant that the alley smelt better than the kitchen bay where the staff congregated on their breaks to smoke and moan about her. That was the other reason she never went there. Her presence would have inhibited their bitch-fests. She had sympathy; everyone needed to sound off about their boss every now and again, and her reputation as a ball-breaker was justified. Everyone had their cross to bear and she was theirs.

Colette found her usual spot, halfway down the passage. She leant against the wall and looked up at the night sky. Only three of the hundreds of distant stars were visible from her narrow, shoddy sliver of paradise. Three would have to do, for the time being. At least it was peaceful and as far away from her family as she could be – for the time being. She breathed in the scent of the rosemary, felt her shoulders relax and her breathing slow.

Alone, surrounded by broken furniture, darkness and rambling rosemary, Colette closed her eyes and lifted the lid on her secret. She had a lover – and that fact, despite the betrayal of her parents and her brother, made her hopeful. For the first time in what felt like forever she wasn't alone, and that meant that what came next didn't seem so difficult. Looking up at the stars, Colette replayed their blossoming relationship. She recalled the bubbling curiosity, the urgent need to know everything, however trivial, about each other, the desire to impress, to please, to seduce. It gave her a warm feeling in her stomach to think how much they laughed. Humour had been an extremely rare commodity in Colette's life, to date – there'd never been much to laugh about in her family – but she was discovering that it was a heady, invigorating property, something to be cherished. She hadn't realised that laughter had the power to reduce anxieties to irrelevancies and adversaries to idiots. Nor had she realised that it could unite people, help them cross boundaries and barriers – emotional, social, physical. Colette wrapped her arms around herself, tried to fill the ache of longing with remembered skin and lips. There *was* someone who cared about her, perhaps more than cared, and that changed everything.

Suddenly she sensed that she was no longer alone. She tensed, opened her eyes. There was someone standing at the end of the passage. They stared at each other. She disciplined herself not to move or say anything. He posed no real threat to her – stupid people didn't. It was the bright ones you had to watch out for. Or at least that was what Colette told herself as she watched him stumble his way down the passage towards her. But clumsy creatures could still be dangerous, perhaps more so because they weren't fully in control. Colette stood her ground, waited. At twenty paces the smell of booze hit her. So, stupid and drunk – the factors indicating a problematic encounter were mounting. Her position, trapped in a dead end in the dead of night, was already less than ideal.

She opened on the offensive. 'Where were you earlier? You were supposed to help with the set-up.'

'I was sorting something for one of the guests.'

'What?'

'That's for me to know,' he tapped the side of his nose, 'and you . . . not to.' He was such a dick. 'Anyhow . . . never mind what I've been up to. I want to know what you're doing lurking around out here at this time of night?'

'I *was* having a few moments of peace.'

'All on your lonesome?'

She looked around. 'So it would appear.'

'You're on your own too much, you.' His syntax was never the best.

'Am I?'

'Yep.' He took another step towards her. She didn't move, but she couldn't, really; her back was literally to the wall. 'Doesn't it get lonely playing the ice queen all the time?'

'No.' And she certainly had no use for the sort of company he was offering. 'Besides, it wouldn't be right for me to socialise with *the staff*.' She knew it was risky reminding him of his lowly place in the hierarchy, but the problem was he seemed to keep forgetting it.

Pissed as he was, Luther picked up on her put-down. 'Fuck you, Colette. I'm not just some employee, and you know it. Why don't you pull the stick out of your arse, just for a second or two.' He rested his hand on the wall beside her head and leant into her. His breath was sour with fags and wine. 'I know what would loosen you up.' His other hand landed heavily on her breast. She didn't react. She refused to give him the satisfaction of knowing that he was scaring her. Any sign of weakness was what creatures like Luther thrived on. He went in for a kiss. She jerked her face away, just in time. He made do with a wet suck on her neck. He was so out of order that it took a couple of seconds for Colette's outrage to fire up. But when the full realisation did kick in that she was pinned against a wall, with Luther's stiff prick digging into her stomach and his wet mouth suctioned onto her neck, her next move was obvious, and decisive. The kneecap is a bony structure and when rammed into a soft, undefended ball-sack it's the perfect weapon with which to remind an old relic just how extinct he is. Luther made a satisfying 'oomph' noise as he doubled over. Even with him head down and groaning she could still make out, 'Ya fucking, frigid witch!' He coughed and a lump of phlegm, or vomit – it was hard to tell in the dark and she wasn't about to check – came up. Jesus, he was disgusting. It was time for Colette to make her exit. She wasn't really frightened of him, but she also didn't want to hang around to find out what sort of mood he'd be in when he got the use of his groin and his senses back. As she stepped around him, she said in a voice that was as cold and steady as she could manage, 'Touch me again, Luther, and you're a dead man.'

His response was another pain-riddled cough and an awkwardly flipped finger.

Chapter 22

MADDIE

Maddie woke and immediately felt troubled. She sat up in bed. The room was in total darkness. When she'd been in the annex with Alex she hadn't realised how little lighting there was around the finca, but in the tower it was very noticeable. Compared to being back at home in light-polluted London, it was like sleeping in a sealed coffin. She clicked on the bedside lamp, felt marginally better for its warm glow. But the light didn't dispel her sense that something was off, not with the room, but with herself. Her face felt weirdly tight, the skin around her eyes and mouth uncomfortable. She raised a hand. Her face was hot – not from the sun, but from inside. She pressed her fingertips into her cheeks. The flesh didn't yield like it should. It was as if her features were expanding, pushing against the limits of her skin. The thought that this was a dream occurred to her. She shoved back the covers and climbed out of bed, hoping that getting up and moving around would wake her. It didn't. Still dream-trapped, she made her way into the bathroom and clicked on the light.

A bloated, engorged creature stared back at her. Thickened lips. Eyes sunk to slits. It looked like a face that had been pumped full of Botox by a vengeful beautician. She told herself that this was an anxiety nightmare. Pre-wedding nerves running riot. She willed herself to wake up, banged her hands against the cold edge of the sink in a bid to break free of the dream. The only response was a sharp pain jangling up her arms. 'No!' The sound of her distorted voice brought home the reality that this was no night fright. She needed help.

Chapter 23

COLETTE

Kissing. There was nothing more intimate. Nothing more powerful. Nothing more soothing after a nasty experience. It was a conversation without words. A welcome home after what felt like an interminable separation. Their kissing contained gentleness, connection, permission, trust, safety, confidence, vulnerability, want, willingness and, of course, desire – all held in a moment that lasted as long as they both stayed with it. It was them against the world. Them in a world of their own making. Just them. No one else. Now, before, or for ever after. Lips, tongue, teeth. A sensory feast that you could never get enough of. Greed elevated by passion. Mutual selfishness. A secret language that silently shouted – *I chose you and you chose me*. Mouth to mouth. Mouth to neck. Mouth to stomach, breast, thighs, legs, ankles, toes and back around again. Always back to the lips. It was life-affirming. Lifesaving.

Chapter 24

MADDIE

Maddie banged on Lou's bedroom door. There was no response. She listened, heard nothing aside from her own panicked breathing. She thumped again. It shouldn't take this long. Someone battering on your door in the early hours of the morning was an alarm call, not a polite request for a late-night chat. Maddie knew she needed to calm down, but she couldn't. She tried the door. It was locked. Why tonight, of all nights, had Lou decided that she cherished her privacy? Unless she wasn't there. Unless she was out somewhere in the finca still drinking. But who would she be with at this hour? She didn't like any of the other guests. Maddie was about to give up when the door suddenly opened and any residual hope that she was dreaming vanished.

Lou looked horrified. 'Maddie, what the hell?'

'I know.'

There was a beat, another. What was she waiting for? Then Lou stepped forward, took Maddie by the arm and led her over to one of the sofas in the lounge. 'Let me see.' She turned on the overhead lights. The brightness was brutal. 'How does it feel?'

'Tight. And getting tighter. And my back is itching like crazy.' A sure sign that the allergic reaction she was having was spreading. It felt like a swarm of ants was crawling all over her, nipping and biting. Lou asked her to turn around. She lifted up Maddie's vest top. Maddie felt Lou trace her fingers lightly across the welts that were brewing and bubbling up beneath her skin. The coolness of her touch and the kindness it contained brought a tiny bit of relief.

'Do you think it was something you ate?'

Maddie shook her head. 'No.' She took a breath, sounding like an asthmatic. 'I think it was the flowers.'

'What flowers?'

'Someone left a bouquet in my room. In my bed.'

Lou made no comment about this revelation; instead she swung into practical mode. 'Okay. I think you should get in the shower. It might wash off whatever triggered this and it might help with the itching. It can't do any harm. I'm going to find someone to help.'

'Who?'

Lou didn't answer, but disappeared into her room. Maddie didn't move. A few seconds later Lou re-emerged, dressed in joggers and a T-shirt, her feet bare. 'Maddie! Go and get in the shower. I'll be as quick as I can.' And then she was gone, leaving the door to their suite wide open. The urge to run to Alex's room was overwhelming, but having a shower was a sensible suggestion. So she did as she'd been told. As she huddled in the cubicle, with the cold water sluicing over her burning skin, Maddie watched herself in the mirror – growing uglier with each passing second.

Chapter 25

COLETTE

Colette took one look at Maddie cowering in the shower and reached for her phone. Lou stepped in between them and passed Maddie a towel – offering her privacy and protection. As Colette clicked on the only number she could think to call she heard Lou say, 'I thought Colette was the best person to tell.'

It was gone 2.00 a.m., but there was supposed be someone awake up at the house 24/7. An overzealous precaution or a necessary one? It was always hard to tell, until something happened that put your security to the test. It took whoever was on duty long enough to answer.

Finally someone picked up. 'What's up?' It was Pete, one of her father's men.

'Maddie's had some sort of allergic reaction.'

'Who?'

'The bride!' Colette didn't give Pete the chance to say anything more, be it stupid or helpful. 'She needs to see a doctor.'

'What, now?' She could almost hear the cogs turning. Pete was thinking about having to wake Ray. Nothing happened without her father's say-so, especially not emergency calls in the middle of the night that involved the family. And Maddie was, very nearly, family.

The bride herself was currently sitting on the toilet, in a world of acute discomfort. 'Yes. It needs to be tonight. He'll be fine about it.' 'He' – a shorthand they all understood. Pete said nothing, trapped between two Archers. For a second Colette felt a flash of sympathy for him. She helped him out by taking responsibility. 'It's my call, Pete, and I'm telling you to wake him up and get him to arrange for one of the lads to get Dr Carizales up to the house ASAP. Tell him that I'm bringing Maddie now.' Decisive was the way to go in a crisis. She needed to be seen to be dealing with this – and she wanted to do it well away from the other guests. Sleeping dogs often sensed drama and stirred, and the last thing Colette – correction – Maddie needed was an audience. 'We'll be with you in fifteen minutes, twenty tops.' She ended the call, reset her expression from irritated back to calm, unflappable mode, and spoke directly to Maddie. 'Lou says it might have been some flowers?' Maddie nodded. 'Okay. I'll go get them. We might need to show the doc what set you off.' There were bin bags and rubber gloves in the cleaning cupboard on the ground floor. 'I'll be back in a minute.' But at the door she stopped. 'Are you on any medication?'

Maddie didn't look up. 'No.' But as Colette turned to leave, she seemed to think better of it and corrected herself. 'Sorry. Yes.' There was a pause. 'They're in my toilet bag.'

Colette returned to the bathroom, grabbed Maddie's toiletries bag and, instead of giving it to Maddie, set off, shouting to Lou over her shoulder as she went, 'Get her into some clothes. Anything will do.'

Chapter 26

MADDIE

Colette's parting question had totally thrown Maddie. Her response had been the worst. A clumsy denial, followed by a stuttered admission, and Colette now had possession of her toilet bag – which meant that Colette would find her collection of painkillers and her epilepsy meds. Well, it was too late to put that cat back in the bag now. Besides, Maddie had more pressing problems. Her whole body seemed to be going into revolt.

Lou guided her into her bedroom. She handed Maddie some of her own clothes to put on, a pair of harem pants and a tie-dyed top. Getting dressed took a huge effort. Lou slipped a pair of sliders onto Maddie's feet for her. Then Colette was back with a bulging black bin bag. She took charge. 'Right, follow me.'

But Maddie didn't want to go anywhere without Alex. Colette seemed to read her mind. 'I think the priority is getting you seen. You can call Alex from my parents' house when we know what we're dealing with.' Maddie looked at Lou. Lou nodded and they followed Colette out into the cool night air. Guided by the light from Colette and Lou's phones, they took the path down to the lake and crossed the bridge. Maddie wondered where the hell they were going – not to the main car park, for sure.

It was very quiet in amongst the trees, except for Maddie's increasingly wheezy breathing. They walked without talking for about five minutes, then Colette stopped abruptly. They'd reached a high wall, wreathed in some sort of vine. What the hell was Colette playing at, leading them to a dead end? Maddie's panic bubbled back up and her breathing worsened. It felt like there was something wrapped around her neck. Her chest was hurting. Maddie felt a wave of despair wash through her. Then she saw that there was a door set deep into the wall. The door was made of wood and had large, brass rivets hammered into it. Maddie was yearning for bright lights and modern medicine, not more quirky fairy-tale touches. Colette didn't need a key to unlock the door; there was a keypad set into the wall. Consciously or unconsciously, she shielded it with her body as she entered the code. There was a buzz, then she pushed the door open.

Chapter 27

LOU

The door opened onto a normal road with tarmac and white lines. Mundane life, just there, on the other side of the wall. It felt like they were escaping some sort of dark fantasy and rejoining good old, boring normality. The sheer ordinariness of it helped to clear Lou's head. Across the road there was a small car park lit by a couple of street lights. There were five cars parked in it. Colette led them to a dusty Audi. Lou and Maddie climbed into the back and they set off.

Colette drove fast. They saw no other cars in the dipped beam of the Audi's headlights, but why would they: they were halfway up a mountain, in the middle of the night. Lou reached out and took Maddie's hand. She looked and sounded terrible. 'How much longer?' Lou asked.

'Ten minutes.'

The news didn't seem to reassure Maddie. She was getting more and more agitated. Her breath was coming in short, puffy rasps. It really didn't sound good. She started clawing at her throat. Lou tried to stop her. 'Mads, it's okay. Try and take some deep breaths.'

'I am!' Maddie gasped.

Lou met Colette's gaze in the rear-view mirror, questioning. 'We're nearly there,' Colette snapped.

She put her foot down and the Audi picked up speed. They barrelled along in the darkness, swooping up and down the unseen dips in the road as Maddie's breathing deteriorated. At one point Colette must have misjudged one of the bends because suddenly the car rocked and tilted. For a second or two, the tyres spun, seeking purchase. A shower of dust and forest floor debris flew up. It sounded like they were being strafed by gunfire. Lou reached out and braced herself against Colette's seat. Colette responded with another sharp glance in the mirror. As the car righted itself, Maddie slumped sideways onto Lou – a dead weight. She'd lost consciousness. She was having a full-blown tonic-clonic seizure. Her body began to spasm. With each fresh wave of muscle contractions her head banged against Lou's chest. They should be going to hospital.

But they weren't. There was nothing but forest all around them.

Lou starting counting. She counted to sixty then to sixty again. And again. And yet again. Four minutes passed and Lou was still counting. A huge seizure, on top of an acute allergic reaction, was bad. It could be fatal.

After what felt like an age, the Audi slewed off onto a much narrower road. Finally, there were lights. Colette pulled the car up outside a huge set of gates. The gates swung open to reveal a sweeping circular drive at the apex of which sat a large villa. There was a Range Rover parked out front. Civilisation, at last. Colette thrashed the Audi up the drive and slammed it to an abrupt stop. She jumped out. At the same time a middle-aged man emerged from the passenger seat of the other car, medical bag in hand – the promised doctor. He ran over to the Audi, yanked open the door and roughly pulled Lou out of the way, then set to work on Maddie, firing questions over his shoulder as he did. Lou answered as best she could, adding, without being asked, 'She has epilepsy. She takes Pregabalin to control it. It normally does. She's been out for about six minutes, maybe seven.'

The doctor manhandled Maddie onto her side on the back seat and repositioned her head, presumably trying to clear her airway. 'Do you have her medication with you?'

'Colette has it.' Lou turned to Colette. For a second she didn't respond; she seemed transfixed by the scene unfolding in the back of the car. 'Colette!' Lou shouted.

'Sorry. Her toilet bag's on the front seat.' Colette still didn't move.

Lou went around to the front of the car and pulled open the passenger door. But the bag wasn't there. No bag. No meds. She searched around in the footwell. Eventually she found it wedged underneath the seat. She passes it to the doctor. While he sifted through Maddie's collection of tablets, Lou looked at her friend. It was a disturbing sight. Lou had seen Maddie have seizures before, but never anything like this. Her face, which was already distorted by the swelling, kept stiffening then going slack as her body convulsed. She looked so vulnerable. The doctor was saying something. Lou tried to focus. 'Sorry, what?'

'I don't see her rescue medicine in here?'

'It should be there. She always has some with her.'

'It isn't.' He tossed the bag aside and went into his own supplies, producing a syringe. He shook it and snapped off the cap, then he leant over Maddie. Lou watched as he parted her swollen lips, forced the syringe into her mouth and pressed the plunger. When the dose had been administered he dropped the syringe and held her jaw shut. The way he was forcing her chin up made it look like he was choking her, not saving her.

Lou retreated – not wanting to see any more – and went to stand silently with Colette. She looked around and noticed a man who was presumably the driver who had fetched the doctor. Also present were Alex's father and, to her surprise, Paul Stainforth. What he was doing up at the villa at this time of night was anyone's guess. Lou risked looking back at the unfolding drama in the Audi. The doctor had let go of Maddie and sat back, all sense of urgency gone, but he continued to stare down at her. The stillness seemed to expand and fill the night air. No one said a word.

Then Lou heard the doctor say, 'It's okay. Take your time.'

Another minute passed, then the doctor backed out of the car and held out his hand. Miraculously, Maddie emerged, under her own steam. The doctor took hold of her arm, looked at Ray and said, 'I think Maddie might need a sit-down and some water.'

Chapter 28

MADDIE

It was night-time. There was a man leading her into a big glass structure. He had a calm voice. She had no idea where she was. Was she dead? It was possible. But it felt too real. Heavenly gravel surely didn't crunch underfoot. She managed the steps, somehow. Her senses started coming back to her and, as they did, so did the pain. Why did her face hurt so much and why was her skin prickling as if it was on fire? She took some deep breaths. The air was soft and cool but it burnt her lungs. Her brain started catching up with her sensations. Someone had sent her flowers. Then . . . then? She'd been in a car. In the dark. With Lou, and Colette. They were here now. As was Alex's father. Then . . . nothing.

They entered a big space. There was something suspended from the ceiling. Maddie stopped and stared at it. It was a human being, made of glass, caught in a web of wires. A modern-day crucifixion. Maddie felt a ripple of sympathy. She swayed. The man by her side held on to her. Colette's voice cut in. 'Bring her through to the lounge.' The next room was again large and soulless. The man – he was a doctor, Maddie knew that now – steered her over to one of the sofas. She stumbled as she sat down. She felt so heavy. Lou appeared and poured her a glass of water. Maddie guided the glass to her mouth with two hands and sipped, like a child. It helped to wash away the bitterness in her mouth. It was that familiar taste that told her what had happened.

She'd had a seizure. A big one. Her first in over a year.

The thought pushed her back against the sofa. No, not now. Not after all this time. Not so close to her wedding. She started to cry. She knew it would make things worse. Crying was a waste of valuable energy, and she had precious little of that left, but it was just so unfair. The people in the room closed in on her. They all started talking at once. She tried to ignore them and breathe. She needed to regain control of her body and her brain – and quickly.

'Please can everyone give Maddie some room,' the doctor commanded. The space around her expanded. She felt a little steadier. 'Good girl. I can see that you're coming back to us.' The doctor had a nice smile. 'We couldn't find your own rescue meds, so I gave you a dose of buccal midazolam. You responded immediately, but I want to give you a steroid injection and some antihistamine as well, to counteract the allergic reaction you've had to the flowers.'

Colette leapt in. 'I brought them with us, if you want to see them.'

The doctor continued to direct his speech at Maddie. 'There's no need. The treatment for acute anaphylactic shock is generic. We just need to make sure that we keep those airways clear.' He took Maddie's hand in his, turned it over and looked at the rash of tiny red blisters that were bubbling up all over her arms. 'Could someone please sort out some cold compresses. Damp, clean towels will do. Iced water, if you have it.' Then the doctor gave Maddie the steroid injection and some tablets to swallow. The towels were brought, and Lou held them against Maddie's arms. Some semblance of normality reasserted itself.

Immediate crisis over, Ray stepped forward. He grasped the doctor's hand and pumped it up and down. 'Thank you so much, Dr Carizales. You literally saved the day, and our dear Maddie. We can't thank you enough.' The doctor made a dismissive gesture. 'And your advice would be, what?'

'To rest. Recover. I'll leave Maddie a course of anti-histamine, some cream to help calm the skin irritation and some more midazolam syringes, to be on the safe side. The swelling will take a few days to settle down, but there shouldn't be any permanent damage. But – should there be any concerns about her breathing she must go straight to the hospital.' He then crouched down and spoke directly to Maddie. 'The seizure was a warning, Maddie. It's not my place to tell you how to manage your condition, but you must listen to your body. You know the risks. Please don't go taking any chances for the sake of a wedding.'

'Thank you,' Maddie croaked.

He rose and started gathering his stuff.

Ray shook his hand again, then guided him to the door. 'Paul, if you can go with Dr Carizales, get together the medicines he wants Maddie to use and sort out payment for his time and expertise, that would be appreciated. Pete is waiting in the car to run you home, doctor.'

At the doorway Dr Carizales bowed courteously, then disappeared.

'How are you feeling?' Lou asked.

'A lot better than I was.' Maddie's skin still felt too small for her body, and she couldn't see properly, but she could see enough. She could see Ray studying her.

There was a pause, then he said, 'You're very welcome to stay here. As long as you need to.' As concern went, it was shockingly minimal. All eyes turned to Maddie. Were they expecting her to recover there and then on the spot?

Colette stepped in. 'Shall I go and wake Mother?'

Her question seemed both to surprise and amuse Ray. 'I'm not sure your mother would be of much assistance in the circumstances. And besides, Maddie is on the mend. Aren't you, my dear?' Then he freaked her out by asking, 'Unless, of course, you would like us to wake Marilyn?'

The thought of Alex's mother being roused from her sleep to come and tend to Maddie was as scary as it was ludicrous. 'No! Please. There's no need to wake her on my account.' Maddie had a sudden very clear image of Marilyn staring in frozen disapproval at the scene taking place in her stylish living room. Maddie hadn't told the Archers about her epilepsy. She knew they had their reservations about her, and adding a medical condition into the mix was, she reasoned, hardly likely to improve her ratings. Well, that secret had been well and truly spilt in dramatic and messy fashion tonight. The thought made Maddie feel even more weary. She simply wanted them all to leave her alone. 'I'll just sit here for a little while, let the tablets work, then I'll go back to the finca and rest.' Ray seemed to approve of the plan. Actual silence now descended on the room. No one said a word. Paul did not return. It was unbearable. 'Please, go back to bed. There's no need for you to stay up.'

Ray didn't need to be asked twice.

The Day Before the Wedding

Chapter 29

COLETTE

It was still dark when they left the villa. It would be another four hours before the sun rose. Lou went to sleep almost immediately. Colette envied her. Silence descended in the car. Colette didn't know what to say to Maddie. She never did.

Unlike their dash up the mountain, Colette took the drive back down steadily. It wasn't a matter of life or death this time. Maddie had been in a really bad way. It had sounded as if she was on her way out. And yet, Lazarus-like, she'd risen from the back seat of the car and, with Dr Carizales's swift intervention, made a remarkable recovery. True, she still looked like shit, but that was to be expected. Equally remarkable was the fact that she seemed to be in the mood for a conversation.

'Where does the road go?' Maddie asked.

Colette couldn't fathom why Maddie was bothering with small talk. 'Sorry, what?'

'The road your parents live on. Where does it lead?'

'It drops down a bit further along the ridge beyond the villa to a farm. It's been derelict for years. That's where it ends.'

'Oh. So you can't get to the next village or town on it?'

'No.'

'It's quite isolated, isn't it?'

'Yes. That's the way they like it.' Tiredness made Colette terse, but she provided the next snippet of information voluntarily. Maddie should know the full extent of what she was marrying into. Yes, the Archers were the type of people who had private roads built, for their own convenience, in areas of outstanding natural beauty. They were the type of people who lived in architect-designed villas full of ground-breaking art with twenty-four-hour security. They were able to summon doctors with access to a panoply of drugs in the middle of the night, no questions asked. They could make anything happen, make any problem go away – if it was in their interests to do so. 'My parents paid for this road to be widened and resurfaced when they bought the finca and built the house. They basically own this side of the mountain.'

Maddie muttered something that sounded like 'right', then shut up – which was what Colette had intended. They turned onto the bigger road; you couldn't really call it a main road. The night had not gone as planned. It had been long, sleepless and stressful. All Colette wanted to do was get back to the finca and crash for a few hours. The next couple of days were going to be even more challenging now. Colette stared out of the windscreen at the darkness. She could sense Maddie looking at her – or more accurately, studying her. Eventually Colette cracked. 'You feeling okay now?'

'I've feel like I've been in a fight.'

'Yeah, I can imagine.'

There was a beat. 'Can you?'

Colette felt caught out. 'Well, obviously, not literally. But I saw how . . . bad it was.'

'Yeah, it was.' There was something in the way Maddie said it that made Colette glance over her shoulder. The face she caught looking at her from the back seat of the car was unnerving, and not simply because it was still so swollen and misshapen. It was the expression in Maddie's eyes that was unsettling. Was she was accusing Colette of something? The tension held. Maddie volunteered nothing more. Colette went back to concentrating on her driving.

She was relieved to see that the car park was coming up on the left. She barely slowed as she pulled hard left into it. The Audi slewed into its space. She killed the engine. Colette reached for the door handle and was about to get out of the car when Maddie asked, 'Did you put those flowers in my room?'

Dawn breaks. I've barely slept. Tired as I am, I get up and go for a walk around the finca.

Last night was a turning point. Time is running out. Tomorrow, Maddie is due to walk down the aisle and become Alex's wife. I had no choice but to up the ante. The flowers were a nice touch, I thought. A bouquet for the bride. How fitting, and how seemingly innocuous. Maddie's gorgeous hothouse blooms even had a secret added extra – a generous spritz of extract of chrysanthemum – otherwise known as synthetic pyrethroid pesticide. As toxins go it's a nasty one, especially for someone with Maddie's physical frailties. It could be a lethal one – given that she's missing her rescue meds. It was easy enough to lift the syringes. I simply asked to use the bathroom before we went down to dinner. She is shockingly lax about some of the things that she really should take better care of.

I pass the tower, the scene of the crime. It's quiet. No signs of life – which is as it should be. I head down to the lake.

As I walk, I reflect on how far I've come. It's interesting, having a hidden agenda, especially one that consumes so much of your time and mental energy. It changes you, makes you look at yourself more clearly, really think about who you are. And that's a worthwhile exercise. Other people would be well advised to give it a go. Were it not for the messy, dangerous aspects to my campaign, it could almost be described as stimulating. It's certainly more challenging than I thought it would be.

I'm very aware that there's a margin of unpredictability in my approach, but that's the price I have to pay in order to remain undetected. Staying hidden while trying to influence other people's feelings and actions isn't easy. But the one thing I am certain of is that I'm not prepared to jeopardise my position, my future, my reputation for someone like Maddie. She's simply not worth it. As a result, my approach has to be innovative and subtle – a sleight of hand, not the thrust of a knife or the press of a pillow. The bad things that keep happening to Maddie are simply terrible accidents. Awful bad luck. And if that's true, how can I, or anyone else, be to blame? There's no crime being committed because there is no perpetrator.

The question is, how much atrocious luck can one woman – and her husband-to-be – take? Well, we're about to find out.

I'm so preoccupied thinking about Maddie that it takes me a second to realise that she is there, right in front of me, sitting on the end of the jetty, looking out over the water. For fuck's sake! This isn't right. She's come into contact with a dangerous toxin, so how come she's sitting there, placidly watching the sun rise as if nothing's happened? She's a bloody limpet, that's why. Have you ever tried to prise a limpet off a rock? It's virtually impossible. They suction themselves on so tightly that you have to use brute force to smash them free.

I'm furious. I have a sudden, intense, overwhelming urge to end it, here and now. Sod caution, sod subtlety, sod finesse. I want to run up behind her, push her in the lake, jump in after her, hold her under and keep pressing down hard until the thrashing and the bubbles stop. That would sort her out, once and for all.

I step out onto the jetty.

She coughs. It's such a small, human noise. But it's enough to shake some sense into me. I won't succumb to such crude violence. There is no need. I have time. I have other options still open to me.

Besides, I am not a murderer. Not yet, anyway.

I back away from her slowly, taking care where I put my feet. She doesn't hear me or turn around. My cover isn't blown.

Although the sensible thing to do would be to go to my room and regroup, I don't. I want to get a proper look at her. I need to assess the extent of the damage I've caused. I head into the trees and make my way around the edge of the lake, praying that she doesn't move. From my new vantage point I study her. God knows, that bouquet took me enough effort and expense to source, have shipped, lace with pesticide and have secreted in her bed (Luther was happy to oblige with the last part of the plan, for a price, although he did query the need for surgical gloves and increased his fee accordingly when I insisted that he wore them). But it's done its job, in so far as she looks terrible. It's as if someone has screwed a bike pump into the back of her head and forced air in between her skull and her skin. With nowhere to go, the air has filled out her features to cartoon proportions. So much for the beautiful bride! She looks monstrous. Surely she can't intend to go ahead with the wedding now. Or so you'd think. But what troubles me is that, despite the state of her, Maddie seems oddly unbowed. As she sits alone and bereft on the jetty she doesn't look beaten. She holds her misshapen head high and her swollen chin level. As a show of bravado it's quietly impressive and deeply irritating. The flowers were supposed to knock the stuffing out of her, not pack it in. Her fucking resilience is still a problem. See, I told you. She's a limpet.

I take a breath. Put things into the correct perspective. Namely, mine. I'm stronger than her, more intelligent, more committed. She will crack. I just need to keep exerting the pressure. And I suspect she's had help this time. How else could she be so calm, so together, so bloody upright? But there are cracks and tensions appearing in her relationships. I've seen how she's been withdrawing into herself and this latest catastrophe isn't going to improve matters. Sow enough seeds of suspicion, and knowing who to turn to in her hour of need is going to become increasingly difficult for our poor beleaguered bride.

Eventually she lumbers to her feet and I watch her walk off in the direction of the main building. I know where she's heading, she's going to Alex – the man she believes will stand by her, no matter what. I almost admire her confidence in his love for her. It would be respect-worthy, if only it weren't the thing that's likely to be the death of her.

I wish I could follow her, catch a glimpse of Alex's face when he opens the door and sees his bride, but that would be too much of a risk. Despite his better self, the one he's been working on so assiduously these past few years, I know that Alex will, secretly, be horrified when he claps eyes on her. Alex likes beautiful things – he grows towards them, like a plant to the light, weakening himself in the process. It's not his fault, it's coded into him. I think it's because beauty is predictable, defined, set in stone, the standards agreed. Beauty makes Alex feel safe, and because of that, like most people, he values it too highly. Anything ugly, be it inside or out, scares him. We all have our codes, however much we try to hide and defy them.

The scene by the lake is perfect now. Humanity-free. The rising sun has burnt off the mist, but the light is still soft. The heat is a whispered promise rather than a harsh fact. I feel awake despite my lack of sleep, calm despite the storm inside me, poised despite the trauma to come.

There's still time.

All I need to do is stick to the plan.

She will break.

And I know what will break her.

Chapter 30

ALEX

Alex woke and knew instantly that it was still early. He could tell by the half-light filtering through the shutters and by the total silence. He was irritated; he'd been looking forward to having a lie-in. More sleep might also take the edge off the hangover that was brewing at the back of his skull. He kept his eyes closed. He was as parched as the Sahara. Bloody Paul with his celebratory cigars and brandy – the props for doing business were so arcane. He knew he should go fetch a bottle of water from the fridge, but he couldn't be bothered.

Still, the deal was done. He had the capital he needed. He was literally in business. Had he sold his soul to secure his future? Yes. But no more so than anyone else. He'd been working in the City long enough to know that morality and ethics played no part in the markets – not if you wanted to be successful. And Alex did want to succeed. Nor was he going to agonise too much about nepotism. Connections and contacts were the currency of the industry he'd gone into – with a firm nudge from his father. If he'd wanted a life of ideals and creativity he'd have chosen a career like Bobby's. And there was a greater good here – by moving the family finances onto a more legit footing he would be protecting them all, including Colette. Not that his sister appeared to see it like that, if the look on her face during Ray's speech was anything to go by. But that was their father's fault. He'd obviously not spoken to Colette about the movement of such a huge chunk of their capital into Archer Asset Management, despite promising to . . . *when the time was right*. Well, in front of everyone at Alex's pre-wedding bash was plainly *not* the right moment. Ray's decision to keep Colette in the dark wasn't, in truth, that much of a surprise. Their father had always played them off against each other. He seemed to take pleasure in it. His oft-repeated 'joke' was, 'What's the point of having kids, if you can't mess with them every now and again?' Alex had made his peace with disliking his father many years ago. Bobby had helped him with that. He'd made Alex see that love was not compulsory within a family, especially when your father was an overbearing egotist. Surprisingly, Colette, for all her seeming toughness, appeared to still be yearning for a more normal parent-child relationship, one that was based on love rather than mutual self-interest. It was never going to happen.

He rolled over, looked at his phone: 6.45 a.m. Although he was fully awake now, there was no way he was getting up. He got comfortable, willed himself sleepy. That was when the knocking started – soft but urgent – at his door. The bloody maid? He wouldn't put it past his sister to have listed his room as first on the cleaning roster out of spite. He waited for Housekeeping to give up and go away. They didn't; they just kept tapping away at the door. He shouted, 'No thanks. I'm good.' They knocked again. Alex was

174

properly awake now. He hauled himself out of bed, crossed the room and yanked open the door. 'Look, I don't need the room servicing right now. Thank you!'

'Alex. It's me, Maddie.'

It was a good job Maddie had identified herself because for a second or two Alex didn't recognise his own bride. She looked like she'd been beaten. Her eyes were slits, the flesh around them a livid pink, and her lips were badly swollen. 'Alex! Please! Let me in.' Even her voice sounded different.

'What in Christ's name?' Her hands flew to her face, trying to hide the damage. 'Sorry, I didn't mean . . . What on earth happened?' He eased her into the room, kicked the door shut behind them and led her over to the bed.

She lowered herself down onto it like an old lady. 'I had an allergic reaction.'

'To what?' She flinched again. He needed to moderate his tone. Patience was what was needed. She seemed very shaky.

'A bouquet.' He didn't leap in, but waited for her to tell the tale. 'Last night, when I got back to the tower, someone had left some flowers in my bedroom. In my bed, to be precise.' Well, that was weird, but Alex kept the thought to himself. 'I obviously handled them when I put them in water. I went to bed. Went to sleep. When I woke up a couple of hours later, I had broken out in a rash, my face was all swollen and my breathing was affected.'

He patted her arm. He was trying really hard not to stare at her, but it was difficult. She looked SO different. It was like when you were dreaming and there was someone in your dream that you didn't recognise, but at the same time you knew, with absolute certainty, that they were really

175

your girlfriend, or sister, or your best friend. But this was no dream, this was Maddie – the day before their wedding.

'We need to get you to a doctor.'

'I've already been seen by a doctor.'

'How?'

'Colette took me up to your parents' house, last night. She called him for me, or your dad did. It's all a bit hazy.'

'In the middle of the night?'

'Yes.'

'Why in God's name didn't you get someone to wake me?'

'There wasn't time.'

Was that really true? Surely Lou or Colette could have come and woken him. Perhaps they'd wanted to keep him away from her. But why? He felt excluded, which wasn't the issue, but it niggled. 'But I . . .'

'Alex! Can you, *please*, just give me a minute.' There was an edge to her voice. He shut up. 'I had a seizure. In the car.'

'What?'

'The reaction to the flowers triggered a seizure.'

'Jesus. Are you all right?'

'I am now. Apart from this,' she gestured at herself, 'obviously.'

'Oh, Mads!'

'The doctor gave me a dose of midazolam, a steroid injection and some antihistamine.' He waited for her to tell him the prognosis. 'The swelling should go down over the next twenty-four to forty-eight hours; the rash may take longer.' As she said it Alex caught himself staring at the cluster of tiny, angry blisters at the corners of her mouth. She saw him looking, let out a sob. 'It's all over my body as well. I tried to get some sleep when we got back, like the doctor said, but the itching was driving me mad. And I wanted to see you.'

So she had gone back to the tower and tried to sleep, instead of coming to him. Again, he felt but fought the ripple of resentment. This was about poor Maddie, not him. He didn't know how to comfort her. He put his arms out and she sort of leant forward into them, but the minute his hands touched her she flinched. 'Sorry. Sorry!' This was an absolute nightmare. She sobbed four more times then stopped. She looked – apart from disturbingly changed – utterly miserable.

'And the doctor was sure that you don't need to go to the hospital to get checked out?'

'Yes, he said the treatment would be the same. I have a week's worth of pills. I know it doesn't look like it, but I'm a lot better than I was a few hours ago.'

'So we have to just wait?'

She nodded. They sat on the bed. Alex saw the wedding they'd planned evaporating. Christ, the photos! And what the hell would their guests make of it? And his mother! Her reaction didn't bear thinking about. On top of which, he couldn't even touch his bride.

Maddie said something.

'Sorry?' He'd been too preoccupied to hear what.

'I said . . . there was no card.' He didn't know what she was talking about. That seemed to irritate her. Her tone was sharper when she next spoke. 'With the flowers. I have no idea who sent them, or who put them in my room.'

'Doesn't Colette know?' Colette knew everything; at least she did in relation to the finca.

'She says she has no idea. She's adamant that the bouquet wasn't in the flower order for the wedding. And she's going to check, but she said none of her staff would ever put anything in a guest's room without her express permission.'

'Okay.' Alex wasn't sure what Maddie was getting at. 'But they were presumably from one of the guests?'

'That would make sense.'

'But?' he queried. He had a bad feeling about where she was going with this.

'I need to find out who sent them. It's a peculiar thing to do – put flowers in someone's bed. And the suite was locked, so how did they get in?'

Alex countered, 'Are you sure? Lou could have left it open. You know how slapdash she is, even when she's sober – and she certainly wasn't that last night.'

It was the wrong thing to say. The set of Maddie's distorted mouth hardened. 'She wouldn't leave the suite unlocked.' She raised her hand and touched her cheek. 'I don't think it's unreasonable for me to be concerned.'

'No,' he agreed in a bid to placate her, but she was no longer listening; she was thinking.

'I need to know whether it was just a horrible fluke that I reacted the way I did.' She stopped talking.

'Or?' he prompted.

'Or if it was deliberate.'

She said it as if it was the most rational thing in the world that someone would try to poison her with a bunch of flowers. 'Surely not,' he countered.

She went quiet and stared at him through her sore, swollen eyes. Her gaze was challenging. He looked away first. 'Why shouldn't I think that, Alex? It's a really strange

178

thing to do, don't you think? Leave flowers in someone's bed with no card? Flowers that were toxic. Flowers that triggered my first seizure . . . in months.'

'Well, yes. But whoever sent them couldn't have known that you'd have such a terrible reaction to them. And no one here, apart from me and Lou, knows you have epilepsy. I'm sure it's just an awful freak accident.' He knew he'd got that wrong before he got to the end of his sentence.

'Why isn't it a reasonable assumption, given everything that's happened?' Her voice hitched up another octave. 'Another freak accident? What is it with me, Alex? Am I cursed or something?'

He wanted to reassure her and to do that he had to share her understandable sense of persecution. 'You really think that somebody here, somebody close to us, would do such a bizarre thing?'

The energy drained out of her and she started shaking and nodding her head at the same time. 'I don't know. I just don't know any more. It certainly feels like someone, or something, doesn't want us to get married.'

Alex felt out of his depth. 'Oh, Mads. I really don't think anyone would do anything to deliberately hurt you. I can't believe it.' She said nothing. He decided that moving forward with sympathy was the only option. 'You must be so tired.'

'I am. I'm exhausted.'

That he could deal with. 'So, let's take this a step at a time. You obviously need to rest. You can sleep in here. I'll look after you. I'll let Colette know that we're not going on the trip to the caves. We'll need to decide what we're going to say to everyone, but . . .'

179

She touched his arm, pausing him mid-flow. 'Alex. Please. Stop. I agree, I need to stay here and rest. Then, hopefully, I'll start feeling, and looking, better. But you don't need to stay with me.' He started to protest. She stopped him. 'No. Listen. I'll sleep if I'm on my own; I won't if you're around.' She must have seen his expression, because she hastily added, 'You, or anyone else. I think you should go on the trip. You can look after everyone, keep the positive atmosphere going and you can make my apologies. It'll be better coming from you. But, please, I want you to keep it low-key. No drama. And don't say anything about the flowers. Lou and Colette won't. We agreed it was better that way.' For who, Alex wondered. Christ, he was starting to think like her. 'Say I've got a touch of heatstroke and I need to stay out of the sun . . . that's what Colette suggested. And while you're all out at the caves, Colette can see what she can find out about how the bouquet got into my room.'

So, the girls had worked it all out in advance. He couldn't help but feel sidelined. 'But I want to stay with you. I feel bad I wasn't there last night.' His admission hung in the air. It was a complicated, twisting thing. He'd been less than attentive the previous night, having been more caught up in the announcement about the deal than in her and their upcoming wedding. And he knew how tricky she found negotiating social occasions when they were all together. But she was the one who had chosen to go back on her own. And how could he have known she'd been taken ill in the night? No one had woken him. She hadn't even come to him when she got back to the finca.

'Alex. Please. I know what I need to do after a seizure, and that's nothing. Me being on my own makes sense. Okay?' she pushed.

'Okay,' he conceded.

Plan reluctantly agreed, Alex stood up and headed into the bathroom to get washed and dressed. When he came out, she was gone.

Chapter 31

LOU

Once again it wasn't the most auspicious of starts – a car park by the side of a busy road with a Portaloo and an overflowing waste bin. Lou was already regretting not staying back at the finca with Maddie – yes, to keep an eye on her, but also for her own reasons, like access to the cooling waters of the lake and the comfortable loungers in the shade on which she could now be fast asleep. But Maddie had insisted that she come. Was it paranoia or justified concern? Either way, she wasn't happy to have been asked to spy on the other guests, especially given how hung-over and sleep-deprived she was.

She and Maddie had shared a bed, briefly, for the first time in ages when they got back to the finca. Maddie had not wanted to return to her own bedroom, for obvious reasons. Over the years the two of them had slept together often; after late shifts and nights out, when Maddie was having one of her many 'technically homeless' spells and sometimes just for comfort. Lou missed it. Whether Maddie did, Lou didn't know. Their few snatched hours obviously hadn't been the same. Maddie's thoughts and energies now lay elsewhere – with Alex. It was as it should be, but Lou still resented it. Then, as if to confirm Lou's demotion in her life, Maddie had woken her up at the ungodly hour of 9.00 a.m. and pushed her into coming on this damn trip. It seemed that Maddie had forgotten what friends were really for.

A battered Renault pulled into the car park and out climbed a man with a head of hair and moustache that were both so luxuriant that they looked false. Luther introduced the man as Raoul, their guide. Then Luther bluntly told them to make sure they were back in the same spot by 3.00 p.m. at the latest – the heavy implication being that if they were late he wouldn't wait. Warning issued, Luther climbed into the minibus and roared away, leaving them coughing in his wake. When the dust had settled, Raoul smiled apologetically and asked everyone to follow him.

Thankfully it was a relatively short walk through the scrubby countryside to the mouth of the caves. The entrance was marked, somewhat surprisingly, by a wrought-iron gate that wouldn't have looked out of place in a suburban English garden. From his pocket Raoul produced a big brass key. Lou was getting used to the props now. Mallorcans seemed to have a thing for a touch of theatre. Raoul unlocked the gate. It gave a plaintive squeal.

'Welcome to the Cuevas Ocultas,' he smiled. 'It means "hidden", before anyone gets worried.' There was a ripple of polite laughter. 'These caves have been here for centuries. They have housed all manner of human and animal kind. Today they welcome us. I have a couple of pieces of advice before we enter. There are sections of the caves where it is very uneven underfoot and patches where it's very slippery, so please take care.' He glanced at their footwear. Colette's very detailed email had recommended sensible, sturdy

183

shoes. Advice that everyone seemed to have heeded, except Ruby, who was wearing espadrilles. Raoul said nothing about her preference for fashion over safety. 'Also, I would ask that we stay together and that you keep your mobiles accessible at all times – for their torches. There's no phone reception, obviously. The caverns run very deep under the mountain and I'd hate to lose any of you.' Another polite ripple. 'Very well. Shall we?' He pulled open the gate and ushered them into an electrically lit concrete tunnel that wouldn't have looked out of place in a war film. The immediate drop in temperature was very welcome. It was a short walk into the cliff face to the first cavern. At the mouth of the cave Raoul asked them to stop and close their eyes. Lou heard a click – the lights being switched off and the squeal of more ironwork. 'Please open your eyes.'

The scale of it stunned them all.

It was a church, peopled with a congregation of ghostly pale stalactites and stalagmites. It felt ancient and organic and – far-fetched as it might sound – spiritual. A place to encourage reflection, which was the effect it seemed to be having on all of them. Even Lily was silent. Lou looked at the others. They were in awe, their faces tilted up, taking in the beauty of it. So much of this wedding seemed to be about theatre and spectacle. Good at his job, Raoul kept quiet. The presence of modern life had been kept to a bare minimum – there was a handrail to guide them down the steep stone steps and a few judiciously placed spotlights, but that was it. The lighting was clever, low-key, designed to make the most of the shadows cast by the rock formations. It didn't take too much of a leap to imagine what the first people to discover these caves must have thought when they stumbled across them. It was 'hand of God' territory.

Having let them marvel for a few minutes, Raoul swung into guide mode. 'The Cuevas Ocultas were officially dis-covered by a Belgian geologist called Eduoard Wouters in 1864, but he was, almost certainly, not the first person to enter these caves. They are known to have provided ref-uge, shelter and resources for the people and livestock of this island for centuries. It's believed that the Arabs hid here, as they did in so many of the caves on Mallorca, dur-ing the Christian conquest in the twelfth century. Because, as you will see – if you would be so kind as to follow me – the Cuevas Ocultas are far more than this one, magnificent natural cathedral.' They descended the steps and followed Raoul into the labyrinth.

For the next hour and a half they wandered through stone corridors and galleries, some large enough to hold a choir, others so small that only two or three of them could enter at once. Raoul explained that the network of tunnels they were travelling through had been created by millennia of water forcing its way through the rock. He was a great guide. He compressed the history of the caves into juicy, easily digestible nuggets. At his prompting they looked at the primitive art gouged into the rock and saw the strange tally marks that, he explained, were the accounting sys-tem adopted by the many crooks and pirates who had used the caves over the years to store their contraband. At the far extremity of one tunnel, they entered a large cave that looked like a bank vault. It had a shaft in the roof that opened out onto a secluded ledge high up the moun-tains. Here Raoul pointed out the graffiti. Compared to the natural, weathered history of many of the caverns this modern defacement was shocking and disturbing. Crude lettering and garish symbols were spray-painted all over the walls, ceiling and floor.

'What's with all the eyes?'

There were eyeballs daubed around the vault, all of them with a single ruby teardrop leaking from the inner corner. Raoul smiled; he'd obviously been expecting Paul's question. 'They're a warning – that the spirits are always watching. They're also a message to anyone contemplating stealing from the Sacra Corona – that's the Mallorcan version of the Mafia. It's rumoured that they used the caves for storing huge quantities of stolen cigarettes, booze and drugs until very recently.' Whether it was Raoul's talk of mob violence or the sensation of hundreds of blood-weeping eyes staring at her, Letty, the flower girl and all-round pain, started to whine. Raoul took it as his cue to bring their tour to a close. He finished off with a descent to one of the underground pools. It was breathtaking. Still, limpid, iridescent with blues, greens and pale pinks. It was like looking into the heart of an opal.

With everyone cleansed of the bad vibes of the Sacra Corona vault, Raoul led them back to the main cavern, where another piece of Finca Encantata magic had been performed. The nameless staff had been busy. Tables covered in white linen had been set up on the cavern floor and lunch had been laid out for them. Each table had a posy of violets in the centre. Having had their fill of natural and human history, they each pulled up a chair and set about filling their bellies.

Chapter 32

MADDIE

Maddie woke with a start. She'd been dreaming, but couldn't remember about what; she only knew that her heart rate was high and she felt tense. The first thing she did was touch her face. It was still swollen and sore. Despite her legs feeling like concrete, she got up and went into Lou's en suite bathroom. The antique mirror did not show the fairest of them all, but she did at least look less grotesque: still puffy and red-eyed, but not inhuman any more. She stood with her bare belly resting against the delicious cool of the porcelain sink for a minute, checking in with herself. For twenty-four hours after a seizure, longer if it was a big one, Maddie could be disorientated, her memory fuzzy – which, ironically, reminded her that she needed to take her meds. But although the collection of pills and potions from Dr Carizales was there – Paul had handed her a plastic bag full of pills and creams when they left the villa – her toilet bag was not. Colette had taken it and not given it back.

Maddie took what drugs were available to her. As she threw the tablets into her mouth and washed them down, she surveyed the damage. The clusters of blisters seemed to be spreading over her body. She thought about her beautiful wedding dress. It was backless, with a plunging V at the front, not the best style for a bride who looked like a burns victim. Maddie felt sadness bubble up inside her, but she pushed it down. It was her only option. There wasn't another wedding dress on stand-by, and you could do a lot with make-up, or so Maddie hoped, although it would probably be the first time that the stylist Colette had booked for her would have been asked to disguise a poisoning victim on the morning of their wedding. Because that was what it had been – a poisoning. Deliberate or inadvertent? That was the million-dollar question. But Alex was right; if it had been deliberate, it was a very contrived and unreliable method to choose. There could only be a one-in-a-whatever-high-figure chance that she was going to be allergic to the bouquet. Just awful bad luck again, then? That explanation was much less scary. Besides, Maddie couldn't let herself think that someone had purposely tried to cause her harm, because if she did believe that darkest of interpretations, it would be a sign of paranoia. And who wanted a paranoid bride? Not Alex. Not the Archers. Not Maddie herself.

To promote calmness, she ran a bath of tepid water – no perfumed oils this time – and lowered herself into it. She closed her eyes to block out the sight of her blotchy skin and practised her yoga breathing. The mantra was . . . one long, slow in-breath on the word 'let' and one long, slow out-breath on the word 'go'. And repeat. She breathed and listened. The finca was quiet, everyone off on the excursion to the caves, Alex and Lou with them, at her insistence. But Colette would be around, somewhere. She was always around, always busy doing something: bollocking the staff, rearranging the furniture, ferrying women who were having seizures up mountains in search of medical assistance in the dead of night, then bringing them home to rest and recuperate while soldiering on bravely herself – without sleep or complaint. Maddie really needed to go and find her and get her toilet bag back. Another long breath in and out. Let ... in, and out ... go. Maddie did not 'get' Colette. She had the distinct impression, despite last night's heroics, that her future sister-in-law did not like her. Colette's 'assistance' had simply been part of the blue-ribbon service, what she would do for any guest paying tens of thousands of pounds for their few days in paradise. Except Maddie wasn't paying, and she guessed that pissed Colette off – royally.

It was always there, in the background. Money. Those who had it – like the Archers – always looked down on those without it, and those without it always resented those who had it. It was the way of the world.

Maddie hadn't realised that she was guilty of being poor until she was nine. It was the kids at her new school who pointed it out to her. Apparently there was plenty of evidence. Her PE kit with the ghost of someone else's name beneath her own. Her school bag that was simply wrong. Likewise her shoes. Her dad, who didn't have an interesting job *that the class might like to hear about on careers day*, and who, unhelpfully, was nowhere to be found. The fact that Maddie and her mother shared bathwater and their food came out of tins. And, according to the other kids, the real giveaway was Maddie's mother in and of herself. The way Kath dressed, spoke, smoked, coughed, laughed – even her name – was, apparently, the biggest indicator of Maddie's lesser status in society.

It hurt Maddie to look at her mum differently. She hadn't changed, but Maddie's sensitivity to appearances and why they mattered had. Before, the stripe of dark hair down her mother's parting that contrasted with her blonde bob was just her style, her thin jackets in the middle of winter were simply what she wore and her collection of sparkly rings, but lack of a simple wedding band, was purely a reflection of her love of jewellery, not a signifier of her lack of taste and her unmarried status.

Having been properly educated in the signs of poverty Maddie went into herself for a few weeks. She felt overwhelmed by the sheer number of things that marked her and her mother out, and she felt doubly stupid that she'd never noticed them before. And the more she looked the more she discovered. Their erratic diet – it was always cheap feast or toast. The letters and calls that her mother ignored, but that kept coming. The amount of mismatched second-hand stuff in their home. By the end of her period of observation Maddie had built quite the inventory. When her mum was out one evening, which she often was – that apparently was another indicator, being home alone – Maddie climbed onto the double bed in her mum's room and reviewed her research.

Maddie's conclusion was that the kids at school were correct. She and her mum did have fewer of the things that other people valued, but they had more than enough of the things that mattered to them. Top of the list was fun. Maddie liked her mum and, crucially, her mum liked her. They spent a lot of time together. Maddie wasn't dumb, she knew it was partly through necessity, but Kath was clear: there was no one in the world that she liked more than Maddie.

And there was another important thing that Maddie appreciated and benefited from – her mother was lucky. Maddie was regularly impressed by her mum's knack for finding things at exactly the point they needed them. Ten-pound notes down the side of seats in cafés, bags of shopping left in trolleys outside supermarkets, perfectly good furniture in skips and, as Maddie grew older and needed more stuff, a surprising number of lost wallets.

By the time Maddie was in secondary school she realised that her mother's luck was made up of one part opportunity and nine parts effort.

Kath was a skilled pickpocket. She stole according to a clear set of rules. Purses belonged to women, and women cared for their kids, therefore you should never lift a purse. Whereas men, especially those drinking in pubs or bars or hanging around in betting shops, were fair game. Likewise with groceries – big stores and supermarkets were a good hunting ground whereas small shops were not, unless you were desperate. Restaurants, especially chain ones – yes. Cafés – no. The list was comprehensive and covered many different types of venues and people. Rich people were a resounding yes. People who were careless with their possessions – likewise yes. People who lived like or near you – no. Thieving wasn't simply a matter of survival, but of principle, for Maddie's mother. She was a one-woman campaign against social inequality.

It was a crusade that fourteen-year-old Maddie had to take up for herself when her mother was diagnosed with bowel cancer at the age of thirty-eight. Maddie's criminal career started with her procuring their groceries and went from there. When the treatment really began to bite, and Kath lost the will and the energy for dipping wallets, Maddie took over the responsibility for the family cash flow as well as their food 'shopping'. It was her turn to tip the scales in their favour, or at least weigh them down enough to ensure that her mum lived out her last few months in reasonable comfort.

Kath died when Maddie was seventeen, two months shy of her sitting her A levels. Maddie had her first seizure on the morning of her English Lit exam. There was a reason Maddie, an intelligent, enterprising young woman, was working in The Shed making coffees for minimum wage when Alex walked through the door that dark January morning.

Maddie's reminiscences were shattered by the sound of loud, sharp, staccato knocking.

She scrambled out of the bath, grabbed one of the towelling gowns and hurried to the door. She opened it, expecting Colette or a member of staff, but instead she came face to face with Marilyn. Without being asked Marilyn moved to step inside. Maddie let her.

'Oh, I'm sorry, my dear. Were you in the bath?' She was scanning the suite.

'No. Well, yes. But I was about to get out. I thought it might help.'

'A good idea.' Marilyn raised her hand and actually touched the underside of Maddie's chin with a manicured fingertip. She lifted her face to the light for inspection. It was all Maddie could do not to knock her hand away. 'How are you? I gather it was all a little traumatic last night.' She let go of Maddie's face and sat down without being invited. But this was her domain.

'I'm okay.' For some reason Maddie added, 'Thank you.'

Marilyn nodded. 'Yes. Dr Carizales is very good. He came to us highly recommended. Such a gentleman ... and his English is excellent.' Maddie knew it was her general uneasiness around Alex's mother, but to her ears Marilyn's comment sounded more like the assessment you would make of a chef or a masseur than a medical professional. An uncomfortable silence descended. Marilyn broke it. 'Can we get you anything?' The royal 'we'.

'No, I'm good.' In truth Maddie was hungry, but she wasn't going to admit that to Marilyn.

'And how is Alex?' she asked.

Maddie didn't really know what she meant by that. 'He's fine.'

Marilyn realigned her bangles. 'But it must have been such a shock for him seeing you ... so affected.' Maddie didn't volunteer a comment. She didn't trust herself to. 'And what shocking bad luck – to discover that you're so *terribly* allergic, so close to the wedding.'

'Yes. Who knew?' Maddie had no intention of feeding Marilyn's superiority complex by giving way to her own anger, but she couldn't stop herself from pushing back at her future mother-in-law, just a touch. 'But I'm sure he'll cope.' They stared at each other. It was the closest they'd come to acknowledging their mutual dislike. This was why they shouldn't be left alone together. Maddie would never be Ruby and Marilyn was never going to forgive her for that.

'I simply can't imagine what it must be like. It must be awful, waiting for the next ... attack. For you and for Alex.' There was a pause. Then, 'Do you fit very often?'

She really was a first-class bitch.

So Colette had told her mother about Maddie's epilepsy. Of course she had. Why not hand a gun to someone already packing grenades? Maddie fought back. 'No. Not normally. I haven't had a tonic-clonic for years. I must be feeling extra stressed for some reason.' She left her own, very long pause. 'Being around people who don't understand or have any sympathy with the condition tends to make it worse.' It was the worst possible time for Maddie to unsheathe her claws, but it made her feel less pathetic.

Marilyn studied her, seemingly totally unembarrassed. 'Well, I'll leave you to get yourself sorted.' She rose elegantly from the sofa. 'Let's hope there are no more incidents in the next twenty-four hours. I think we've had quite enough drama for one wedding.' She did a weird little chuckle at her own joke, but Maddie could tell that she was deadly serious. 'Do ring if you need anything.' And with that she glided out.

'Fuck you!' Maddie hissed, hopefully loud enough for her future mother-in-law to hear.

Chapter 33

COLETTE

They kept the wine cellar locked at all times, for security, but also for safety. An incident, not long after they opened, when one of the waiters tripped down the stairs onto the unforgiving floor and smashed three vertebrae, had been tricky to smooth over. It had taken a generous amount of 'off-books' compensation and Colette's vigorous assertion that the man in question had been drunk on the job, which was not strictly true, to make the problem go away. But when Colette went through to the old pantry she found the cellar unlocked, the padlock missing. Bloody Luther. His firm belief that the rules didn't apply to him infuriated Colette on a daily, almost hourly, basis. More so because it was true. His long association with her father afforded him a degree of protection that was way out of proportion to his actual usefulness. Her pissed-offness hitched up another notch. She slammed open the unlocked door and started to descend, her knackered anger audible in her footsteps.

There was a series of cellars beneath the Finca Encantata. Back in the day it had been the only place cool enough to store food. Over the years more and more sections of the cellar had been fitted out with wine racks and the large oak stands that held the barrels. The higgledy-piggledy network of interconnecting rooms was now exclusively used for storing the Archers' considerable wine and whisky collection. The cheaper stuff they passed off as 'specially selected' to the paying guests, the actual good stuff her mother and father drank and the investment cases and casks were traded. The cellar was the most un-modernised part of the castle. Dimly lit, deliciously cool even on the hottest of days, steeped in spilt wine – the finca cellar was a unique, extremely asset-rich underworld.

Colette paused halfway down the stone steps, alerted by the sound of grunting. It was a distinctly animal-like sound, but she knew, without a shadow of a doubt, that the noise was coming from a human being, not a beast. Her stomach contracted with disgust, and yet she carried on down, advancing more stealthily.

She found them in the second chamber on the left, too engrossed to notice her approach. He'd fashioned some sort of platform out of crates and pallets, covered it with a tarp. For comfort or for ease? So this wasn't the first time. She wasn't surprised. The girl – it took Colette a moment to identify her as Maria – was the youngest of the waitresses. He was so predictable. Maria sat astride him, her back to Colette. She was bouncing up and down, working up a sweat, while Luther lay back, his hands behind his head. He was even a lazy bastard when it came to screwing. Colette took a few steps backwards, out of sight, then shouted, 'Is there someone down here?'

Maria let out a squeal which coincided with the sound of breaking glass. 'For fuck's sake,' was Luther's eloquent contribution. Colette waited – but not for long. Maria rushed around the corner carrying her shoes and clutching her blouse closed at the front. On seeing Colette, she stuttered to a halt. She looked mortified.

'Good morning, Miss Diaz.' Colette left a painful pause. 'I assume there's something more constructive that you're supposed to be doing upstairs.' The poor girl nodded and went an even darker shade of red, but she seemed rooted to the spot. 'Well, I suggest you go and get on with it. And Maria, I'd advise against coming down here again. There are rats in these cellars, and they're riddled with nasty diseases.' Maria might not have understood every word, but she'd obviously got the gist. She fled. Colette rounded the corner. Luther was sitting in his makeshift shag-pad studying a large red patch on his white chinos. He was scowling. She was pleased he'd not escaped unscathed. Colette looked from the puddle of broken glass and wine to his soiled trousers. 'Well, if you will grub around down here, what do you expect?'

'Did you want something?' Even caught with his trousers literally down he was still a smug prick.

'Me?' She shrugged. 'Nah. Apart from you actually doing your job. For some peculiar reason, despite all the evidence to the contrary, I can't stop myself believing that one of these days you might actually do some work around here.' She turned to go, threw over her shoulder, at the last minute, 'Oh, and by the way, my mother's been looking for you, for the past half-hour. Apparently she has some errand she wants you to run.' It was gratifying to hear Luther scramble to his feet in a panic at the mention of her mother.

Chapter 34

MADDIE

After Marilyn's visit Maddie felt motivated to get up and out. She needed to eat and to retrieve, and take, her epilepsy meds. She also wanted an opportunity to test out reactions to her appearance with the finca staff before having to face their guests. Secretly, she was hoping to find a little human sympathy to counterbalance Marilyn's chilly contempt. The real reason for Marilyn's fly-by had obviously been to check out how bad Maddie looked rather than to enquire after her health or her mental state. It was almost a relief that Alex's mother hadn't bothered to disguise her true feelings this time. When it came to the marriage of her son, Marilyn had obviously planned for the perfect wedding in this most perfect of settings with as close to perfect a bride as possible. Well, she was going to have to put up with a blistered and bloated Maddie instead.

Maddie chose a bench in the shade in the courtyard, hoping to bump into one of the many nameless staff who quietly and efficiently kept the finca running. A simple sandwich and a glass of milk would sort her out. Once she'd eaten, she would seek out Colette.

As if thinking made it so, it was Colette who appeared first. She burst around the corner like a bullet – everything Colette did was at speed – but instead of shooting off to her next task, she stopped stone dead. Maddie waited for Colette to spot her and come over – she seemed to be looking straight at Maddie – but her staring was obviously sightless, because what Colette did next was the most unconscious thing Maddie had ever seen her do. She turned to face one of the huge windows that punctuated the ground floor of the main building and rested her head against it. Even from way across the courtyard it was clear that she was taking deep breaths. Then, shockingly, she lifted her head and banged her forehead against the glass. One short, hard, unflinching blow – an act of pure frustration. Maddie waited, dreading but anticipating another head bang, but something must have caught Colette's attention because instead of repeating the assault she glanced down to her left. She scowled then she whipped around, grabbed a stone from the top of one of the big pots and hurled it. The pebble hit the flags with a loud crack and skittered away, but the noise wasn't loud enough to drown out Colette's shout of, 'And you can fuck off out of it too!'

It was at this point that Colette realised she had an audience. Maddie had no option other than to stand up and walk over to her. 'I will, if you want me to, but I was wondering if I could get my toilet bag back from you first.'

There was some pleasure in seeing Colette struggling to regain her composure and her usual position on the higher ground. 'Sorry. Yes.' She was obviously flustered. 'It's in my locker. I meant to drop it round, but I got caught up with other things.' The Archers really didn't do TLC. But

Colette still seemed distracted. 'Whatever I do, I can't get rid of the damn thing.' Maddie followed the direction of her gaze. There was a cat sitting near one of the huge terracotta pots. A scrawny black cat with yellow eyes. It seemed to be watching them as much as they were staring at it. 'It's a total pest. It just keeps coming back.'

Maddie had no feelings either way about the cat. 'My toilet bag?'

Colette shook herself. 'Yeah. I'll fetch it now.' Maddie followed her towards the staff quarters. She was keen to see the other, less glamorous side of the finca, the side that was normally kept hidden.

Chapter 35

BOBBY

Bobby and Lily sat with Lou and Priya for lunch in the caves. Bobby felt he should be making more of an effort with Lou. He knew from conversations he'd had with Maddie how important their friendship was. Lou was *the* person Maddie trusted above all others. The lack of parents from such a young age must have compounded that reliance. Bobby could identify with that. People banged on about how important family was to a person's well-being, but he knew that a good friend could be even more valuable, because they were there for you through choice, not obligation.

It didn't take a psychologist to realise that this whole fancy wedding weekend was not Lou's natural habit. Everything about her, from her clothes and her battered Converse to her estuary accent, shouted 'not me'. Although, to be fair, Bobby doubted that many of the assembled guests had been served luncheon in a magical underground cavern with real linen tablecloths and ebony-handled cutlery before. 'Raoul was great, wasn't he?' Bobby felt compelled to get the small talk rolling. They all looked around for their guide. He'd taken himself away from their pop-up picnic, and was sitting with his back to them, his head tilted back, gazing placidly at the rock fingers that reached down from the ceiling of the cave. Bobby remembered Raoul saying that it would take another century at least before some of the stalagmites and stalactites touched. It put things into perspective.

'Yeah, he was, but the stuff about the Mafia was a bit on the nose. The way they'd defaced that cave was heartbreaking.' Lily reached for a panade then hesitated. She beckoned over one of the waiting staff. 'Are any of these vegan?' As the waitress pointed out the 'safe' panades – there was a choice of pea and caramelised onion or sundried tomato with vegan cheese – Bobby watched Lou. She wasn't very good at keeping her thoughts off her face, or maybe it was that she simply didn't bother trying. She swallowed whatever was in her mouth, joined the conversational fray.

'Oh, I liked all the Sacra Corona curse stuff. All those eyes. It was dead creepy. It makes you realise that this isn't ... or wasn't always ... just a tourist attraction.' So Lou thought they were behaving like crass, over-indulged tourists. Well, again, her views were no great surprise and she did have a point. The tour had been good, but their lunch was a step too far. As was her habit, it was Priya who tried to smooth the atmosphere by changing the topic – to the schedule for the following day. Lou seemed to lose interest and went back to eating. It didn't take long for the speculation about Maddie to surface. The explanation for her absence had, unsurprisingly, not been taken at face value by everyone, especially not Lily.

'It's such a pity Maddie couldn't be here.' Fly cast. Lou

202

didn't bite. Lily tried again. 'How was she this morning when you saw her?'

Lou ripped off a hunk of bread and chewed it. 'Okay.'

'But not up to coming with us?'

Lou pretended to look around the cavern for her friend. She was taking the piss out of Lily. 'Obviously not.'

But Lily was resilient. 'I really hope she's feeling better soon. She must be worrying with it being so close to the ceremony. I'd be in a total state.' She flicked a glance at Bobby. He avoided its message by suddenly becoming interested in the salad on his plate. Bobby had been seeing Lily for eight months. They'd met at a book launch. She'd been taking photos, doing a favour for a friend who worked on the marketing team for the publisher. A rival outfit. Bobby was only there to snoop and because he'd had nothing better to do with his evening. He'd approached Lily, which was unlike him, but seeing Alex so resolutely and happily paired up had encouraged Bobby to be more proactive in terms of his own social life. They'd got on. The conversation had flowed, Lily had ensured that. They started seeing each other. Soon they were an item. Being in a couple himself had made it far easier to socialise with Alex and Maddie. It was a win-win situation. It had gone from there to here. Talk around the table turned to speculation about Maddie's wedding dress. Lou kept her counsel and glugged down half a pint of water. Bobby tuned out Lily and Priya's chatter.

It was as the waitress came round offering drinks topups that Bobby noticed Raoul get to his feet. He stared at the gathered diners, his stance tense and alert. Bobby knew what he was doing. Lou caught on quickly as well.

Bobby watched her scan the tables and the assembled guests. The two empty chairs obviously confirmed her suspicion. It was the sound of Raoul scrambling down towards the lunch party that drew everyone else's attention. His voice had a distinct edge. 'Have any of you seen the other two guests? The pretty lady with the espadrilles and the tall gentleman.'

'Alex and Ruby,' Lou added, just to be clear. There was a general swinging of heads and mumbling. The consensus was that they had not seen the groom or Ruby, not for a while, now that they thought about it.

'When was the last time anyone saw them, please?' The urgency of Raoul's question curdled the atmosphere.

'They were at the pool with us,' Paul said.

'Yes, I saw them there too,' Lily chipped in.

'I thought they were following on behind us.' Priya. There were more mutters of agreement from Mateus Torres and his wife.

'Okay.' Raoul hesitated, but only for a second. Eleven people, safely seated at tables, with staff in attendance, near the cavern exit, or two people gone rogue in the caves on their own. It was a clear choice. 'I must insist that you all stay here, together. I do not want anyone to leave. Or to follow me. I'm sure they have simply been delayed by the beauty of the caves. I will be back very soon.'

They all watched him make his way over to the steps, expecting him to disappear off on his hunt, but at the top he stopped. They realised why after a few seconds. The sound of voices bounced up the tunnel in the rock and spilt out into the void of the main chamber. Ruby emerged first, followed by Alex. They stuttered to a halt when confronted by Raoul and the scrutiny of their guests. There was an awkward beat – which was eventually filled by Raoul. 'Ah. It is good you have joined us. I was about to come searching for you. I was . . . concerned.' It was a polite rebuke.

A look passed between Alex and Ruby. Ruby took the lead. 'No need. We were simply enjoying the tranquillity of the pool, weren't we, Alex? It is mesmerising.' She wafted past Raoul. It was the only apology he was going to get. 'Oh yummy, lunch. I'm starving.'

Alex looked much less blasé, in fact he looked quite embarrassed. 'Sorry. Didn't mean to cause a panic. Our bad.' He hurried past Raoul.

Ruby and Alex's reappearance allowed the feasting and chatting to recommence, but Bobby contributed little to the revived conversation. There was no need; Lily and Priya had moved on to speculating about where the happy couple might be heading for their honeymoon. The excitement in Lily's voice gave him pause. This whole wedding, with its no-expense-spared glamour, was going to Lily's head. As they twittered away Bobby watched Ruby sweep into a seat next to Paul and start holding court, while Alex stood looking uncertain. Bobby pulled the chair next to him out from under the table and beckoned Alex over, but he turned away and went to sit with Charlie and Tom. His first action was to wave over the waitress and request a beer. When it appeared he downed it in a few gulps and immediately ordered another.

Bobby looked away and once more caught Lou's intent gaze. In that moment he was grateful for Lily's wedding prattle.

Chapter 36

ALEX

Alex was relieved to get out of the caves, to be on the bus, to be heading back to the finca and Maddie. He was even more relieved that there was a spare seat. He put his rucksack on it, deterring company. There was no one he wanted to talk to or sit beside. He stared out of the window at the scenery, not seeing it.

Ruby had always had the power to throw him off kilter; it was part of her appeal, but this was a total curveball. True, it was her life, her decision. She'd always been very clear about forging her own path. No one told Ruby what to do, or even offered an opinion. She didn't respond well to advice. But this? This did affect him. She couldn't expect him not to be surprised. No, shocked was a more accurate description. It would change their relationship, complicate it, just at the point he'd hoped it would become simpler. And he did have an opinion, whether she wanted to hear it or not. He felt a burst of anger. Ruby had a knack for making him feel impotent – which was ironic. Not that he was in the mood to see any irony in the situation. As she'd talked he'd simply stared into the shimmering waters of the underground lake. The setting for her announcement also troubled him. Had she chosen it for its privacy or its beauty? If the latter, what the hell was he supposed to read into that? He couldn't remember what he'd said in response; she'd done most of the talking, laying it out – a fait accompli. He did recall her reassuring him that she'd say and do nothing to disrupt his 'big weekend'. There it was again, that stab of sarcasm. Indeed, she'd gone further, told him that she intended to keep her news quiet for as long as possible ... 'mainly for work reasons'. It was, she'd reminded him, no one else's business but her own.

Alex glanced up at the driver's mirror, seeking out Bobby, but he was sitting in a window seat, out of his eyeline. Did Bobby know? Was this a Three Musketeers moment, or had she told only him?

As the minibus sped along, Alex tried to think more clearly and less emotionally about Ruby's bombshell. And the more he thought the more questions he had. Top of the list was – why now? The timing was odd – the day before his marriage. Was this her way of telling him something? Or was this simply her messing with him, for the hell of it? Her last hurrah before, to quote her, he 'did the evil deed'. Was it a classically self-centred Ruby footnote to his wedding? Or was it somehow a dig at Maddie?

Maddie. Shit! She'd better not find out. If she did, she'd go crazy. She was already fragile. This would tip her off the ledge, and for no good reason. Certainly not one that was relevant. Well, she would, obviously, find out eventually, but he would deal with that after the ceremony. When they were man and wife and they were back home and everything was on a firm footing.

As the bus neared the finca, Alex vowed to dedicate himself to Maddie for the remaining hours and minutes leading up to their wedding. She deserved his undivided attention. Ruby, his new business associates, his parents, his sister, even his best mate, none of them mattered.

Maddie did.

Chapter 37

LOU

When they got back from the caves, Alex announced to everyone that he was going to check on Maddie. It was what you'd expect of an attentive fiancé, but it ticked Lou off; she'd had quite enough of him for one day. After sulking like a teenager on the bus, he was all easy charm once again. On the walk over to the tower he made a concerted effort to get her talking. He asked her if she'd enjoyed the trip, he chatted about their lavish lunch and, when he got really desperate, he repeated snippets of Raoul's commentary. He made no mention of his little excursion with Ruby, of course, but it was there, pulsing away in the background. He had to know that she would tell Maddie about their liaison by the lake. That had, after all, been Lou's brief – to keep her eyes peeled for any signs of Ruby-on-Alex action and for any indicators that they had a fiendishly clever poisoner in their midst. This wedding was screwing with more than just Maddie's physical health.

Maddie looked noticeably better when they got back to the suite. Not ready for three thousand wedding photos, perhaps, but she no longer looked like the victim of a botched Botox incident. Lou left them to it. She went for a shower, stayed in the bathroom as long as she could, then thought, *sod it!* This was her last night with Maddie; Alex was going to be spending the rest of his life with her. Lou wandered into the sitting room area in her knickers and T-shirt, plonked herself on the sofa opposite them and proceeded to towel-dry her hair, sitting in a very unladylike position. He got the message. 'So I'll come and collect you at 7.00 p.m. We'll walk down to the lake together? Don't look so worried. It'll be fine. I bet people won't even notice.' He kissed her, gently, as if she was one of those broken and repaired Japanese vases. 'See you in a little while. I love you.'

Did Maddie really like all this OTT lovey-dovey bullshit? Lou thought that Maddie's 'I love you' reply was muted. Was that because she was still feeling rough, or was it because she was reserving judgement on her beloved fiancé until she'd heard Lou's debrief from the trip to the caves? Behind Alex's back Lou mimed putting her fingers down her throat. Maddie didn't respond. Alex pulled the door closed gently behind him as if he genuinely thought she might shatter if there was a loud noise. It was finally Lou time. Her opening gambit was sympathy. 'How are you feeling, honestly?'

'Okay.'

'But you don't fancy round two of "weddings under the stars" tonight?' Maddie shrugged. 'Text him. Tell him you've changed your mind and you're not up to it.'

'I can't.'

That shocked and infuriated Lou. 'Yes you can! You had a seizure. A bad one. You need to rest. Here.' She picked up Maddie's phone and tossed it to her. 'He can entertain them on his own. He's good at it!'

210

Maddie shook her head. 'No. I need to be there.'

Lou was sick of all these bloody anachronistic wedding traditions, sick to the back teeth of all of the showy socialising and performance loveliness and, in truth, she was sick of this vapid version of her used-to-be-feisty best friend. 'For God's sake, Mads, you can say "no", you know. You're going to need to with his lot.'

'What do you mean by that?'

'You know what I mean.'

'No, go on. Please, enlighten me.' This was more like it. Here was a glint of the old Maddie spirit. Unfortunately, its sharp edge was being turned on Lou. But Lou wasn't one to back down from a fight, and this fight needed to happen – maybe if the gloves came off some home truths might actually land and wake Maddie up.

Lou went for direct provocation. 'Tell me again why you're getting married.'

'Do you mean to Alex, or at all?' Maddie knew Lou's views on marriage. The pause Lou left was long enough to imply both. 'I love him.'

The way Maddie said it was full of defiance. It made Lou wonder who she was trying to convince – Lou or herself. Lou mimed pressing a gameshow buzzer. 'Uh-ahh! Too vanilla. *Nul points*.'

'And I want kids.'

'So? You don't need a ring on your finger for that.' Lou didn't add that neither did you require a man, just his sperm.

Maddie picked up a tube of concealer and started dotting it on her arms. It took Lou a second to realise that what she was doing was trying to cover up the rash.

211

She really had got it bad. 'I'd never have a child on my own.'

Lou wanted to shake Maddie back into the shape of the woman she used to be before Alex came along, although Lou had to concede that even before lover boy rocked up and rocked her world, Maddie had been blind to some things, including the feelings of the people who were closest to her. She wouldn't have had to raise any child on her own if she'd only been willing to see what was staring her in the face. But that boat had sailed, or more accurately it had never really floated. Sadness made Lou strike out. 'Christ, have you started reading the *Daily Mail*?'

'It's not a moral thing.'

'What, then?'

'Being the child of a single parent leaves you vulnerable.'

Lou got it. Maddie had had to survive on her own from the age of seventeen, parentless, penniless, protectorless. But that didn't mean you had to sacrifice who you were to get what you thought would make you safe – not in this day and age. Maddie had been standing up straight and strong on her own for years until bloody Alex Archer had come along and done his 'sweeping her off her feet' thing.

Maddie screwed the top back on the tube of concealer and threw it aside. 'You can sit in judgement all you want, Lou, but being settled matters to me. With Alex I'll have proper security. It's not why I'm with him, or why I'm marrying him, but it is a huge bonus. And I refuse to feel bad about that.'

'I'm not trying to make you feel bad,' Lou protested

– falsely. She would've loved Maddie to feel bad about abandoning her because if she felt really bad, she might change her mind and call off the wedding.

Maddie was fired up now. She came out swinging. 'Aren't you?' Her eyes glittered. 'From the minute I told you Alex and I were getting married, all you've done is snipe.'

'That's just the way I am. About everything.'

'No, it's not. About some things, the things you care about and that you think matter, you're impassioned and enthusiastic and lovely. You've been anything but lovely about this wedding or about Alex.'

'This is Alex, the man of your dreams, who you asked me to spy on.'

That punch definitely landed. Maddie took a couple of shallow, snatched breaths. 'I was in a state after everything that happened. I've spoken to Alex. It's all okay now.'

Lou paused. She studied the woman she'd loved for years. She didn't recognise her. Lou wasn't sure she even liked her any more. 'So you don't want to know what happened in the caves, then?' It was pin-drop silent. Lou could see a battery of emotions warring inside Maddie.

Anger got the upper hand. Maddie stood up. 'Stop it!'

'Stop what?'

'Messing with my head.'

Lou stood up as well, adversaries across a three-hundred-euro coffee table. 'I'm not the one messing with your head.'

Maddie's breathing was loud and fast. 'Go on, then. I can tell you're itching to say something. Go ahead, knock yourself out. Spill your poison. Cause more trouble.'

Had she really just accused Lou of having something

to do with the bouquet in her bed? Lou sat down. It was her way of trying to tilt the balance back in her favour. She waited. After what felt like an age Maddie sat down as well. 'You asked me to keep my eyes on your fiancé.' It was possible to pollute a supposedly nice word with a nasty taint. 'So I did. He was his usual charming self for the majority of the trip. He made sure everyone was having a good time, was uber polite to Raoul, our guide.' Maddie barely blinked. 'Raoul told us to stay together at all times. We all followed his instructions.' Lou paused. 'Except Alex and Ruby.' Now Maddie did blink. Cruelty bred cruelty, and Maddie had hurt Lou. 'There was this really beautiful underground lake in one of the deepest caverns. It was the last stop on the tour. After the lake we climbed back up to the main chamber to have lunch. It was proper fancy, tables and napkin rings and all that guff. It distracted everyone.' Maddie was getting impatient. 'We'd been eating for about ten, maybe fifteen minutes when we noticed that Alex and Ruby hadn't returned to the main cave with us. The guide was quite angry about it. He was about to go searching for them when they appeared.' Maddie said nothing. 'Ruby breezed in, claiming the lake had cast a spell on them and that they'd stayed to appreciate its beauty – together.' Lou stopped talking.

Maddie's question was predictable. 'And Alex?'

'He was embarrassed. He sat down, not with Ruby, picked at his lunch, wasn't the life and soul of the party any more. In fact, he seemed in a right funk. His priority seemed to be necking as many beers as possible before we got back on the bus.'

'That's it?' Maddie asked.

'Yes. That's it. Oh, and if you're still interested, no one confessed to planting a bunch of poisonous flowers in your bed, before you ask.'

'So nothing really happened?'

Lou gave up. She stood up and without another word went into her room. She closed the door, softly. The time for home truths was over. Maddie was a lost cause.

Chapter 38

COLETTE

Somehow it wasn't as good an atmosphere as the previous evening. After the grandeur of the picnic in the caves, maybe anything was going to be a let-down. Colette hadn't been on the trip – too busy exposing Luther for the creep he was, deflecting her mother, running around after Maddie and chasing off feral cats – but the photos that Antonio, the head waiter, had taken proved that the considerable effort had been worth it. The cave picnic never failed to wow guests. It was one of *the* set pieces of a wedding at the Finca Encantata, along with the arrival dinner in the olive grove and the wedding ceremony itself, of course. Perhaps the somewhat forced mood tonight was because the guests were having to serve themselves from a cold buffet, the kitchen having been given over to the mountain of preparation for the following day. Despite appearances, Colette had only a small staff to call on. She couldn't have them working all day and night on the Friday if she wanted them to put in a fourteen-hour shift on the day of the wedding itself. So self-serve meat, cheese and salad with fresh bread and fruit, accompanied by whatever they wanted to drink, set out down by the lake, with her on hand for any additional requests, it was. It was hardly slumming it.

Despite there being no need for his attendance, she saw Luther making his way down to the terrace. Her expression should have warned him off, but in what was obviously an act of deliberate provocation, he came and stood next her. Too close for comfort. She refused to acknowledge his presence.

He lit a cigarette, in direct contravention of the rules – staff were not supposed to smoke anywhere other than in the designated areas, all of which were out of sight of the paying guests. Colette refused to react. He launched in with no preamble. 'You do know that, however hard you work, no matter how often you do his bidding, no matter how much shit you shovel ... Ray will never let you have a seat at the table, don't you?' She didn't deign to answer, but Luther didn't need her to; he simply wanted her to listen to his bile. 'Never.' He took another drag on his cigarette. 'Maybe I am just the hired help, but at least I know *what* I am. I'm not delusional – not like you.' He took another drag. She imagined the carcinogenic smoke travelling deep into his lungs, sticking blackly to his insides, storing up trouble for later. She could but hope. 'And,' he threw in a dramatic pause for effect, 'I know how to get my due – plus some.' He leered. The image of Maria riding him in the cellar resurfaced in Colette's brain. He was obnoxiously proud of his little side hustles. She knew he was skimming off the booze deliveries – had raised it with her father months back, but Ray had said to leave it. He saw it as an old-school tax that was worth paying in return for Luther's loyalty. The problem was that with a taker like Luther, unless you slammed

217

the till drawer shut on their fingers every so often, they would just keep on dipping. Colette refused to turn her head so much as a millimetre. Luther was beneath her attention and she wanted him to know it. For once, staring at the beautiful people getting ugly drunk was a better option. He let out a short, harsh laugh then flicked his fag stub onto the ground. 'The sad thing is that you, Ms Colette Archer, don't realise how insignificant you are. Well, let me help you. You are nothing but a glorified maid.' Mike-dropped, Luther strolled back up the path to the main building, his hands buried deep in his pockets, no doubt holding onto his dick.

Colette stared at the glowing tab end, then stepped on it and ground it out beneath the sole of her shoe. It left a dirty black smear on the flagstone. She would need to get that removed before tomorrow. Perhaps alerted to her presence by the movement, her brother caught her eye. He was sitting so close to Maddie that they looked fused together. He waved and smiled. He was as oblivious as ever to the undercurrents that swirled beneath the surface of the whole enterprise. Such ignorance must be bliss. Colette didn't wave back. In that moment she hated him as much as she hated Luther. Why should he get to have everything he wanted in life, while she didn't?

She looked away, worried that her feelings might be writ large on her face. She watched Maria weaving between the tables, clearing plates with real grace. Maria hadn't been in any position to refuse the extra shift after being caught in flagrante in the cellar. Despite her dreadful taste in men, Colette thought that Maria had the makings of a good waitress. The guests responded well to her quiet efficiency

218

and her youthful beauty. Here was something Colette could do – she could try to keep Luther away from Maria. Perhaps a word in the girl's ear about his recent appointment at the clap clinic in Palma would do the trick. Retribution, served cold and in small portions, was the way to go.

As Colette pondered sexual proclivities and disease the guests lounged, drank and socialised. She was sickened by them all. By it all. By her own role in it. She stared at the eyesore of the fag mark. Luther was right about one thing; she was little more than a housemaid. But he was wrong about her prospects. Because Colette wasn't going to wait around for a fairy godmother to appear in a puff of smoke, rustle up a coach and horses and whisk her off to the ball – where she would meet a prince who would save her from a life of drudgery. Hell, no! Colette was going to rescue herself.

Chapter 39

MADDIE

They'd actually clapped when Maddie appeared on the terrace. It had been deeply disconcerting. She'd been glad that Alex was by her side. He'd held her hand so tightly that her engagement ring had bitten into her finger. Fuck Lou. She was a jealous old maid. An old maid who was currently sulking back in the suite. Let her stew. If she didn't have the good grace to be happy for Maddie, then it was better she stayed away.

Everyone was very solicitous. There was a great deal of fuss about finding the best spot for Maddie to sit in and asking what they could do to make her comfortable – which was actually to be left alone, but that wasn't on offer. The story that Colette had spun and Alex had cast – that she'd felt unwell after being out in the sun for too long the previous day – had obviously been accepted. Far better that her indisposition be down to her own stupidity than due to a poisoned bouquet left in her bed. That tale was way too gothic for the night before a wedding. Besides, Maddie didn't want to draw any more attention to herself. The maxi dress that Colette had dropped round for her was a good cover-up. And wearing sunglasses in the dark? Well, they did feel, and probably look, ridiculous, but they hid her still-puffy eyes. Hay fever was mentioned in passing.

When she was finally settled to everyone's satisfaction, people started drifting back into their little groups. It might have been her slightly weird appearance, but Maddie could have sworn that the atmosphere felt off. Even when the drinking and chatting recommenced, the mood felt different, more forced somehow. She obviously wasn't the only one to sense the low energy because she overheard Bobby mentioning to Priya that some music might be nice. And Priya – kind, accommodating Priya – immediately got up and went to fetch her speaker from her room. When she returned, she suggested that everyone take turns picking the track that reminded them of the happiest times in their lives. Priya's intention was good, but the result wasn't. Their impromptu jukebox session turned into a bizarre one-upmanship exercise.

Paul set the tone by starting with 'At Last' by Etta James, which apparently reminded him of his honeymoon in Bali. Paul's wife, Yvette, went next. She chose Bill Withers's 'Lovely Day', a track from her birthing playlist. 'After Letty was born and we'd both been checked out and passed A-OK, the staff lowered the lights and left us alone. I'll never forget it. Paul climbed into the bed with me and we simply held Letty, marvelling that this tiny but absolutely perfect child was ours.' Yvette reached out and grasped Paul's hand. A chorus of muted 'aah's rippled through the assembled guests. As the couple sat in blissed-out harmony, said perfect child was throwing rocks into the lake. They then had to sit through Craig David's '7 Days' – that was Tom and Charlie's choice, something to do with a 'very successful' lads' week in Zante and the surprising friendliness of Northern girls. The next person to choose was Lou, who had finally put in an appearance. But, true to form, she declined to pick a track. The abrupt way she said no prompted Priya to move swiftly on to Lily. They were all wary of Lou now, given her past performances. Lily picked Adele's 'To Make You Feel My Love'. Her choice should have been followed by Bobby's, but he, by coincidence or good planning, had at that moment gone to use the facilities. Priya went for Roberta Flack: 'The First Time Ever I Saw Your Face', which proved to be oddly embarrassing. It seemed too intimate a song to be played to a group of pissed-up wedding guests. Maddie could feel her turn drawing closer. As bride, she would be expected to pick something romantic, a track that captured the moment that she and Alex realised they were destined to be together. In her current state her mind was blank. The Torres couple dragged things back onto an even keel with an Al Green number and Teddy passed, pleading a tin ear, which did not go down well with his plus-one. Next up was Ruby. Maddie sipped her water and waited. Ruby refused at first, which seemed unlike her, but under pressure from the others she eventually chose a classic – 'When a Man Loves a Woman' by Percy Sledge. The ping-pong of glances while it was played was painful.

Throughout it all Alex stayed by Maddie's side, only leaving to fetch her food that she didn't eat and glasses of water that she did drink. The antihistamine pills were making her very thirsty. He also insisted on asking Colette to go and fetch her a throw to keep out the chill, although Maddie was plenty warm enough in her borrowed maxi dress. The thought of a blanket made her skin itch. Time was up.

'So, what's your song, Maddie?' Priya asked, all wide-eyed expectation.

Maddie still had nothing. The pause teetered on the edge of awkwardness, then Alex stepped in. 'Our song is Labrinth: "Beneath Your Beautiful".'

Priya blinked. 'Oh, I love that song.' She dropped her face to her phone and found the track. It started softly, just Labrinth's voice to begin with followed by the piano then the orchestra, until finally Emeli Sandé joined in. The music and the emotion built, creating a canopy of sound. It was the perfect choice, full of vulnerability, tension and passion. It silenced the guests. When the song finished no one asked why he'd picked it. Maddie knew – it was the track he'd played when he proposed.

Alex asked her to marry him on a rainy mid-week evening in August. It had been a totally uneventful day; both of them had been to work and they'd had no plans for the evening other than something to eat, some TV and an early night. That's why it had come as a complete surprise. Maddie had just got out of the shower. She'd pulled on a pair of joggers and a T-shirt. No bra. Her hair was only towel-dry. When she came into the lounge Alex was sitting looking out of the window at the rain. There was music on, low. 'You all right?' He was doing nothing, which was very unlike him.

He turned. 'Me? Yes, I'm fine. Will you come and sit with me?'

That had freaked her out. Why so formal? Her first thought was that he'd been offered a job abroad – New

York or Hong Kong? An opportunity that was *simply too good to turn down*. Their time was up. He'd decided that she wasn't right for him after all. She steeled herself. He looked serious. 'I was going do this differently, but I've thought long and hard about it and I think . . . I hope . . . that this is better than what I had planned.' He seemed nervous. 'We're good together, aren't we?'

'I think we are.'

He rubbed his hand over his face, obscuring his expression for a few seconds. Where was he going with this? 'It's been eight months.'

'Sorry?'

'We've been together eight months, exactly.'

'You checked?'

'I did.'

'Okay.' And?

'I want to ask you something.'

'Go on.'

He slipped his hand in his pocket and pulled out a small box. He slid it across the table to her. On the track Emeli and Labrinth sang of their love for each other. 'Maddie, will you marry me?'

She was so taken aback that she was silent. As a distraction she picked up the ring box. It was beautifully made out of some sort of wood. She opened it. It was empty. She looked up, feeling utterly confused, saw the tension in his face. The track ended. Alex scrambled for his phone and cut off the next song. The silence deepened. 'I thought, if you said yes, that you'd prefer to pick your own ring.' By now he looked panicked. 'I've fucked this up, haven't I? You wanted a proper proposal.'

'No!' It was she who dropped to her knees and reached up to hold him. 'It's perfect.'

'So is that a "yes", then?'

'Yes . . . it's a "yes".' She realised that it was what she wanted as she said it. His proposal had shocked her. She'd thought their relationship had a time stamp on it, the expiration of which would be determined by Alex. She'd believed that he simply didn't see her as wife material. But clearly he did.

They both had a cry, then Alex had made her a mug of tea and they'd gone to bed. It seemed that Alex could see beneath the beautiful and be happy with her after all.

Romantic peak reached and surpassed, Priya surreptitiously wiped away a tear. She was so soft-hearted. Charlie snatched her phone from her and stuck on a party playlist, and the serious business of getting even drunker began. As the attention moved off them, Maddie leant over and kissed Alex, feeling pure love for him for the first time in days. With perfect timing, he asked, 'Cup of tea?'

'No. It's okay. I'm fine. It'll be a hassle to make.'

'Please. I want to get you one. I want to do anything and everything I can to make you happy.' He took her hand in his and stroked it. They could both feel the bubble of blisters from the bouquet along the top of her thumb.

'Okay, then. Thank you. That would be lovely.'

Pleased to be allowed to play her knight in shining armour, he bounded off. She wanted to relax into his concern for her, forget her awful conversation with Lou, get over her grubby suspicions about Ruby and her poor relationship with Colette and the Archers, let go of her

225

paranoia about the flowers, get past all the bad stuff that had happened. Forget and just be.

But it was hard.

Alex's current behaviour was such a stark contrast to the previous evening. Then, he'd belonged to his family and friends, whereas tonight there was nothing he wouldn't do for her – which was making her question whether his attentiveness sprang from love or guilt. She turned that thought over in her mind and came to no solid conclusion. Maddie looked over at Ruby. Alex hadn't been anywhere near her all night. They'd not so much as exchanged a hello. That was odd. Wasn't it? Lou had said his mood had changed after their tryst by the lake in the caves.

Someone plonked themselves down in Alex's vacated seat. It was Bobby. She could tell that he was drunk, which was unlike him. He never seemed to get pissed; it just wasn't his style. He liked to stay in control. 'Hi, there.'

'Hi.'

'You okay now?'

'Yes.'

'That's good. We missed you today. At the caves.'

'It sounded like an interesting trip.'

'It was.' But he must have picked up something in her tone because he leant closer to her, wine on his breath, and added, 'It was something and nothing.'

'What was?'

He flushed, caught out. 'Ruby and Alex, being late back for lunch. The guide was being a bit overzealous about safety, that's all.'

They watched Tom and Charlie cajoling Priya and Lily to dance. Lily didn't take much persuading, but they had to literally drag Priya to her feet. The music spread out over the black waters of the lake. Yvette, Teddy and his plus-one joined in. Ruby wasn't dancing. She was talking to Paul – the adults at the grown-up table. They kept glancing over at the wavering, drunken figures on the terrace.

'Bobby.'

'What?' He was drumming his fingers on his leg to the beat.

She didn't have him down as someone into dance music, assuming his tastes to be more classical, but there again, what did she really know about Bobby, apart from what Alex had told her and what she'd observed over the past year? 'Bobby, look at me.' He did. 'Is there something going on that I should know about?'

'I don't know what you mean.'

'You do.'

He sighed. 'I've told you. They're friends – that means they talk. It's what friends do.'

'So what were they talking about today when they went off on their own?'

'How would I know? I wasn't there.'

'But you can hazard an educated guess?' He made an exasperated sound. She pushed it. 'They're behaving strangely. They've not said a word to each other all evening. And that's not normal. Something happened in that cave.'

Instinctively, they both looked over at Ruby. She was listening to Paul hold forth. She looked bored. Or did she look sad, distracted, worried, angry? Whatever she was feeling, it was obviously putting a damper on her mood. Maddie had never seen her so subdued.

'It's nothing for you to worry about.'

So there was something. 'Bobby!'

'Please, Maddie. I don't want to break any confidences.'

'But if it's going to reassure me, and if it really is nothing to worry about, on the eve of my wedding, why not tell me?'

Bobby interlaced his fingers behind his head and stretched. She was pressing him to choose between his loyalty to his friends and her. It was an emotional squeeze that was unreasonable – but all was fair in love and war. Eventually he said, 'Ask Alex.'

'I can't.'

'Why not?'

'Because he already thinks I'm paranoid about him and Ruby.'

Bobby let his hands drop. 'Okay. Okay.' But he said nothing else. He seemed to have slipped into a trance. He stared past the dancers out over the lake. Eventually he said, 'Ruby didn't want to say anything, not until after the wedding. She didn't . . . doesn't . . . want to steal your thunder.'

'How would she do that?'

'By being pregnant.' An invisible punch hit Maddie in the gut. And Bobby thought this wasn't something to worry about? He went on. 'It's come as a bit of a surprise. It's not planned, as far as I can make out, but she seems pleased.'

'She's keeping it?' Maddie's immediate assumption had been abortion. How would a baby fit with Ruby's high-powered lifestyle, and with Ruby herself? She simply didn't seem like mother material.

'Yes. Apparently. It's early days. So you can see why she doesn't want people knowing yet.'

'Except you and Alex.'

'Well, yes. We're her closest friends.'

'When did she tell you?'

'A couple of weeks ago.'

'So why not tell Alex then?'

Bobby was looking at Maddie now like she was mad. 'Presumably because he was in full wedding planning mode and she didn't think it was the best timing.'

'So why tell him today?' The day before he gets married.

Bobby shook his head. 'That I don't know.' Then, bizarrely, he went wistful. 'The caves were kind of special. The pool was breathtaking, calming. Maybe it was the first chance they had to be on their own together and she felt moved to share the good news with him.'

She had to ask. 'What about the father?'

At that Bobby pushed himself upright. 'Maddie, that's none of our damn business. I've said too much as it is.' He stood up, saved from any further questions by Alex's reappearance with her tea.

The musical interlude down by the lake is nauseating. Romance is such a con and yet people persist in believing in it, and pursuing it, at considerable cost to themselves.

This wedding is taking its toll on me. The need to be involved in every gathering and to be seen to be delighted 24/7 is wearing. It's also a total waste of my time – and I have precious little of that left. Look at tonight, attendance was compulsory, participation likewise. A wedding is a fascist regime wrapped up in a satin bow.

The only upside of this evening is seeing how fragile Maddie looks. The bouquet may not have incapacitated her, but it has weakened her – physically and mentally. She looks awful and is obviously uncomfortable and on edge. She holds herself stiff as if anticipating the next blow.

She's right to be anxious. My next move will do little to improve her state of mind. The first chance I get, I slip away and head for the tower. It's time to wreak more havoc.

Chapter 40

ALEX

Maddie gulped the tea that he'd made for her, then said she was tired. Alex suspected that it was the rowdiness that was getting on her nerves. When Tom pushed Charlie into the lake, that decided it. Lou announced that she would turn in too. Was that consideration for Maddie, or a similar desire to get away from his friends? Lou had looked miserable all night. Alex was glad that Maddie was sleeping with Lou close by. She might not be his first choice of companion, but he didn't want Maddie to spend the night on her own. Despite her much-improved appearance, Maddie was still shaky. He would never have said anything, of course, but he was mightily relieved that the swelling and the redness had gone down so much – for her sake as much as for their big day. She wouldn't have wanted to be photographed in the state she was in that morning. It had been worrying and oddly disturbing seeing her like that.

Maddie said she wanted to leave without making a fuss; not that the others were likely to notice her departure, they were far too drunk and preoccupied. Tom had joined Charlie in the lake. They were hitting the water with the flats of their hands, sending arcs of it up onto the jetty. It was an odd tactic if, as appeared to be the case, their aim was to encourage the girls to get in with them. As Alex and Maddie stood up to leave, Paul's wife, Yvette, shocked everyone by stripping off her dress, kicking it aside and taking a running jump off the jetty. For a second she hung like a thin starfish above the lake, then she plummeted. Her scream as she hit the water was piercing. Tom and Charlie whooped with delight and Paul scrambled to his feet, a look of shock on his face. It was definitely time to make their exit.

By the time they made it back to the finca, the only sounds were Maddie's still raspy breathing and the skitter of the occasional gecko. As they neared the tower Alex felt Maddie tense. 'What is it?'

'There are bats, in the eaves.' She glanced at the tower up ahead.

'I've never seen any.' That was a lie – Alex had spotted the occasional bat flitting between the tower and the trees, but that was to be expected. However manicured the finca might appear, it still roosted in the wilderness. Still, he wanted to do whatever he could to reassure Maddie, so he let go of her hand and ran up the last section of the path shouting 'Yah, Yah', waving his arms around like a mad-man. The things we do for love. There was no response, other than the faint murmur of 'dickhead!' – Lou's contri-bution – as he swept past her. At least Lou had the good grace to head straight into the tower, leaving them to say their goodnights in peace. Alex gently pulled Maddie into his embrace and was relieved when she didn't wince or flinch. As he held her close, he was shocked to feel her heart thudding inside her chest. 'Sorry. I didn't mean to startle you. I was trying to scare the little bloodsuckers off.' She leant into him and despite her evident rattled state it felt good. He was protecting his bride as a proper man should. Holding her tight, he said, 'I know things haven't exactly gone as planned so far and that it's been a rough twenty-four hours, but tomorrow we're getting married. How mad is that? Mr and Mrs Archer! I can't wait. Not to see you in your dress – although that will be special, and I'm sure you're going to look absolutely beautiful – not for the service or the party afterwards, but to marry you. Maddie, I love you with all my heart. Tomorrow will be the start of the rest of our lives together.'

He kissed her gently, pouring as much emotion as he could into it. He felt her relax and respond. Their lips created a small, tight world of sensation and safety made up purely of themselves. Eventually, reluctantly, he broke the spell. He stepped back. 'Goodnight, Maddie. I'll see you tomorrow.' One last kiss, and he left.

Chapter 41

LOU

How long did it take to say goodnight? They weren't teenagers copping a last feel on the doorstep before the front room light went on. Lou felt stupid. She wasn't Maddie's keeper. As Maddie had made crystal clear during their argument, Lou was now auxiliary to her life. Another few minutes passed and still she didn't appear. Should she move Maddie's stuff back into her own room? Leave her on her own, given that was what she seemed to want? Lou went into the bathroom intending to collect Maddie's stuff, but the sight of the various pills and potions scattered on the side gave her pause. There were her painkillers, her Pregabalin, the antihistamines and steroids that the Archers' doctor had given her, her contraceptive pill and a full blister pack of some small orange tablets with no name or dosage instructions on it. It was one hell of a concoction to have swilling around in your system. No wonder she wasn't thinking straight.

Lou wandered back into the lounge, her brain ticking. Where the hell was she? There was no point looking out of the window – due to the weird construction of the tower it was impossible to see the base, unless of course you were prepared to lean way out and risk death by broken neck. Lou gave it another couple of minutes, then she did what any good friend would do, even a pissed-off one who was surplus to requirements – she went looking for her mate.

She didn't need to go far because when she opened the door Maddie was standing on the landing, her back to Lou. She appeared to be staring at the ribbon draped across the stairwell. 'You okay?' They were the first words she'd spoken to Maddie since their spat. Maddie didn't respond. 'Mads?' Nothing. 'Are you coming in?'

Finally, Lou got a response. 'No. Not yet.' There was a long pause, then Maddie said, 'I want to see my dress.'

Lou didn't ask why. She didn't know what was going on inside Maddie's head or her heart any more. She was a bride now, and they were alien creatures. 'Okay then, why don't you?' But the dependent wifey shit had really got to Maddie, because she didn't move. A satin bow was enough to defeat her. This was why Lou was never getting married. Ever. Enough. She slipped past Maddie, yanked free the ribbon and threw it on the floor. 'Come on. It's your dress. Your wedding.' *Your funeral*, she added, in her head. They clattered up the stairs, Lou leading the way. She'd imagined that the dressing suite – for crying out loud, who came up with these descriptions? – might be barred with a portcullis and guarded by ravens in hoods, but the only thing in their way was another length of ribbon, tied in another sodding bow. Lou ripped that off as well and discarded it. Everything was gift-wrapped at the Finca Encantata. The door, oddly, was already ajar. Lou pushed it fully open then stepped aside so that Maddie could enter first.

Moonlight silvered the room. Lou caught sight of herself and Maddie in the triple mirror on the dressing table. There was another huge, full-length mirror propped up against the wall. The effect of seeing repeated images of themselves reflected in so many surfaces was disorientating. It was like being trapped in a fairground attraction. Lou was shocked to see that there was a third person in the room, standing tall and slender by the window. What the hell were they doing wearing Maddie's wedding gown? She told herself to get a grip. It wasn't a person. It was a mannequin. But with the veil falling in a swirl of tulle to the floor and a pair of shoes peeping out from beneath the hem it had, momentarily, looked like an actual person – albeit a headless one. Lou noticed that Maddie hadn't moved. She was stuck a few feet inside the room. Decisively, Lou flicked on the light switch and rid the room of its gothic overtones. Still Maddie didn't move. 'Mads?' Even to her own ears Lou's voice sounded impatient. 'You okay?' Maddie shook her head. 'What's wrong? It was only the moonlight.'

Wordlessly, Maddie pointed at the mannequin.

All Lou saw was a beautiful, incredibly expensive gown that was going to look stunning on Maddie's slim figure – skin rash or no. Lou had hated the dress the moment she'd set eyes on it, when Maddie had emerged from the changing room in the bridal shop in Fulham. It was a sight that had taken Lou's breath away and crushed her heart.

Maddie was still rigid. 'Look!' She was pointing at the pool of tulle heaped at the side of the dress.

Lou looked, and saw what was troubling Maddie. The veil was moving. It wasn't a trick of the moonlight; there was something dark writhing around underneath the layers of material. Lou marched over to the dress.

Maddie tried to pull her back. 'Don't!'

'I've had enough of this nonsense.' Lou bent down and lifted the veil. It took a huge effort not to scream. It was a nest, not of vipers, but of blood-smeared hairless creatures. They were scrambling over each other blindly, making a weird creaking noise. It took Lou a couple of seconds to register that they were kittens. Freshly born. Some of them appeared to have black string wrapped around their bellies. Lou's own stomach heaved. It wasn't string, it was umbilical cord.

Lou felt Maddie step up behind her. 'Jesus!'

'Kittens,' Lou said, in case Maddie hadn't realised. Lou looked at Maddie. She'd gone deathly pale. Her hand was pressed against her mouth. It made her look like a distressed child. She said something that Lou didn't catch. 'What?'

Maddie lowered her hand. 'My dress.' It came out as a wail.

Lou wasn't surprised that Maddie was struggling. She was right: the train and the hem of the dress were wrecked, the delicate fabrics covered in blood and afterbirth. The end of the veil itself had been ripped to tatters – by the mother cat, presumably. Lou's stomach heaved again, but she made herself sound calm. 'I think the dress might have escaped the worst of it. Look.' Maddie seemed to want to do anything but look. She started to sob. Lou had to do something – and that something was get rid of the kittens and the veil so that they could properly assess the damage. The things we do for the people we love – even when they don't love us back, or even seem to like us any more. Lou scanned the room, looking for something to put the kittens in. There was nothing obvious. Her eyes fell on a stack of presents. They were all beautifully wrapped in an array of silver and white paper and tied with more fucking ribbon. Amongst the parcels there were a number of what looked like decent-sized boxes. Lou guided Maddie away from the mewling kittens to the gift pile. She grabbed one of the box-shaped parcels and handed it to her friend. 'Open it.' Maddie looked confused. 'So I can get rid of them.' She jerked her head in the direction of the kittens.

'Without Alex?'

Lou was firm. 'Yes, without Alex.' She glanced at the tag. 'It's from Mr and Mr Salentos. Whoever the fuck they are when they're at home.' She didn't give Maddie a chance to answer. 'Just rip the damn thing open.' Still Maddie hesitated. Lou moved the action along by grabbing the parcel and tearing a big strip of paper off it, then she passed it back to Maddie to finish unwrapping. It turned out to be a pasta and noodle maker – the perfect gift for the couple you didn't know. Lou decanted the machine and the polystyrene packing curls onto the floor. It was going to be a tight squeeze, but it would have to do. Now came the tricky bit. Armed with the box, she turned to face her task. The thought of touching the kittens made Lou nauseous. She advanced slowly and knelt down. They were still scrambling around and their eyes looked glued shut. She reached out, but couldn't bring herself to go any further. It was the veins bulging beneath their papery thin skin and the noise they were making. Then a solution occurred to her. The veil was fucked either way. 'Mads, go and get me some scissors.'

'No!' This time it was a full-on wail.

'If you want my help, you will go and find some scissors and bring them to me.'

Lou stayed kneeling on the floor, trying not to breathe in the weird, yeasty smell that was rising up off the kittens' squirming bodies. She heard Maddie leave. The minute she was gone Lou fled to the far side of the room herself. As she waited, she scanned the room. If there was a litter of newborn kittens then surely the cat that had given birth to them should be close by. The last thing Lou wanted was the enraged mother launching herself at her as she bent down and tried to move her offspring. But there seemed to be no sign of the creature. Maddie eventually returned, bearing a pair of nail scissors. They would have to do. Lou took a deep breath, advanced again and went to work.

It took ten minutes of snipping through the gossamer tulle to cut the bloodied section of the veil free. Another deep breath, and Lou lifted up the kittens. They tumbled on top of each other as she lowered them into the box. By this point she was past caring if they got hurt or not.

Chapter 42

MADDIE

It was another sign. One that Maddie couldn't ignore. The most glamorous, luxurious thing she'd ever owned was ruined. Her dream of walking down the aisle as a radiant, happy bride to take her rightful place by Alex's side, shattered. The desecration of her wedding dress seemed a random act, but Maddie knew that it wasn't. It was a warning. Someone or something was determined to stop her marrying Alex, and they weren't going to give up until they succeeded. There would be no happy ending – not for Maddie.

Lou was talking, rushing around, making out like she could fix this, but it wasn't fixable. Her beautiful dress was covered in blood. Her path to the altar strewn with sick, scary obstacles. The room tilted and slid away, taking Lou with it.

Maddie closed her eyes and tried to centre herself, but her imaginings were as disturbing as the carnage in the suite. In her mind's eye she saw a figure creeping into the tower carrying the cat. Maddie could hear the creature mewling and crying in pain. The figure climbed the stairs and slid into the suite. They knelt down and lowered the cat onto her dress. Had they tethered it to the mannequin so that it couldn't escape? Had they been that cruel? Had they stayed to watch or had they crept away, job done, into the night? Had someone really been that sick and malicious? And if so, who?

Was it Ruby, acting out of pure jealousy? Could she really want rid of Maddie that badly? What about Colette? Were all these 'terrible accidents' actually her warped way of wrecking things for the brother who had everything? Or could this nightmare be Marilyn and Ray's doing because they simply couldn't countenance Maddie becoming their daughter-in-law? Or was it Lou? The non-believer in weddings, in love and in Alex? Or why not Bobby because he saw his friendship with Alex being relegated to the background by their marriage? Or was it Lily, who resented being a bit-part player at the most lavish wedding of the year? Or why not sweet, accommodating Priya, who looked at Alex with such desperate yearning?

It could be any of them.

Or none of them.

It could be her losing her grip on reality because she was so exhausted and drugged up and stressed out.

The madness reached out and embraced Maddie. She let it. She felt its tendrils ripple over her brain, poking and probing, searching for the weak spots, of which there were many.

Out of nowhere Colette appeared. Her lips were moving, words pouring out of her, but Maddie couldn't make sense of them. Then Colette's hands were on her, gripping her arms. 'Maddie. Can you hear me?'

241

She nodded, but only because she wanted the shaking to stop. Colette lost patience and cast Maddie aside, then set about stripping the dress from the mannequin. Maddie wanted to tell her to be gentle, but it was too late for that. A dress bag appeared from somewhere and Colette stuffed Maddie's gown into it. She zipped it up as if disposing of a corpse.

The floor tilted again. Maddie knew what was about to happen. Colette's voice faded away and the room darkened. Maddie felt her legs and spine stiffen. Her eyesight blurred. The last thing she saw was the bare mannequin standing bereft in the moonlight.

I go to bed happy. The cat did my work for me. All I had to do was let her in. I have to admit that her violation of Maddie's wedding dress was much more impressive than what I had planned. Where I brought a knife, she brought claws and gore.

As I lie in bed listening to the bats flit around the finca I feel an unfamiliar sense of contentment descend on me. It's rare for me to find anyone who looks at the world the way I do. Unheard of, actually. Are the cat and I kindred spirits? It's a fanciful but appealing thought, but perhaps our moment by the lake really did forge a connection. True, the fact that my counterpart is a feral stray might be seen as worrying, but I can't think of an animal more self-sufficient than a cat. They are singular creatures who stalk and dispose of their prey ruthlessly.

Tomorrow I'll find out whether I have the stomach to be as effective as my familiar.

The Day of the Wedding

Chapter 43

MADDIE

Unsurprisingly, Maddie slept poorly. She was too wired, too confused, too overwhelmed. A second tonic-clonic seizure in twenty-four hours – her body had gone into battle with her, which was bad enough, but far worse was her growing conviction that one of their guests was also attacking her. The little sleep that Maddie had managed to snatch had been dream-ridden and exhausting. She'd been watching a wedding video: smart guests, amazing flower arrangements, burnished wedding rings, champagne fizzing over the lip of fine flutes. Alex had been in her dream looking handsome and expectant, the perfect groom; Bobby alongside him, performing his best man duties. Lou had been there, stony-faced, unreadable. Lily, Ruby and Letty were in attendance, all dressed up, ready to follow her down the aisle. The Archers were also present, their backs to her. And there had been glimpses of Colette bobbing in and out of each frame. But the one person missing from this scene of loveliness had been the bride. Because Maddie had been nowhere to be seen at her own wedding. As she'd watched, Maddie had become aware that beneath the soundtrack of glasses clinking and excited chatter she could hear a voice pleading, over and over again, for help. No one else in the dream seemed to hear it, or if they did, they didn't respond.

When Maddie woke again, for what felt like the hundredth time, she sat up, too weary to dream any more. It was 6.30 a.m. on her wedding day. It didn't seem real. She slid out of bed, pulled on her borrowed dress – she'd spent the past couple of days wearing other people's clothes, none of which had fitted her – and crept out of the room. She felt no desire to wake Lou. It would trigger another exhausting conversation about whether she was doing the right thing, for the right reason.

She sat in the lounge and watched the rose-tinted light slant though the shutters. What did she feel? She was no longer sure. Unbelievably unlucky? Targeted? Vulnerable? Confused? Frightened? Ill? All of that and more. The one thing she did not feel was bridal.

She lowered her head and pressed her fingertips into her temples, seeking relief. She didn't find any. It was as she raised her head that she saw the envelope. It was on the floor near the door.

Maddie tried to convince herself that it was a good luck card or a note from Colette with some last-minute instructions, but the sick feeling in her stomach warned her that it wasn't. She picked up the envelope. It was light. Her name was printed on it. She ripped it open where she stood. Inside there was a folded sheet of notepaper. Finca Encantata stationery. It *was* something innocuous. She was being paranoid. She unfolded the note. There was one line of type. ASK ALEX ABOUT THIS. She shook the envelope. A pregnancy test landed in her palm. One glance. Two small blue lines. Her world fell apart.

Chapter 44

COLETTE

Colette had left Lou and a stable but groggy Maddie at 1.15 a.m. She'd not got back to the villa until after 2.00 a.m. Her alarm had gone off at 6.30 a.m.

Her first task was trying to resurrect Maddie's ruined wedding dress. Colette had already messaged Gabriela, and asked her to come in extra early. She'd explained the problem as best she could. Gabriela had made both of her daughters' wedding dresses – Colette had seen the photos. Sure, her parents' housekeeper wasn't a high-end couturier, but there again, the dresses sold in the salons of Chelsea and Fulham were probably made by women just like Gabriela somewhere in the world.

Colette went down to the back kitchen and lifted the dress bag onto the table. She unzipped it. In the pearly early-morning light Maddie's dress looked fine, until your eyes moved downwards. It was the contrast between the pristine, exquisitely tailored loveliness of the bodice and the tattered, soiled hem and train that made it look so bad. The cat had not only bled on the lace, it appeared to have ripped or chewed quite a large section of it as well. What was left of the balled-up veil was in an even worse state.

Gabriela was going to have a job on her small hands fixing it. Colette heard footsteps approaching, but by the familiar slap of heeled mules she knew it wasn't Gabriela. She would never wear something so impractical on her feet. What her mother was doing up this early was anyone's guess. Marilyn swept in, her silk robe fluttering. No matter how often Colette saw her mother without her make-up, it was always a shock. The woman who came into the kitchen was old, her eyes sunken, her skin thin, likewise her lips. The lack of eyebrows added to the crypt-ready appearance. Colette looked away, back at the ruin of the dress.

'Jesus Christ! What in God's name happened?' Marilyn exclaimed. Already this was shaping up to be Colette's fault – which in some ways it was. She had left the room unlocked. Her mother reached out her hand to touch the dress, then thought better of it.

'How on earth did it get into that state?'

'That cat I told you about.' Marilyn looked blank. 'It got into the dressing suite and gave birth on it.'

'What a fucking waste. We should have just bought one of those hideous off-the-peg dresses from that awful shop in Shoreditch – saved ourselves a lot of time and money. Well, I suppose one more disaster is no great surprise, given the shitshow this wedding has been so far.' Marilyn had a foul mouth, but she tended only to use it in front of members of the family and the staff. 'I'll see you later. Much later.' And with that she departed. No offer of help and, interestingly, not an iota of interest in whether Maddie knew her dress had been wrecked, and if she did, how she'd reacted. In other words, not the slightest bit of sympathy or concern for her future daughter-in-law.

251

Chapter 45

MADDIE

It was only when Maddie got out into the stairwell that she realised she was barefoot. She didn't go back for her sandals – such small details were an irrelevance. A tiny sliver of her old self registered that it was a glorious morning. It was cool and there were wisps of cloud in the just-lightening sky. She could hear birdsong, and voices. The voices belonged to the florists who were already at work dressing the courtyard. One woman was up a ladder threading cream roses into a greenery arch while another was hand-tying cascades of peonies, heavily scented gardenia and gypsophila to edge the aisle. Maddie remembered agonising about what flowers to choose a lifetime ago, when such things had seemed important. There was another woman ferrying more crates of blooms into the courtyard. Maddie briefly considered asking them about her toxic bouquet, but decided that what energy and fight she had left she needed to keep for her showdown with Alex. Had he been playing her all this time? Or was that just what someone wanted her to think?

It was when Maddie stepped into the archway to the

main building that she saw the cat. The sight of it made her heart thump. It was curled up, its head and paws tucked inside its body, a curl of darkness at the base of one of the terracotta pots. The disgust that the newborn kittens had provoked in Maddie the night before returned, but, bizarrely, with it came a shiver of sympathy and a sense of shared suffering. Maddie wondered whether the cat was distressed about being separated from its litter. Could an animal feel love and loss? Perhaps a cat that had just given birth could. Maddie didn't know what Lou and/or Colette had done with the kittens. It hadn't been a priority at the time. But they had, evidently, not reunited them with their mother. Had they simply left them to die in a cardboard box, a soiled wedding veil acting as their shroud? Or had Colette drowned them in the lake? Maddie couldn't bear to think about it. The cat must have heard or sensed her approach because it went from inert to alert in a second. But it didn't run away. Instead, it slowly got to its feet. It sniffed the air and yawned. Only then did it turn and look at her. Its eyes were glittering, its tail vibrating. For some strange reason it reminded Maddie of a tuning fork. Maddie crouched down, keeping her distance. She was wary, and yet curiously drawn to the cat.

'I'm sorry. I know it's not your fault.' The cat's paper-thin ears quivered. Was it listening? Encouraged, Maddie stretched out her hand. 'Any of it.'

She didn't see the cat move, but she did feel the sting of its claws on her forearm. Maddie recoiled. A thin line of blood appeared on her skin, a string of tiny black seed pearls. She rubbed. The pearls turned into an ugly pink smear. It was eerily similar to the stain on the flagstone that was all that remained to show that the cat had been there at all.

There isn't much more I can do now, other than let it all play out.

It's come down to me or Maddie.

One of us will get what we deserve today.

The burning question is who?

Chapter 46

MADDIE

Maddie stood outside Alex's room. Two futures lay on the other side of that door. One loving and honest, the other a travesty. Was Alex lying in bed wide awake, unable to sleep because he was so excited about Maddie becoming his wife? Was he still the man who loved her, and only her? She blinked. Or was he fast asleep, a naked, slumbering Ruby by his side? Had he spent the night before his wedding with his lover, thereby proving, despite the vows he was about to make to his bride, that he still belonged to her? And always would – now there was a baby on the way.

She didn't knock. It was time to face it. Here and now. She opened the door and stepped inside. Alex sat bolt upright as if mounted on a spring. The bed beside him was empty. 'Maddie! What are you doing here? I thought it was bad luck for the groom to see the bride on their wedding day.'

'It's too late for that.'

Her tone obviously helped to wake him up. She came further into his room, looked for somewhere to sit. She couldn't countenance the bed, despite the absence of any evidence of Ruby's presence. She saw a stool, dragged it into the middle of the room and sat on it. Alex – obviously thrown by her sudden appearance, her odd mood and by her obvious desire to keep her distance – perched on the edge of the mattress facing her. 'What's wrong?'

'Everything.'

'What do you mean?'

'I mean ... everything is wrong.' She couldn't say any more. She rubbed at her forearm. It began seeping blood again.

He noticed. 'Christ. Now what?' He made to move towards her, but she held up her hand, warning him off.

'It's nothing. Just a scratch.'

'Maddie, please, talk to me.'

She looked at him. At his oh-so-familiar loveliness. At his strong body and his handsome face. At this very physical vessel that he was about to dedicate to her in front of a small, select group of guests in the most romantic setting for a wedding that any bride could wish for, thereby kick-starting a life of love, beauty and security. Then she thought about him and Ruby and the baby. 'Are you sleeping with Ruby?'

He actually threw his hands up in the air. 'Oh, for Christ's sake, Maddie, not this again. How many times do I have to tell you? Ruby and I are friends. And that's all we are.' He was angry, but was it anger designed to deflect her away from his guilt or anger sparked by his justified fatigue with her persistent accusations? Her persistent *false* accusations? He sounded weary. 'I love you, you know that, but this has to stop. This obsession you have with Ruby simply isn't healthy. It isn't good for you. And to drag this all back up again, on the morning of our wedding.' He shook his

257

head. 'Do you ever stop to think how it makes me feel? It's not a great basis for a marriage, is it, Mads?' He was right, it wasn't, but there were too many questions swirling around Maddie's brain for her to sleepwalk into marrying him. And his failure to see that was worrying. His next question compounded her sense of being misunderstood. 'What set this off?'

How to answer that?

Was it the mewling ball of bloody kittens nestled in the delicate lace of her wedding gown? Alex's hand lingering on Ruby's bare shoulder at the party? The way his father had welcomed Ruby like the rightful daughter-in-law that first night? Was it Alex's failure to tell her that he was taking his father's money – and that of a couple of his dodgy associates – to set up his business, despite swearing that he wanted to be his own man? Was it a pair of borrowed high heels that broke her leg, scarred her back and crushed her confidence? Was it Bobby's face when he told her that Ruby was pregnant, father unknown or, more accurately, unspecified? Or was it the sight of the naked mannequin in the moonlight before she lost consciousness?

'Mads! Are you in there?'

'Yes. Just wait.' She couldn't have another seizure. Not now. She needed to calm down and get her scrambled thoughts together, but it was difficult with him staring at her with such a frustrated look on his face. Then he shocked her by throwing aside the covers and getting out of bed. She assumed he was coming to comfort her, but instead he walked towards the bathroom. 'I need to pee. I'll be back in a minute or two and then we'll sort this out, once and for all.'

Once the bathroom door shut, she stood up and paced. It was something to do, and it allowed her to scour the room for any clues that Ruby might have been there after all. She approached the bed. There was a floating shelf either side of it. On his side were his wallet – the self-same one that had started them on this journey when she'd been just a girl looking for an easy ride – his watch, a half-drunk bottle of water and a slim volume of poems. An echo came back to her of the happy, calm, loving days they'd spent together at the finca before their guests, and the awfulness, had arrived. *Shine here to us, and thou art everywhere; This bed thy centre is, these walls, thy sphere.* He'd learnt poetry for her. Alex loved her and she loved him. Would he really cheat on her, father a child with another woman and still go ahead with their wedding? Or did someone want her to think that? And in believing it get her to self-sabotage her one chance of happiness?

She heard the toilet in the en suite flush.

Either way – she had to find out.

Chapter 47

ALEX

Alex took longer than he needed to in the bathroom in the hope that Maddie would be calmer and more rational when he came out. He loved her, he really did, but these past few days had been worrying. They'd been fine before everyone else had arrived: more than fine, they'd been happy. He hadn't had the slightest doubt about getting married, then, or before. Now? He washed his hands. He didn't love anyone else, never had. But it was hard to prove a negative. Could he convince Maddie that this obsession she had with Ruby was damaging, to her and to them? He didn't know. But if he didn't put an end to her suspicions, where did that leave them? They were supposed to be getting married in six hours' time. He took a deep breath, smoothed down his hair and opened the bathroom door.

She was standing next to his bed holding something. She was very still. He was halfway across the room when she threw whatever was in her hands at him. It bounced off his chest harmlessly and fell to the floor with a light clatter. He bent down to pick it up. It was a plastic stick with a small window at one end inside which were two thin, but very clear blue lines. She'd thrown a positive pregnancy test at him. 'What the hell!' He bent down and picked it up, held it away from him as if it was dangerous – because it was. He was shocked and confused. 'What?' He got no further.

'Exactly. Or more accurately, what the fuck?'

He went towards her, intending to give her a hug, but she moved away, as if she was afraid of him. He stuttered, 'But isn't this . . . a good thing? Sooner than we'd planned, obviously. But we did say that we didn't want to wait too long before we started trying, didn't we? I know we'll have to be extra careful because of your health, but . . .'

Her expression hardened. 'It's not mine, you idiot!'

Now it was his turn to take a step back. 'I don't understand.'

'Don't you?'

'Maddie, please. I don't know what the hell's going on. What exactly are you accusing me of?'

'It's quite simple. I'm accusing you of fathering another woman's child.'

'That's ludicrous. Is this some sort of sick wedding day prank?' He looked around the room, expecting, and hoping, that Lou would suddenly leap out, cackling.

'Prank?' Maddie's voice wobbled. 'No, it's not a prank. It's a positive pregnancy test.'

'That belongs to who, if it's not yours?'

'You know who! Ruby!'

He sat down on the bed with a thump and said nothing for a few seconds. He was between a rock and a hard place. The allegation was ridiculous, but Ruby's pregnancy was real enough and if Maddie found that out now, in the state she was in, so close to the wedding – well, God knows what

261

she'd do. His priority was calming her down. Full disclosure could come later, after the ceremony, when they were on the opposite side of the world to Ruby. 'Who has been putting this garbage into your head?'

She was prowling to and fro. She was more agitated than he'd ever seen her before. 'No one.'

'Was it Lou?' he blurted out. She'd never liked him.

Maddie's expression was stony. 'Don't try and throw me off by attacking other people. This is about you and Ruby.'

He took a couple of deep breaths. 'There is no ... *me and Ruby*.' His effortful calmness only served to infuriate her further.

'I know you went off with her, at the caves.'

He fought back. 'Oh, there you go then – bang to rights. I was seen talking to my friend of fourteen years, surrounded by loads of other people.'

She ploughed on. 'You weren't with *loads of other people*, you went off on your own with her. Then, last night, you were both acting weird.'

'How?'

'You didn't say a word to each other.'

He made an exasperated noise, but Maddie carried on. 'You barely looked at her. And that's not how you are together. Normally, you can't get enough of each other.'

He shook his head in despair. 'This is nonsense.'

'Is it, Alex? Is it really?'

He had no answer to that question other than 'Yes, it is', but she was in no mood for listening. 'Okay.' He ran his hands through his hair. 'Let's just take this a step at a time. But before we do, I want you to know that *I am not*

262

having a sexual relationship, of any description, with Ruby or anyone else. Please, will you at least sit down?' She refused with an impatient shake of her head, leaving him to plough on regardless. 'First off. How come you've got hold of Ruby's pregnancy test?'

'So you concede it is Ruby's?'

'Maddie, please, this isn't going to work if we aren't *both* straight with each other.'

'No, it isn't.' She said it with accusation, not agreement, in her voice.

'So, I ask you again, how come you have it?'

'Someone posted it under my door last night . . . or this morning . . . with a note.'

'A note that said what?'

'To ask you about it.'

'Show me.'

'I left it in my room.'

'Did you recognise the handwriting?'

'It was typed.'

'Which is odd, don't you think?' She slowed her pacing, but refused to answer him. 'Why did you assume it was Ruby's?'

She flared, 'Because I know she's pregnant.'

'How do you know?'

She stopped pacing and faced him. 'Bobby told me.'

That threw Alex. 'Bobby told you, or you overheard him talking?'

'What is this, twenty questions? Don't you believe me?'

It didn't add up. Bobby wouldn't break a confidence, especially not one that would put Alex in a tricky situation. It wasn't the way he operated. 'But why would he tell *you*?'

'Why would your best friend talk to crazy old me?! Oh, I don't know. Maybe because I asked him what was going on and he seemed to think, God knows why, that I had a right to know – given I'm supposed to be your fiancée.'

'Bobby had no right telling you and stirring up all this shit so close to the wedding.'

'Don't blame this on Bobby. I made him tell me.'

'And what exactly did he tell you, Maddie?'

'That she was pregnant and that she didn't want to say who the father was.'

'And your immediate conclusion was . . . that it was my child?'

'No,' Maddie said, but she followed up with another salvo. 'And yet we have a secret pregnancy, a mystery father, and Ruby talking to you in private, after which you avoid each other like the plague. And then a little white stick is delivered to my room, on the morning of our wedding.' She was breathing hard and her colour wasn't good. Alex waited and here it came. 'I need to know. Is the baby yours?'

'Christ, Maddie, how many times? Of course it isn't! How can you even think that of me?'

'Because I have eyes. I see how you are together. Everyone sees it.'

This was pointless. It was a never-ending cycle of accusations and recriminations. 'Well everyone is sick, then. We're getting married, today, in a few hours' time.'

'Are we?'

They stared at each other, on the cusp of no return.

The only route back to each other was to accept that she was right – not about Ruby, but that there was someone playing God with their lives. 'Maddie, you're the one

264

who's been saying that someone is intent on stopping us getting married. Well, isn't this precisely the sort of thing that someone might do if they wanted to guarantee that we don't make it to the altar?'

By way of response, she finally stopped pacing and stood still. The heat seemed to leave her and finally she softened. 'So you believe me?'

It was a last roll of the dice. 'Yes, I do.' Alex stood up, crossed the room and took hold of her hands. 'And I think that the best thing we can do is show them, whoever they are, that we are unbreakable. We go ahead with the wedding. We stand in front of our friends, my family and them – whoever they are – and we declare our love for each other. We make our vows. We become man and wife. We don't let them win. What do you say?' He got down on one knee. 'Will you marry me, Miss Maddie Laughton? For better for worse, for richer for poorer, in sickness and in health, till death us do part?'

Chapter 48

COLETTE

Gabriela had worked miracles. True, the train of Maddie's wedding dress was now a good ten centimetres shorter and the dress itself was still a touch damp along the hemline, but it was a vast improvement on how it had looked a few hours ago. The veil, unsurprisingly, had been beyond repair. Whether Gabriela's efforts had been worth it, time would tell. Colette returned the rescued dress to its bag and hung it on the kitchen door. She had a few last-minute things to sort out and her own bag to pack before she could dedicate her full attention to the bride and groom.

An hour later, loose ends tied up before her parents had even risen – or in her mother's case, re-risen – from their respective beds, Colette collected the dress and left the villa. When she arrived at the finca she was pleased to see that the flowers were nearly finished. Sofia, the head florist, knew the property well and, more importantly, she knew and met Colette's high standards. And Josef was already setting out the chairs for the guests. He would be rolling out the specially commissioned carpet that served as the aisle and adding more flowers later on.

They did these jobs in the last hour or so, in a bid to stop the sun from bleaching out the roses that had been woven along the edge of the runner and wilting the peonies and gardenias in the aisle pieces. Yes, the courtyard was, as planned, shaping up to be the most Instagrammable outdoor wedding setting imaginable. It was all as it should be – at least, the elements that she could control were – so she made her way up to the staff quarters to stow her bag. She lugged Maddie's wedding dress with her. It seemed to grow heavier in her arms with each step. In Colette's overnight bag there were some clothes and a few essentials. She hadn't packed much, but it would be enough. As she glanced around the spartan staff bedroom she felt a range of emotions, uppermost of which was nerves. It was showtime – in more ways than one. She was about to swing by the kitchen when her phone pinged. It was a text message from Lou asking if Colette had any paracetamol, and if she had, to bring it to the suite ASAP. Surely more drugs in the circumstances were not a good idea. But Colette's job was to fulfil the bride's every wish, so who was she to argue? She found a packet of ibuprofen in the bathroom cabinet, shoved the box in her pocket, picked up the dress bag yet again, and set off for the tower, curious to see how the bride was holding up.

There were thirty steps up to the second floor. By the time Colette got to the landing she was blowing. She knocked and waited, but no one appeared to hear her. Colette had witnessed wedding-morning hysteria plenty of times before. It was as if the bride was some sort of sacrifice that had to be ritualistically prepared by her gaggle of female attendants. Hair had to be tortured, make-up applied, sexy underwear sutured on, virginal dress reverentially lowered, perfume sprayed, body adorned with specially bought jewellery. Old, new, borrowed, blue – it was an elaborate ritual that went on for hours. Another knock, then Colette let herself in.

But the room Colette stepped into didn't contain the usual frenzy of bridal activity. There was no clink of bottle against glass, no music playing, no chat, no anecdotes and no last-minute advice – although the make-up woman did appear to be having a rather relaxing time drinking her coffee and flicking through the feed on her phone. At least the hairdresser and his assistant were busy. They were working on Ruby's and Priya's hair, creating similar elaborate, pearl-studded up-dos. Ruby met Colette's gaze in the mirror. She answered Colette's unasked question. 'She's in the bathroom, with Lou. Has been for a while. She wants to have a word with you.'

Colette couldn't imagine what about. Besides, the dress was Colette's immediate responsibility, not the bride. She laid the bag on one of the sofas, unzipped it, slid out the gown and proceeded to try to put it on the mannequin. It was harder than she'd expected. Loath as she was to ask for assistance, Colette did eventually have to request that the make-up woman get off her toned ass and help. Together they managed to ease the fragile gown back onto its stand. Colette glanced at the time. The chamber orchestra would be arriving any minute now and she still hadn't been anywhere near the kitchen. She headed for the exit, but Ruby spotted her. She swivelled around and pinned Colette with her beautifully made-up eyes. 'You really should speak to her.' There was no other option. Colette crossed the room.

268

But if Maddie didn't open up straight away, Colette was going to leave the ibuprofen and run; she needed to get on. Just as she was about to make her escape, the bathroom door opened and a firm grip pulled her inside.

Chapter 49

ALEX

Alex looked at himself in the mirror. His wedding suit was the colour of smoke, his shirt pristine white. He'd decided against a tie – a concession to the heat, a nod to informality and a small but satisfying act of defiance against his mother's wishes. His suit fitted perfectly, but there again it would, having been handmade by a tailor with a royal crest above the door of his Jermyn Street shop. Objectively, Alex looked every inch the groom, but appearances can be deceptive.

His thoughts turned to Maddie. She should also be nearing the end of her transformation from a normal person into his princess bride. He hoped with all his heart that she was all right. Their long, difficult conversation had been like a purge, horrible and depleting, but it had – he prayed – ultimately been worth it. He'd borne her accusations because he loved her. He'd managed to calm her shattered nerves because he loved her. He'd convinced her that he was not the father of Ruby's baby, because he loved her and no one else. He'd been able to reunite them, in the face of their unknown adversary, who she believed in, but he still had his doubts about, because he loved her. He'd persuaded her to go ahead with the ceremony because he loved her. And now he was about to prove that love by marrying her.

'A couple of hundred quid for them?' Bobby appeared at his side in the mirror. 'I assume the price for your thoughts has gone up, now you're minted.'

Alex deflected him. 'Nothing worth sharing.'

Bobby's smile flickered and dimmed. 'You sure? As your best man my duties include calming any last-minute nerves . . .' he left a pause, 'or doubts.'

It sometimes felt as if Bobby could see right through him. 'It's just not been the build-up to the wedding that I was expecting or hoping for.'

'I get that.'

How could he? Bobby had no idea of the scale and weirdness of the problems he and Maddie had encountered over the past few days. Bobby said nothing, which was his way of inviting Alex to say more, which was possibly why he blurted out, 'It wasn't sunstroke. She had a seizure. She's had a couple in the past twenty-four hours.' It was a secret he'd promised to keep – shared with the one person that Alex would have sworn could keep his mouth zipped at all times, about everything, up until a few hours ago.

'Jeez. Is she all right?' Bobby looked shocked. 'I didn't know she had epilepsy.'

'No, most people don't. She doesn't like to talk about it. It's under control, normally.'

'What triggered it? The stress of the wedding?'

Alex smoothed his hair, not that it needed it. 'That, and other stuff.'

Bobby didn't hesitate. 'Like Ruby's pregnancy.'

That was one of the things Alex appreciated about Bobby – whereas most people skirted around tricky issues, especially when they involved themselves, Bobby went straight there, which gave Alex the opportunity to challenge him. 'Why on earth did you tell her?'

Again Bobby didn't fluff or obfuscate. 'I was drunk, and she kept badgering me. And I suppose I thought that telling her was better than what she was imagining. She was getting really worked up about your and Ruby's relationship. If I got that wrong, I'm sorry.'

Alex quit looking at himself in the mirror and turned to Bobby. 'It's okay.' He appreciated Bobby's honesty – knew it came from a good place. 'It did cause one hell of an argument, but it forced us to get things out in the open. Things that needed dealing with.'

'And that helped?' Bobby seemed genuinely interested.

'Yeah, I think it did. Although the timing was, obviously, not great.' Alex's phone dinged. It was a message from Colette requesting their presence in the courtyard. The guests were assembled, the orchestra was playing, the sun was shining – it was time. 'Right. They're ready for us.'

'Just a minute.' They faced each other. Bobby's expression was serious. 'Before you do this, I want to say something.'

Bobby's evident emotion set Alex off. It drew him back seventeen years to the dusty floor of the craft cupboard at King Henry's – to the day he realised that he hadn't a clue who he really was, but that Bobby did, and that together they could conquer anything. Alex smiled at his best friend. 'Can't this wait till the speeches, Bob? I've a wedding to go to, you know.'

But Bobby reached out and touched Alex's sleeve, requiring him to wait. 'No, what I want to say isn't for public consumption.'

'Shit, now you've really got me worried. You're not about to declare your undying love and plead with me to dump Maddie at the altar and run away with you, are you? You know I love you, man, but not like that.'

There was a beat. Bobby's serious expression held for a split second, then he smiled. 'No, you prat. I just wanted to say . . . I really hope that you'll be happy with Maddie and that being married is everything you want it to be.'

They hugged, enveloped in a cloud of brotherly love and Vetiver Extraordinaire.

Chapter 50

COLETTE

Colette looked out over what she had created and felt satisfied. The stage was set and it was, as planned, immaculate. The guests looked like so many jewel-coloured butterflies basking in the sun. Ruby and Priya were sheltering from the heat in the doorway like two delicate hothouse flowers. The verdant arch of roses, gardenias and ivy stood ready to frame the happy couple as they made their vows. Beneath it waited the celebrant, a slim column of black, upright and unwavering.

It was fairy-tale worthy.

She zoned in on her brother. He was standing, as directed, at the front, to the right of the altar, with Bobby by his side. They looked like two elegant statues that had been added to a garden to give it structure and gravitas. She felt a sudden stab of pity for him, but there was nothing she could do about it now. It was too late to explain and justify her actions.

It was showtime.

Love really is deaf, blind and stupid. Surely if the gods throw that many obstacles in your way the only sensible thing to do is concede defeat and accept that it was never meant to be? And yet here we all are, dressed up to the nines, about to witness the union of Alexander George Archer and Maddie Laughton.

Why they still want to go through with this charade is beyond me. Haven't I done enough?

I've destroyed her beauty.

I've weakened her body.

I've proved that she is irrational, riven with jealousy, prone to hysterics, with a real temper on her when provoked.

I've shown that he is untrustworthy, in the thrall of Ruby, still beholden to his father.

I've rendered them both utterly unlovable.

I've sucked every last ounce of promise and joy out of this wedding.

And yet, they persist.

Chapter 51

COLETTE

The butterflies were getting restless. They were fluttering and stirring, straining against the compulsion to stay put. It might be traditional for the bride to be late on her wedding day, but in thirty degrees of heat it did seem a little selfish. Colette saw Bobby lay a reassuring hand on Alex's broad shoulder. He leant in close and said something in her brother's ear. A joke to break the tension, perhaps, or some last words of reassurance? Colette wished she knew.

They all heard the approaching footsteps. The guests' anticipation was visible in a myriad of tiny gestures and sounds. Trouser creases were straightened, skirts redraped over long tanned legs, zippers checked, rings realigned and throats cleared. Then a general resettling occurred. *Yes*, they all seemed to silently concur – *we're good to go*. But the vision that appeared through the archway and shot into the courtyard was not the blushing bride; it was Lou, the visibly flustered maid of honour. There was a perceptible sag in the mood and posture of the congregation. Lou ran down the aisle and pulled Alex and Bobby to one side. The guests all watched, intrigued, as a hurried conversation took place.

Colette waited to be summoned. She saw Alex run his fingers through his hair – a sure sign of stress. He used to do it as a boy, although at the time she'd thought it more an affectation than a tell. It was Bobby who signalled for her to join them. She tried to look calm and composed as she made her way to the front. It would only cause more anxiety among the by-now impatient guests if she gave any sign that there was going to be a further delay. She did, however, glance at her parents. Her father looked hot and pissed off. Her mother merely raised a redrawn eyebrow and continued to cool herself with her small electric fan.

'I can't get into the tower,' Lou blurted.

'That's not a problem, I can let you in.' Colette had the key on her. She always did.

'So Maddie's in there on her own?' Alex's voice carried an undertone of worry.

'Well, yes.' Lou looked and sounded rattled.

Colette made an executive decision. She turned to face the expectant guests. 'Ladies and gentlemen, I'm afraid we're going to have to ask for your patience. There's going to be an unavoidable short delay before the ceremony can commence. Given the heat, my suggestion is that we all retire to the lounge.' She pointed, showing them the way. 'There's champagne on ice and plenty of cold soft drinks available. We'll let you know as soon as we're able to gather again – for Alex and Maddie's much-anticipated nuptials.' She tried to put an upward lilt on the last few words. No one moved. Colette scanned the courtyard and caught Maria's eye. She was lurking in the shade of the main building, no doubt hoping to catch a glimpse of the bride. 'Maria...' Colette beckoned the girl forward, 'will show you the way.'

With no other choice, Maria stepped out into the sunshine and started directing the guests back inside. Once Tom and Charlie stood up – they were always keen to get to the booze first – everyone else started to follow. The reluctant exodus allowed Colette to return to the matter in hand – an emotionally unstable bride, alone in a high tower, after a stressful and physically punishing two days. 'How was she – in herself?' It was the obvious question to ask.

Lou paused. 'Okay – I suppose. As you saw, we managed to persuade her to get her hair and make-up done.' Alex's frown deepened. 'When she was finished she said she wanted to go and look at the view from the top of the tower – to clear her head before the ceremony. Ruby and Priya set off to wait for her down here. I went up to the bridal suite with her. She was nervous, but that's what you'd expect, isn't it? She didn't say much. She just stood and stared out of the window to start with, but she got agitated when she realised that the girls had taken her bouquet with them. She said she wanted it, asked me to run after them and fetch it back.' Lou paused. They all knew what was coming next. 'So I did.' Alex was looking at Lou as if he couldn't quite believe her stupidity. 'I was halfway down the path when I got a bad feeling about leaving her on her own. I ran back to the tower, but the door was locked.'

'You idiot!' Alex set off. They followed him. The final act was underway.

As they hurried out of the courtyard Colette heard her father shout, 'I'll send Nige.' As if a musclebound driver from Croydon was going to be any sort of a solution to what lay ahead.

Chapter 52

BOBBY

Alex was already banging on the door, yelling Maddie's name, when Bobby arrived at the tower, having run as fast as he could – which was obviously not as fast as a groom who is worried that he's about to be stood up on his wedding day. Bobby's lungs were screaming. He wasn't used to sprinting, and certainly not in thirty degrees of Mediterranean heat. Ruby arrived next, which was a surprise. She hadn't been party to the conversation at the altar, yet here she was clutching her shoes in one hand, holding her bridesmaid dress up out of the dust with the other, her normally pristine face coated in sweat. Lou joined them. 'It is locked, isn't it? I wasn't imagining it?' Bobby confirmed that the door was indeed locked. Lou's relief seemed misplaced in the circumstances. Ruby and Lou joined in shouting Maddie's name. It went on for what felt like ages, but in reality was probably only a minute or two. There was no response. One by one they stopped shouting – Alex was the last to give up. They stood around, breathing hard with exertion and worry, until Colette finally arrived.

'Get it open,' Alex barked.

'Okay. Okay.' She slid the key into the lock. 'But Maddie never had a key for the downstairs door, so I don't see how . . .' The key turned. Colette tried the handle. The door didn't budge. 'She must have bolted it on the inside.'

'Why in God's name can you lock it from the inside?' Bobby knew that the sharp edge in Alex's voice was a sign of his deepening anxiety.

Colette spoke without turning around. 'Because towers were built to protect the people inside them.'

'So what do we do now?' Alex asked.

'Has anyone tried calling her?' Colette asked.

'We've been yelling,' Lou said.

Colette shook her head, disgust at their pathetic efforts evident on her face. She drew her mobile out of her pocket and dialled Maddie's number. They all heard the ringtone at the other end. No response. Then Colette tried the numbers for the phones in Maddie and Lou's rooms, the dressing suite and the bridal suite. Still there was no response.

'Is there another way in?' Alex was sounding increasingly stressed.

'No,' Colette responded coldly.

'So what the fuck do you suggest?' Alex bit back.

Colette turned away from the tower. One of Ray's drivers was wandering up the path, looking for all the world like he was out for a stroll. 'Brute force,' Colette replied. 'Nigel!' she shouted and beckoned him. He sped up, but only a touch. 'I need you to break the door down.'

If Nigel was surprised by Colette's request, he gave no sign of it. He took off his jacket and draped it over a bush. So fastidious, and built like a brick outhouse. 'Okay. Step back, folks.' Nigel launched himself at the door, shoulder down. The noise of the impact reverberated up Bobby's spine. The door pinged open and Nigel fell through the gap. He got up, dusted off his trousers and grinned.

'Thanks, Nige.'

'Do you want me to wait around?' he asked.

Colette nodded. 'Yeah. For the time being.'

He wandered over to the bush to retrieve his jacket. Job done.

Alex took a step forward, but Bobby put out his hand. 'No, Alex. I think someone else should go.'

He responded vehemently. 'Oh, we're not still on with all that crap, are we? I think it's a bit late to be worrying about the groom seeing his bride before the wedding. I want to check she's all right.' And yet he didn't go any further. Did he not want to face Maddie, fearing that she'd changed her mind? Or was he worried about something else? Was he actually frightened of Maddie?

'I think Lou should go,' Colette said.

But Lou responded negatively. 'I don't think I should, she doesn't seem to want me around any more.'

'What about you going up to talk to her, Colette?' Ruby asked.

'Oh no, I don't think it's my place,' Colette said. 'I don't know her well enough.'

No one suggested Ruby, for obvious reasons.

Alex had plainly had enough. 'If one of you doesn't go and check on Maddie in the next five seconds, I swear to God I'll . . .'

He didn't get to finish his sentence.

I have sixty steps to make up my mind.

Fate has handed me one last opportunity, but it isn't much of one. There are four witnesses, five, if you count big Nige. I would be the last person to see Maddie alive, which would make me the prime suspect. It's a big risk to take.

I reach the first floor.

If I'm going to do this, I need to do it quickly. I would have to rush her, take her by surprise, push her onto the floor, grab a cushion or a pillow, press it over her face. Can I do it? Am I capable of pinning down her flailing arms and thrashing legs? I would need to press hard enough to cut off her oxygen supply, but not so hard that I break her nose or cause any bruising. I have, of course, researched smothering, so I know how to do it.

I reach the second floor. The door to the dressing suite is wide open. I glance inside. The naked mannequin greets me.

There's another option. It's dramatic and would be upsetting, especially for those gathered below, but a flutter of lace as she falls through the balmy air would be a nice touch. I would say that she was by the window when I got up there, that I tried to talk to her, but that she wasn't rational. That I was worried about her mental state – which, as we've all observed, has been deteriorating over the past forty-eight hours. I would describe how I took a step towards her, meaning to reach out to comfort her, and how she simply leant backwards. It's a long way down and there are stone flags below.

I take the remaining stairs up to the third floor.

But there are no guarantees that her plunge to earth would result in instant death. She might survive, be incapacitated for life. The Archers with a disabled daughter-in-law? Alex with a dependent wife? Me in prison? I simply can't see it.

I reach the top floor.

I stand outside the bridal suite and listen. Despite being out of breath and out of time, I'm excited. It's decision time. How badly do I want to keep Alex from Maddie – and for myself? Enough to commit cold-blooded murder? I unlock the door with the card Colette gave me. It swings open in a nice smooth arc. The views up here really are something. There's a delicious breeze rippling through the room. But Maddie is not conveniently standing by the open window waiting to be turfed through it to her death or permanent injury. I scan the suite. I shout her name, for the benefit of the gang gathered below – they may be able to hear me, I can't know for sure – and to summon her. If this is going to happen it needs to happen now. I only have a few minutes. Alex is not a patient person.

I shout her name again. There's no response.

Hallelujah. She's gone. Run away. Been vanquished. My considerable efforts have not been in vain. Euphoria sluices through my body. I'm incandescent with triumph. My campaign to rid Alex of the clingy bitch has finally worked. That must have been why she sent everyone away. She didn't want anyone to try and talk her out of it. I briefly wonder how she made her escape.

Did she ask one of Ray's flunkeys to drive her? No, she wouldn't have risked approaching someone on the payroll, they would've reported straight back to the Archers. An old-fashioned taxi, then. How gloriously prosaic. It's all a total head rush. I have finally succeeded in driving her away. Her infatuation – it was never love – wasn't strong enough in the face of a few nasty rumours, a poisonous bouquet, a faked pregnancy test and, let's not forget, the assistance of a feral cat. I've won. I have finally levered free the limpet.

Fuck.

She's not gone.

She's in the bedroom, lying on her side in the marital bed, her back to me. From my position in the doorway, she looks like a child curled up beneath the covers. The euphoria drains away, leaving me ice cold. She doesn't move, doesn't react to my presence as I enter the room. I glance around. Her wedding dress lies dumped on the floor, discarded like a skin that was too tight to bear. Lying beside the heap of lace I spot one of her wedding slippers. They're beautiful – the exact same shade as the inside of an oyster. The shoe looks tiny. Did she kick it off in a hissy fit? The second shoe is nowhere to be seen. Under the bed, perhaps, gathering dust and marks. Not that a discarded slipper is my immediate priority, but I have a thing about shoes being separated. It bothers me. Small things do. A pair is just that, two things that are meant to stay together.

'Maddie?' I whisper. The concern in my voice sounds genuine. I sometimes convince myself that I have the feelings that I've become so adept at mimicking. No reaction. There's no shift in the creases of the sheet, not the lift of a wisp of hair in the tender breeze. She is absolutely immobile. I cross the room, walk around the bed and look down on her.

She looks composed. The stylist hasn't done a bad job with the make-up, considering what they had to work with. There's a sheen of highlighter on her cheekbones, her lips are peachy pink and her lashes are rimed in grey – a nice touch: black is so harsh and ageing – but the swelling is still there, pushing her cheeks and eyes out of shape, making her look wrong, a parody of a bride.

The blister packs are scattered across the bed. They glint prettily in the sun. Each one has been punched through, their perfectly smooth pearls of pain relief removed and swallowed. Washed down, presumably, with water from the nearly empty bottle on the nightstand. As I step closer my foot sends an empty box of ibuprofen skittering across the floor. I do a quick calculation. Three boxes, six blister packs, forty-eight tablets. Probably enough – especially on top of her epilepsy meds and whatever she was taking to reduce the swelling. And we are a long way from a hospital. The tension that I've been carrying around inside me for months snaps. I laugh with sheer, wonderful, liberating relief.

She is done.

I have won.

Outside, the Greek chorus finds its voice again. I'm taking too long. They're getting anxious, which is apt given the tragedy that's unfolding in the bridal suite. This time it's my name they shout, which is as it should be. I will be the bearer of the worst possible news, but I will also be the still point in a crazily spinning world for Alex. I shall be there for him, not simply by his side, but inside his pain, as I have been before, and will be again.

I kneel on the bed and take one last look at her, before the audience arrives and the final act begins. Staring at her once-pretty face and her comatose body, I feel a tiny bud of pity form inside me. It's small and crystal clear – a perfect teardrop. It wobbles, threatens to fall, but clings on. It is a shame. If only she'd

285

left him alone, not strayed so far outside her natural habitat, she could have been happy with someone else, with anyone else. There's no such thing as 'the one' for people like Maddie. She simply doesn't have the depth. The tear gives way under its own tender weight and drops, leaving no mark.

I reach for the pillow.

Chapter 53

ALEX

What was he playing at? Why the hell was he hanging around at the foot of the tower like a coward? Whatever fate lay in store for him, he needed to man up and face it.

He set off running, taking the steps two at a time. The thudding of his heart was as loud as his footsteps. Halfway up he tripped and smashed his chin on the unforgiving stone stairs. He tasted blood in his mouth as he got up. Adrenaline coursed through him. He knew in his bones that this was going to be bad. This wasn't a case of last-minute nerves – something awful had happened to Maddie. There *was* someone at the finca, one of the guests or, God forbid, one of his own flesh and blood, who was dead set against their marriage, and that someone *had* been trying to do her real harm.

And while he'd stood at the altar, surrounded by family and friends, soaking up the adulation and the atmosphere, blindly hopeful that he was about to get married – they'd tried again.

This was his fault.

Maddie had been right all along – and he hadn't believed

her. He'd dismissed her fears, belittled her worries, told her it was paranoia to think that they – that she – was in any danger.

Well, she was in danger now.

They're coming. Time is up.

I allow myself one last glance at the pitiful scene, then I pull the bedroom door closed behind me. How I handle the next few minutes will be important – for me, as much as for Alex. This is my moment to shine, with empathy, compassion and love.

Their footsteps are thunderous. The sound bounces and kicks its way up the stairwell. Alex arrives on the landing. Mine is the face he sees through the open door. He runs into the bridal suite. I must have got my expression right, because he brakes suddenly and cannons into me. I catch hold of him and pull him into my orbit. 'Wait. Alex, just wait a minute.' I feel his heart thumping against mine. I worry for a moment that he'll hear or, more accurately, sense the absolute calm at my centre, but he's too caught up in his own panic to be aware of other people's feelings. He rights himself, pulls free of my embrace.

'What's happened?' He's sweating. His hair is flattened against his forehead in a really unflattering way. The urge to reach out and rectify it is momentarily distracting. An unintentional fringe is not a good look on a groom. But, of course, he is no longer a groom. 'Tell me,' he hisses.

I reconfigure my features. Channel shock at the appalling

289

cruelty of life. 'Oh, Alex. I'm so sorry. I've called for an ambulance.' I haven't yet, but I will. Cover – it's always best to have some. I don't get to use any more of my hastily prepared script because he pushes me off.

'Bobby, if you don't get out of my way this fucking second I swear to God I'm going to punch you.'

I step aside. It's time he faced his future.

The rest of the gang have arrived now. They all run into the bedroom after Alex. They squawk. The sound reminds me of chickens fluttering and scrambling over each other. I can't see the poignant scene any more, there are too many bodies in the way. I take the opportunity to phone for the ambulance. I stumble through my pleas for assistance – making sure I repeat 'Finca Encantata' and 'emergency' a number of times. I don't know the Spanish word for suicide. As I end the call, I sense someone closing the door to the suite. It's my first inkling there's something wrong. If all of them are in the bedroom, who's behind me? I turn around and see Nigel, the door-destroyer. He's blocking the doorway. His beefy arms are crossed and his legs are planted in a ridiculously masculine stance. He very consciously looks through me. He appears to be guarding the exit – whether he's there to stop people entering or leaving is unclear. I'm confused. Who asked him to come up? Colette, perhaps? Ever one to protect the reputation of the Archer family. My unease coalesces. It becomes a worm, filled with undulating, gritty suspicion. I sense that things are about to get away from me. How? I don't know.

I head into the bedroom. There's a wall of backs in front of me. Colette, in her understated aqua two-piece; Lou, in her ill-fitting maid of honour get-up; and Ruby, who still manages to look like sex on legs in a simple silk bridesmaid dress. It strikes me what a well-dressed bunch we are to be attending the bedside of a tragic suicide. The room falls quiet. I expect to hear Alex, weeping, wailing and generally lamenting the loss of his love. I should be at his side. His comfort in his darkest hour. I'm about to push my way, gently and politely of course, through their obstructive bodies to reach my friend, when, on cue – and as if choreographed – the well-dressed human curtain moves aside to reveal the heartbreaking tableau.

Except Maddie is no longer dead.

Or dying.

Or even unconscious.

She's sitting up, staring straight at me. Her face is no longer slack and lifeless. It's full of life. Her eyes blaze with anger. She looks, for the first time ever, like a fully formed person. She holds my gaze with an intensity that surprises and almost intimidates me. I find it difficult to look away. But I do. My instinct, as always, is to seek out Alex, my lodestar. He's kneeling on the floor at the foot of the bed, crushing still further the fallen wedding dress. He looks shell-shocked. As well he might. I don't know what sort of shitshow this is, but it's not right.

Colette pulls the chair from the dressing table into the middle of the room. The floor protests by letting out a nerve-shredding cry. Colette directs me to sit. The chair is too low and my legs stick out awkwardly. I feel deeply uncomfortable, but I'm guessing that is the point. The rest of them sit on the bed, flanking Maddie, like harpies. I experience a stab of irritated confusion – since when were the four of them best buddies? They not-so-secretly all hate each other. The only other chair in the room is brought for Alex. He looks like he needs it. His chair is placed alongside the bed, within grasping distance of his now not-dead bride. His sister helps him into it.

The battle lines are drawn.

The echo of a courtroom is hard to ignore. We have the accused (me), the accuser (Maddie), with the rest of them making up the jury. I shall not recognise this kangaroo court's jurisdiction. I lift my chin. No one can judge me. I opt for an expression of hurt confusion – which, in truth, is what I'm feeling. Why is Alex allowing this? I've done nothing wrong. Well, not in this room, not in the last five minutes. I didn't have time to. The same cannot be said of Maddie. Who fakes their own suicide on their wedding day? A madwoman, that's who. I shuffle around on the chair, trying to regain my composure.

The first person to speak is ever-practical Colette. 'Before we start, I suggest that I radio Xavier and get him to buy some time with the guests. I'll ask him to say that Maddie is . . . having issues with her dress.' Involuntarily, we all glance at the trampled heap on the floor. 'Agreed?' There's a murmur of consent. I say nothing. Colette produces a radio from her pocket and we all listen while she relays her instructions coolly and efficiently in Spanish. Event managed, for now, she turns down the volume on her radio and pockets it. There's a long, slow beat. It's filled with so many questions and raging emotions that the air feels unbreathable. They are waiting for me.

I give them what they expect and take for granted, which is – Bobby, their friend, their confidante, the all-round thoroughly decent, conscientious, caring guy who they all know and like, but do not love. I give them the best man. 'The ambulance is on its way.'

'Is it really, Bobby?' Maddie asks.

'Yes.'

'Well, there's no need for an ambulance.' No hint of shame. She glances at Colette, who steps away to make the call to cancel it.

They are working together. It's a worrying development. 'But . . .' I gesture at the empty pill packets.

'They're props.' Her voice is full of flint.

I hold my nerve. 'I don't understand.' Neither does Alex, by the look of him. What he actually looks is shattered. I lock eyes with him. He latches on and stays with me for a few precious seconds before glancing away. He scans the room, seemingly hoping that it might contain some clue as to what the fuck is going on. There's another theatrical pause.

'I'll give you an explanation, shall I, Bobby?' Is she enjoying this?

'I think you should.' I have no intention of lying down and letting her walk all over me.

'Okay.' She actually sits up straighter. 'There are a few gaps that we might need your help with, but we think we have most of it.' The harpies exchange glances.

I resettle myself on the shockingly uncomfortable chair and gesture for her to proceed. I'm interested in what she has to say.

Chapter 54

MADDIE

Maddie felt surprisingly calm. She knew why. It was the first time in a very long time that other people had listened to her. She'd been right all along. Someone had been prepared to go to extreme lengths to stop her marrying Alex – which meant she wasn't going insane, she wasn't being paranoid and, crucially, her brain, although wired differently, was not breaking down.

And now she knew who that person was – Bobby.

He had such a convincing look of hurt and confusion on his face, but she wasn't buying what he was selling any more. She was done with being played. And she wasn't the only one. 'You made the mistake of forgetting that women talk, even women who don't particularly like each other.'

'Maddie. I don't know what you think I've done. There's obviously been a serious misunderstanding. But whatever you . . . or anyone else . . . may believe I've said, done or even felt, I want to get this resolved as much as you do.' The bastard actually looked at Lou, then Colette, apportioning blame elsewhere.

Where to begin? There was so much to unravel.

Maddie decided to start at the very end, with his response to the trap they'd set for him. The trap he'd walked straight into. 'Okay, Bobby. What I want, or perhaps *I need* you to explain is your reaction when you found me lying unconscious on this bed, surrounded by empty pain-killer packets.'

'I was horrified and distressed.'

'Really?'

'Yes.'

'So why did you laugh?'

'I did no such thing.'

She ignored his lie. He was full of them. 'After you laughed, you came into the room and, in spite of your sup-posed "horror and distress", you didn't check for a pulse. Try mouth-to-mouth. Pour water down my throat to make me vomit. I'm not even convinced that you rang for an ambulance. What you actually did was climb onto the bed, lean over me, really close, and study me. Why did you do that, Bobby? Why didn't you try and save me?'

'I did. But when I first saw what you'd done – or what I thought you'd done – I was in shock. We must remember that you were totally unresponsive at this point.' Here he glanced at Alex. 'The shock immobilised me for a few sec-onds, but I quickly realised that I needed to act. I leant over you so that I could check to see if you were breathing. I was so relieved that you were. And I *did* ring for an ambulance.'

Maddie stared at him. He was going to deny it all. The thought infuriated her. 'So you're claiming that you did everything you could to save me?'

'Of course. Oh, Maddie, please, this is . . . madness.'

There it was! His insistence on her mental instability. He was, once again, trying to gaslight her. But she wasn't going to let him get away with it, not any more. 'All this time I thought you were a decent person. How wrong can you be? You've been trying to get rid of me since the day we met, haven't you, Bobby? You've been lying and scheming for months. And you did it cleverly, stealthily, so that it all looked coincidental. Or better still, as if it was all in my head. But the truth is . . . you've done nothing but try to hurt me.'

His expression of sympathetic bemusement didn't flicker. 'That's simply not true.'

But Maddie was determined to make him admit to his role in the nightmare that her life had become. 'Isn't it? From the very beginning you fed my anxieties about Alex and Ruby. It was you who was always pointing out how special their relationship was, how close, what a good couple they'd have been if they'd got together.'

He shook his head. 'Maddie, *you* came to *me* with your concerns. I distinctly remember reassuring you that there was nothing for you to worry about.'

She talked over his denial. 'I'll give you credit. It was all very slickly done, imperceptible, really. And I bought it. More fool me. But that's your MO, isn't it? Manipulation. Only it didn't work, did it? Alex and I stuck together, we got engaged, planned our wedding. That must have infuriated you.' He opened his mouth to argue, but she stopped him. 'No. It's your turn to listen! That's why you ramped it up once we got here, isn't it? The flowers, the messing with my meds, my dress, the positive pregnancy test. It was all you, wasn't it, Bobby? You hate me, don't you?'

296

He sighed and said softly and oh-so-calmly, 'Of course I don't.'

It was classic Bobby; everything under control – his control. Maddie suddenly thought back to her accident at the Valentine's party, about lying at the bottom of the stairwell at Blink. She recalled the pain and the panic, and Bobby's preternatural calm. How had she not seen that his composure was a clue? Real people panicked when faced with trauma. Bobby never did. And he wasn't panicking now. He really was a psychopath. 'So you deny it all?'

His expression shifted slightly. 'Yes, I do deny ever wanting to harm you, like any rational person would. As to your allegations, that's all they are – allegations.' He stood up. 'I don't want your wedding day to be a disaster, Maddie, but I'm afraid that seems inevitable now. How could this ever be the happiest day of your lives after this bizarre charade?' He waved to indicate the bedroom and the pills. 'This is obviously some sort of cry for help.'

'Sit down!' Maddie heard the anger in her own voice. It sounded ugly, but that was his fault. He hesitated, looked at Alex, then sat down again. 'I haven't finished.' Maddie drew breath and tried to control her rage. 'Don't you want to know how I eventually worked it out?' He refused to say anything. She wasn't bothered. This was her story to tell. 'It was Ruby. There's a nice dose of irony for you. Yep, it was the person you'd schooled me to be most suspicious of who gave me the key. After I left Alex's room this morning, I was a mess. I didn't know whether I was going to go through with the wedding or not. It really was that touch and go. Ruby was in the corridor waiting for me. She'd heard Alex and me arguing, heard her name being used, wanted to

297

help – despite what a bitch I'd been to her. We went for a walk and we talked, properly, for the first time ever. And the more we talked the more your role in things became clear – to both of us. You're always there in the background, aren't you, Bobby? Saying one thing to one person and something else to the other – orchestrating everything, making things happen the way you want them to. Ruby had noticed it as well, hadn't you, Ruby?'

Maddie nodded at her new ally, inviting her to weigh in, which she did in typical Ruby style.

'First of all, I didn't *tell* you I was pregnant. I'm guessing that you found out by snooping around my apartment. I think you make a habit of that, don't you, Bobby? And it was you who advised me not to say anything to Alex given how close it was to his and Maddie's wedding. Then you changed your tune when we got here. I thought that was odd.' She leant forward, seeking out Alex. 'He said that you'd been asking questions about why I wasn't drinking. It was Bobby who pushed me to tell you rather than risk upsetting you by keeping it a secret – hence our conversation by the pool. And Maddie was right to pick up that something was "off" between the two of us. I was upset about how you reacted. You didn't seem pleased for me, you were more worried about how she would react if she found out. But, as we now know, that was Bobby's doing as well.' She turned her gaze back to Bobby. 'Where you got this from . . .' she placed the pregnancy test that had been delivered to Maddie on the bed, 'I don't know. Because it's not mine. You made a mistake there, Mr Genius – it's a different brand.' Ruby sat back and crossed her arms.

Maddie leant forward. She was exhilarated to have finally outed him. They had him bang to rights. 'So Bobby? Is there anything you want to say now?'

Tall, twisted tale spun. Bile spewed. Mutual self-congratulation indulged in. Girl power exerted. Maddie sits on the bed surrounded by her newfound bosom buddies. We have arrived at the ta-dah moment in the story.

They expect me to play my part now, which is to fall on my sword. I'm supposed to confess my sins, in a state of well-deserved distress but with startling clarity and surprising powers of self-diagnosis. That's how trite and clichéd this is. I will do no such thing.

Their error, and my opportunity, is that no one has noticed how quiet Alex has been while Maddie and disloyal Ruby have been making the case for the prosecution. He hasn't spoken a single word and no one has thought to ask him if he's okay, not even his bride. It takes me back to our King Henry's days and the 'plays'. No one ever worried about collateral damage then either. But it's obvious, to anyone paying attention, that Alex is not okay. In stark contrast to their self-righteous zeal, he is shell-shocked. He's shut down, emotionally and intellectually, overwhelmed by their sick little plan and Maddie's litany of wild allegations. I understand his response. I always have. He can't stand ugliness, in any form. It makes him feel unsafe. That's why he let me come up here in the first place. He was afraid of what was waiting for him at the top of the tower. He wanted me to deal with it for him. And that's why I may still be able to salvage something from this train wreck.

Why? Because he trusts me.

How much? I'm about to find out.

They're still waiting. I draw myself upright. Rise above this, and them. 'I honestly have no idea what you're talking about.' I turn my attention to the only person in the room who matters. 'Alex?' I fix him with my gaze, reminding him who has always had his back. 'You can't possibly think that any of this is true.'

The howl of indignation they let out is loud enough to lift the birds from the trees.

Chapter 55

ALEX

His head was going to burst. 'Stop! Can you all just shut up for a fucking minute.' They looked startled. They'd obviously forgotten he was even there. All of them except for Bobby. 'This has gone too far.'

'Yes, it fucking has!' Lou chimed in. She looked happy for the first time since she'd arrived at the finca. Had she been the one to come up with this God-awful set-up? She'd certainly put in a convincing performance in the courtyard, sowing the seeds of panic and getting them all to rush to the tower, expecting the worst. Surely it couldn't have been Maddie's idea. What sort of bride fakes their own suicide on the morning of their wedding? And how had Ruby got involved? Up until a few hours ago Maddie had hated her.

He had thought Maddie was dead. And she had let him. It was too much.

'I can't believe you could be so cruel.' Finally they were listening to him. Bobby sat with his chin lowered but his eyes fixed on Alex. Maddie shifted position at the sound of his voice. The pill packets slid off the bedcover onto the floor with a soft patter. Alex stared at his bride-to-be. She looked – what was the right word – glowing, strong, justified? No, what she looked was triumphant, like she'd won something, and that something was him. Was that all he was to her – a prize? 'I don't know how you could have come up with something so warped.'

Maddie misunderstood. She was still fixated on Bobby. 'Yes! Finally!' She didn't actually do a fist pump, but she might as well have.

In that moment Alex knew it was over. 'Not him! You!' She winced as if slapped. They were all looking at him now. Alex had found his voice again and with his words came a tsunami of hurt and anger. 'How could you?'

'What?' she stuttered.

He laughed, bitterly. 'You don't even realise what you've done, do you?'

'Alex, please. We needed to expose him for what he is.'

'What HE is!' Alex's voice cracked. 'What about what YOU are? You let me think you had taken your own life, on our wedding day, because of me.'

'No! That wasn't our intention. Not at all. But the only way to catch him out was to play him at his own game.'

'Game! You think this is a game?' He was shouting now. 'There's no sane reason for pretending to have killed yourself. It's a terrible thing to do.'

'Alex. No! Please! We thought you'd just come into the room and see that I was fine. This . . .' she gestured at the pills on the floor, 'was for him to see, not you.' The triumphant queen was gone now.

'But Bobby told me you were dead.' She started crying. 'And I believed him – because that's exactly the way you'd set it up. That's unforgivable. You must see that.' He stood up. Maddie tried to scramble off the bed, but he held out his

303

hand, warding her off. 'I don't want to hear it. I don't want to be anywhere near you or any of this ... cruel, sadistic shit. We're done.' She collapsed back onto the bed. Ruby started to say something. That infuriated him even more. 'And you! I thought we were friends. Obviously not. Good luck with the baby, Ruby. The poor thing's going to need it.' She blinked, stung. They had all hurt him, all three of them, with their weird, secret alliance. His sister had obviously been in on the plan as well. But there again, when wasn't Colette poking her sticky fingers into things? And Lou? She was loving this. He swayed. An arm pulled him close, providing strength and support.

'Come on, Alex. We need to get you out of here.'

Alex let Bobby lead him out of the room, out of the bridal suite, out of the tower, and out of his life with Maddie.

Chapter 56

COLETTE

It was carnage. But even as Colette watched her brother walk out on Maddie with Bobby, she was already thinking about what needed to be done. It would appear that you could take the bride out of her own wedding, but you couldn't take the planner out of Colette. Even when there was no wedding to plan.

In priority order, she needed to find her parents and inform them that Alex and Maddie's marriage was off, then she'd have to break the news to the guests, and manage their disappointment. That wasn't going to be a simple task. They'd come to Mallorca for a lavish wedding and a lavish wedding was what they wanted – although some of them would, no doubt, find the current drama equally, if not more, compelling. It would be a good story to take home to the UK . . . if they could get some juicy details. She would have to brief Nige, tell him in no uncertain terms to keep his mouth shut about what he'd witnessed in the tower. Then she would need to get the staff started on clearing the courtyard. The aisle, the chairs, the altar and the floral arch needed to come down ASAP. And she'd have to speak to the celebrant. Colette wondered if this would be the first time that he'd had a ceremony cancelled at such short notice. Next, the food! Christ, Aiden, the head chef, would go ballistic. What a total waste of time and effort. But they would still have to feed the guests. Some sort of late lunch composed of the less fancy elements of what would have been the wedding feast would suffice. Yes, there was a lot to do. Colette looked at her watch. In an alternate universe, Alex and Maddie would be husband and wife by now.

As for the emotional aftermath of the scene in the tower – Colette was happy to leave that to other people. The truth about Bobby and Ruby and Maddie and Alex's complex, interwoven, perverted relationship didn't really interest her. She had other priorities. If that sounded harsh, so be it. It was time for her to fulfil her own needs, rather than cater to everyone else's. Another twelve hours of diligence and she would be done – with the Finca Encantata, with her family and with the Archer empire.

She instructed Lou to take Maddie back down to their suite, away from the reminders that it was still her wedding day. Ruby and Lou guided Maddie out between them. She had to be held up. It gave Colette pause – love could be a curse as well as a blessing. But despite what she'd just witnessed, she was going to take the risk. If she didn't, she might not get another chance. Room cleared of redundant bride, glamorous pregnant bridesmaid and loyal maid of honour, Colette surveyed the scene. In among all the debris her eyes snagged on Maddie's discarded wedding dress. Poor Gabriela! All that work and look at it now, trampled underfoot in the stampede. Colette bent down, picked it up and tenderly laid it over a chair. It was a small, pointless gesture in the midst of such disorder, but it made her feel a little better to indulge in sentimentality for a moment. Switching back to manager mode, she signalled to Nige to follow her. They were going to need all hands on deck.

Colette was under no illusion – cancelling a wedding was going to be nearly as much work as hosting one.

Chapter 57

LOU

Shit! That had not gone to plan.

Okay, in retrospect, a fake overdose hadn't been the smartest move, but Lou had never claimed it was fool-proof. She'd been improvising, and under a lot of pressure. Maddie had been adamant that they needed to expose Bobby before the wedding could go ahead. Lou got it – Maddie had felt that she needed to reclaim some of the power that he'd taken from her – but it left them with only a couple of hours to come up with something. And, let's be real here, none of them had any previous experience in flushing out a psycho.

In contrast to Lou's atypical hesitation, Ruby had been well up for trying to set a trap for Bobby, especially after she found out that her pregnancy was being used as a weapon. It transpired that, contrary to received wisdom, Ruby wasn't Bobby's biggest fan after all. The three amigos shit was his spin on their friendship, not hers. The way Ruby told it, Bobby had always been way too intense for her liking. She described how, even back in the day, Bobby had always wanted to know more than was normal, or healthy, about her and Alex's lives. Unfortunately, she hadn't realised just how deep his obsession went until her heart-to-heart with Maddie.

And once Ruby was involved the whole thing had gathered a momentum that had been impossible to stop. Before they knew it they were scattering wedding dresses and shoes around a bridal suite, popping pills onto bedcovers, roping in Colette to add some theatre with the supposed locked door and plotting how to get Bobby up to the bridal suite for his final showdown with Maddie. But there was one part – or, more accurately, one player – that they'd neglected, badly. Alex. He was never supposed to believe that any of it was real. The consequences of that carelessness were now all too apparent.

Having navigated the treacherous stairs, they manoeuvred a weeping Maddie onto the sofa and Ruby fetched her a glass of water. She didn't drink any. She was too upset. A weird calm descended on the room. Lou and Ruby sat and listened to her cry. What else could they do? Any which way you looked at it, their plan had backfired horribly. Sure, they had confronted Bobby, proved that they knew what he'd been up to, but that had not had the desired effect. He'd not been shamed, not confessed, not so much as blinked in the face of their allegations. Instead, he'd faced them down, ridden the storm and somehow managed to convince Alex that they were the ones in the wrong – which in Lou's book just went to show what a waste of space Alex was. If he was prepared to believe his old school chum rather than the woman he claimed to love, then Maddie was – as Lou had always believed – better off without him.

But although she thought that her friend had dodged a bullet, Maddie herself looked like she'd been hit by one.

309

The crying changed to gulps, then to snotty sniffs, then finally stopped. There was total silence.

Maddie eventually broke it by asking, 'What am I supposed to do now?'

Chapter 58

MARILYN

They needed to get Alex away from the prying eyes and insensitive questions of the guests. The obvious move was to take her boy back to the villa – correction – *boys*, because Bobby, of course, needed to come as well.

They left via the back route. Ray drove. They didn't want any of the staff seeing the state Alex was in. As they made their way up the mountain Marilyn watched her son in the rear-view mirror. He looked traumatised. In contrast, Bobby looked as composed as ever. When they got home, they headed into the back lounge. Ray poured brandies for everyone, with an extra-large measure for Alex. He drained it in one. Ray refilled his glass. Marilyn noticed that Bobby barely touched his drink.

As Ray started in on his lecture about resilience Marilyn sipped her Courvoisier and consulted her own feelings about the aborted wedding. Yes, she was irritated – by the wasted effort and expense, although in reality very little of the work had fallen on her and the money wasn't really a problem; and she was embarrassed – she disliked being the subject of gossip, and a no-show bride was a juicy anecdote; but she was not sorry that the wedding hadn't gone ahead.

Maddie had been an unexpected and unwelcome choice as Alex's fiancée. His previous girlfriends had all been posh girls from the home counties who he'd met through work. They'd been beautiful and ambitious. Maddie, in comparison, was a rough diamond. Or, more honestly, a cubic zirconia. Marilyn had not been happy. And her opinion had not improved the more she'd got to know her future daughter-in-law. Maddie had seemed wholly uninterested in Alex's career – she held some very strange views when it came to wealth – she'd been socially awkward, and, as clearly demonstrated in the past forty-eight hours, she'd appeared to be hiding a bundle of mental and physical frailties. All of which made her wholly ill-suited to becoming an Archer, in Marilyn's opinion. But frustratingly, for the first time in his life, her son had been adamant. He claimed he loved Maddie and stated that he was going to marry her, with or without their blessing . . . although their financial support would be appreciated, of course.

Well, perhaps this messy, costly, embarrassing episode would be a lesson to him.

But it was one that he would have to learn quickly.

Marilyn looked across at Ray. His foot was jiggling up and down, pent-up energy surging through him. Marilyn knew that his primary concern was not their son's emotional state – he would leave that to her and Bobby to address – it was the business. Her husband often failed to see how the two issues were interlinked, but that was why they made such a good team. Ray was right to be concerned. It was a critical time. Wheels had been set in motion. No matter how upset their son might be, Archer Asset Management had to start trading in three weeks' time. The lease for the building just off Moorgate had been signed months ago – they'd gone for 'old money' rather 'modern thrust' styling for the offices. Good set dressing influenced investors as much as it did brides-to-be. The decorators had finished the previous week and the IT and security systems were being installed over the coming fortnight – all ready for Alex's return from what would have been his honeymoon – at which point they needed him to hit the ground running. There was a lot of cash waiting to be cleaned, their own and other people's. Teddy Largos and Mateus Torres were both rich men, with more money than they knew what to do with, but that didn't mean that they were patient. Quite the opposite. Heartbreak could not be allowed to hinder performance. And for that performance to be good, Alex needed be put back together as good as new ASAP.

Which was where Bobby came in, as he had in the past.

Marilyn and Bobby's curious mutual understanding had begun many years ago. It had been Bobby who approached her. He'd been an awkward teenager at the time, but had looked younger with his baby face and skinny frame. Marilyn had been secretly impressed, not only by his balls, but by the fact that he was smart enough to approach her and not Ray, the more obvious head of the family. It happened during one of the boys' interminable school holidays. Alex had invited Bobby to the house in Deal. Bobby's home life at this point was more than a little rocky – a recently dead father and a flaky mother, apparently. Marilyn had forgotten that she'd agreed to the boy coming until she ran into him in the library – the shock was that he was actually reading. The books had been bought as a job-lot by an interior designer – Ray and Marilyn used the room for smoking.

Bobby had made Marilyn jump by saying 'Good afternoon.' She'd taken a drag on her freshly lit cigarette and nodded noncommittally. She wasn't remotely interested in this boy, other than as proof that Alex was building a network of friends who might prove useful in later life. Bobby had closed his book and said, 'I'm pleased to have run into you, Mrs Archer. I wanted to say how much I appreciate you allowing me to come and stay in your beautiful home.' 'Pompous arse-licker' was the thought that came to Marilyn's mind, but then Bobby had wrong-footed her. 'And it's lovely to see Alex in a much better frame of mind.' Despite herself, Marilyn had found her interest piqued. What was wrong with her son's mind? She volunteered nothing. That didn't seem to intimidate Bobby in the slightest. Marilyn's silence normally did, even fully grown men. 'The incident on Founders' Day was obviously a symptom of the difficulties he was experiencing.' Marilyn still said nothing. But it transpired that Bobby had a lot to say.

In the time it took Marilyn to finish her cigarette Bobby filled her in on Alex's struggles to fit in at King Henry's, his unwise attempts to rectify that social anxiety by getting involved in some low-key bullying, and the impact that this behaviour had been having on his academic performance and his 'standing' at the school. Apparently 'the Founders' Day debacle' had been coming for months. The boy certainly liked the sound of his own voice. Marilyn had listened and been intrigued. Bobby was doing something that was extremely difficult: he was expressing sympathy and understanding while at the same giving his alleged best friend a complete kicking. The question was why?

Like all good long-con artists, Bobby kept his powder dry. He brought the conversation to a close with a no-strings-attached promise to keep an eye out for Alex when they returned to school. In many ways it was gross pre-sumption from a weedy boy from a broken home who was a guest in their house. Marilyn didn't nod her assent, but as Bobby walked past her out of the library, she remembered feeling that they'd entered into some sort of pact – one that acknowledged her son's weakness and gave Bobby some sort of purchase. As an opening gambit it had been impressive.

Over the subsequent years, Bobby and Alex had stayed friends. Indeed, they'd grown ever closer. As a result, Bobby visited the house in Deal a lot. And, although Marilyn never spent much time with either of them, there was always an occasion when she would find herself alone with Bobby and a conversation would take place where he would update her on her son's progress and the areas of his life where 'there was room for improvement'.

The request for financial help wasn't made until towards the end of the boys' time in the sixth form. The trigger was university application. The ground had already been laid by Alex, who'd rung home distressed that Bobby was talking about not going to university, despite his obvious intelligence. 'It's the cost, especially in London. He sim-ply can't afford it,' Alex explained. Here it comes, Marilyn thought. But, proficient at silent bargaining as ever, Bobby kept her waiting. And during that prolonged hiatus, Alex became more and more upset by the thought that his best friend would not be going to UCL with him. By the time they all came to the house at Christmas – because by now Ruby was also part of the gang – the door was already ajar. Appropriately enough, and probably by design, the 'ask' came in the library. All Bobby had to do was to remind Marilyn of Alex's past social integration difficulties and ongoing academic struggles – and Bobby's role in smoothing those 'lumps' out – and the door swung open. Marilyn spoke to Ray and they paid up. Accommodation costs in the first year, then a rent-free room in the Bayswater flat with Alex in years two and three, plus a monthly living allowance. Alex never knew anything about their agreement. It would have damaged their friendship. Bobby simply spun some tall tale about a legacy from a distant uncle to cover their tracks.

From Marilyn's perspective it was money well spent. Their investment in Bobby ensured that Alex stuck at university and, with Bobby's guidance, that he continued to make the right sort of friends and pick up the attitudes and habits that were going to be essential for the life he was destined to lead.

When the 'asks' continued beyond university Ray had questioned the need to comply with such extortion, but Marilyn had reassured him that it was worth it. What that said about her lack of faith in her own son she didn't like to dwell on. Hence, even now that Bobby was a fully grown man, Ray and Marilyn still subsidised his rent and helped out with expenses. Bobby had a penchant for the finer things in life that his publishing salary simply could not buy. Marilyn's 'asks', well, they were the same as they'd always been – to keep a window open on her son's life and to provide a heads-up if there was anything on the horizon that might jeopardise the long-term plan. Which was to embed Alex in a job in the heart of the City from where he would secure, and build, their capital and make it safe from sequestration.

But that plan was at risk now, and in no small part because Bobby had failed to see the danger that Maddie represented.

Marilyn looked across the pool at the mountains and the wide blue sky beyond. It was a view that had been bought with decades of hard work, risk and ruthlessness and it was in jeopardy because of fucking, flaky Maddie Laughton.

It was time for Bobby to pay back some of the investment that had been made in him.

As Alex lifts his second brandy to his lips the feeding frenzy begins. Ray and Marilyn are like sharks taking alternate bites out of their prey – sorry, correction – their son. At King Henry's, Alex and I bonded over the awfulness of our respective parents. We both lived with an acute awareness that our worth was dependent on fulfilling their expectations rather than as people in our own right. Our friendship is based on the belief that we are alike. We are not.

Why am I willing to bite back when Alex is not?

The answer is shockingly simple. I learnt, at an early age, that people can only have power over you if you let them.

My father, like Ray, was a bully – although he didn't look like one. He was tall and slim, with a fine head of curly black hair. He wore suits for work – he was a university lecturer, mechanical engineering. At home he favoured chinos and neatly pressed polo shirts. His eyes, behind his wire-rimmed glasses, were shiny and bright. (My mother recently commented on how much I'm beginning to remind her of him. I can't see any shadow of resemblance myself.) But beneath the shell of this normal man there lurked an altogether different beast, one that was impatient and dispassionate to the point of cruelty. He was singularly unable to contemplate, never mind accommodate, anyone else's viewpoint or feelings. Any display of emotion deeply irritated him – laughing, crying, even talking with too much passion or enthusiasm about anything that he was not interested in, was shut down immediately. He had my mother whipped early on in their relationship. He believed he was well on the way to cowing me. He was wrong.

Things came to a head during the summer holidays the year I turned fourteen. He'd been building up to one of his epic meltdowns for days. During the holidays he was always more vicious and unpredictable. In hindsight I think he found the absence of deference that he was used to being surrounded by at the university intolerable. My mother and I were simply not enough to feed his endlessly demanding ego. Me being at home from school for such a long period also irritated him.

It was a hot day in August when the power balance between us shifted forever. I'd already been reprimanded twice, once for my idleness, getting up gone 8.00 a.m., and once for leaving the lid off the jam. My next affront was making an 'unconscionable' amount of noise by throwing a tennis ball against the side of the house. My father summoned me into his study – he liked to be comfortable while lecturing me. He sat behind his huge desk and launched into his tirade. I stood perfectly still, head down, eyes lowered, seemingly compliant, but I didn't listen to a word of his ranting. I never did. Mulish silence was the only defiance open to me and I made full use of it. As he started in on the need for me to have more respect for our home and for my mother, I fantasised about what he would look like if his true character was reflected in his appearance. I saw bumps forming on his forehead and horns breaking through his brow. I imagined his skin turning *green, his eyes glowing red, his tongue swelling, filling his mouth, choking off his vitriol.*

It took me a moment to realise that my imaginings were coming true. I looked up. His face had gone a strange colour. Not green, but a deathly white, and instead of horns there were beads of sweat on his forehead. And the choking noise was not inside my head. It was real. Through the gargling I heard him gasp, 'Fetch your mother.' The words were snatched, but clear enough. He must have thought I hadn't understood him, or more likely that I was too shocked to react, because he took a struggling, stuttering breath and repeated, 'Go . . . fetch . . . your mother.'

I stayed exactly where I was and watched. His arms flopped down on his leather-topped desk and he started to arch backwards at an odd angle. His face seemed to be sliding down into his neck. His glasses were askew, but, and this was gratifying, I could see in his eyes that he knew what was happening to him. We'd all seen the TV adverts alerting people to the signs and emphasising the need for swift action. He was having a stroke. His attempt at speech was now nothing more than a series of painful grunts. Loud enough for my mother to hear? I doubted it, she was upstairs having a rest. She had a lot of naps when my father was around. But it was better to be safe than sorry. I closed the study door.

I started counting. He stared at me, whether in panic, anger, pain or bewildered disbelief I couldn't really tell because by that point his face was a melted mask, his body an unwieldy corpse. I like to think it was disbelief. I like to think that finally I'd surprised him. He lost consciousness on the count of seventy-nine. Luck was on my side because he didn't fall off his chair. He was too wedged up against his huge desk. I kept counting. At one hundred I approached him, still a little wary, but the creature was definitely dead. I spat in his face then went to raise the alarm.

The funeral was everything he would have loved – which is why it was such a pity he missed it. There were mountains of floral tributes and lots and lots of words – all about him. Mum wept and I wailed: her with grief, me with relief. I composed and read the eulogy. There wasn't a dry eye in the house. We sang his praises and paid him the respect he did not deserve, then we lowered him into the ground. I would have danced on his grave, but there were too many people present.

My mother and I never spoke about him again. Not once.

But it was no happily-ever-after, at least not for me. Because the restless spirit inside my mother – that my father had repressed for so long and I thought had been smothered – took a deep breath, and fuelled by the sizeable financial settlement from my father's pension and life assurance policies, she went off travelling in search of a new husband. Which left me to fend for myself. King Henry's, for all its faults, became the one place of security I had. There, and the Archers' house in Deal. In reality my mother's search for Prince Charming was a tawdry affair. Kissed frogs remained slimy toads – many of whom departed with more in their knapsacks than they'd arrived with. Potions in dark-green glass bottles turned out not to be the elixir of life but bog-standard gin, and wherever she lived – and she moved around a lot – she always complained about the forest growing up and pressing against the windows.

That makes it sound like she's dead. She's not. As I sit watching Marilyn and Ray harangue Alex about his poor choices, my mother is living in a small rented cottage on Jersey, paid for by yours truly. She's currently trying to decide whether 'island life' is for her and while she does she's been making 'some lovely new

321

friends'. Most of them will, I suspect, be male and all of them will be younger than her. Larkin was right and wrong – your parents really do fuck you up, but they also shape who you are and what you're capable of.

I zone back into the here and now. I can see that Alex is sinking, battered by the booze and the barrage. If Ray and Marilyn aren't careful there won't be anything left of him for me to resuscitate. Marilyn keeps glancing at me. I hold my gaze steady. She's waiting for me to get involved.

The consensus that Ray and Marilyn eventually arrive at, and brutally state, is that marriage to someone so evidently unstable as Maddie would have been a mistake. Ray crassly adds that Maddie would have proved a liability to Alex's career, which is very on the nose, but true. The sun slides lower in the sky. Ray pours a fourth brandy for Alex and himself. I haven't finished my first. Marilyn is not drinking hers.

It's Marilyn who finally puts a stop to it. She points out that they're going round in circles and that Alex is tired. She doesn't add, but I hear, 'and emotional'. She suggests that she and Ray 'leave us boys to it'. She says she'll get some food rustled up for us. Not by herself, obviously. She rises to her feet and Ray lumbers to his. Marilyn's capacity to direct Ray's movements is impressive. He leaves the room first. At the doorway she beckons me over. I'm interested to find out what level of responsibility she will ascribe to me for this whole debacle.

'You'll stay with him.' It's an instruction, not a question. We both watch Alex reach for the brandy bottle and top up his glass.

'Of course.' I wait for her to say more.

She studies me, calculating. 'This…' she indicates Alex's drinking and generally unravelled state, 'is understandable and acceptable tonight. But tomorrow, the work starts.' I nod, wait

for the blame to be laid at my door. But as she stares at me I realise
that even Marilyn, with her unique insight into my personality
and motivations, can't see my fingerprints on the events leading
up to today. Is that a compliment or an insult? It's both, but it's
no surprise. The Archers have never had any finesse and, there-
fore, they can't see it in others. While Marilyn appreciates and
utilises my skills, she's always underestimated me. 'Tomorrow,
then.' She leans in and I realise that she's expecting me to kiss her
powdery cheek. I comply. It costs me nothing to feign subservi-
ence. Marilyn knows that I hold sway over her son. She believes
I will continue to use that influence to further her and Ray's
ends in return for my cash rewards. But what Marilyn has spec-
tacularly failed to appreciate is just how far the pendulum has
swung in my favour over the past few days.

Alex belongs to me now.

His future is mine to decide.

Chapter 59

LOU

Lou looked out of the window. It was impossible to tell what was going on; the tower was too isolated from the rest of the finca, but perhaps that was a good thing. Watching the wedding being dismantled flower arch by crystal flute by expensive wedding favour would only have added to Maddie's pain.

The toilet flushed. The tap ran. Lou waited. Maddie came out of the bathroom. She'd changed into shorts and a T-shirt and had washed her face. She looked beautiful. Sure, she also looked wrecked and distraught, but she did at least look herself again. 'How are you doing?' Maddie shrugged. She flopped down on one of the sofas and stared at her feet. Lou came and sat next to her. They both studied Maddie's pearly toenails. 'Colette says it's all being handled.' Maddie nodded. Lou didn't know what to say next. Whatever she said was going to be wrong. She ventured some sour humour. 'Can you imagine Marilyn's reaction? I wonder if she managed to crack an actual facial expression!' Lou meant it as a comfort.

But Maddie put her hands up to her face 'Don't, Lou. Please.'

'Too soon?'

'Yes. Way too soon.'

'Colette has offered to sort out getting you a flight home.'

'I can't think about that now.'

'I know.' Lou paused. 'But you should. The quicker you get out of this make-believe nightmare and away from Alex the better.'

'Lou. Stop!'

Lou paused, then went for it. Out of love, not malice. 'Sorry Maddie, but, no, I won't. You've got to face up to the fact that it's over. Your fiancé chose his conniving, warped, dangerous best friend over you. That's harsh, but it's the truth. And I know you're hurting, but thank God you found out how toxic Bobby and Alex's relationship really is before it was too late.' Lou waited for a response, and when Maddie said nothing she carried on. 'I know you don't want to hear this, but you must see that you've had a narrow escape.' Still nothing from Maddie. 'You'll survive this. I know you will. You're the girl who looked after her mum, and herself – and me – for years. You've always been strong and tough and resilient. Being with Alex made you forget that, but it'll come back. It already is.'

'I don't want to have to be tough and resilient.' She sounded so flattened.

Lou took hold of Maddie's hand and squeezed it. 'I know, but it's far better to stand on your own two feet than be anywhere near this lot.' Finally, there was a glimmer of something other than defeat in her friend's expression. Lou pushed it. She turned Maddie's hand over and touched the big rock on her ring finger. 'You can always pawn this monstrosity to get you started.'

Maddie slipped the ring off her finger. At least that was a step in the right direction – tacit acknowledgement that the fairy tale was over. She passed it from hand to hand as if weighing up its value, or perhaps she was thinking more about what it had cost her. Without looking at Lou she quietly said, 'I couldn't.' She held the ring up to the light. The diamond sent sparkles shooting around the room. 'But if I ever did, I'd say that – at a conservative estimate – it must be worth at least four grand.'

Lou was delighted to see that tiny glimpse of her old friend peeping out from beneath the ruins.

Chapter 60

COLETTE

A wedding day without a wedding, even in paradise, was simply another day followed by another long, empty evening.

As Colette took a turn around the finca she was amused to see how unsettled Alex and Maddie's guests were. They simply didn't know what to do with themselves. They clearly didn't want to spend their last night on the island in their rooms and yet there was no focal point for them to gather around, so they drifted from the courtyard to the terrace, into the long room and back out again like people suffering from dementia. The dynamic was fractured, conversations forced; even their drinking seemed half-hearted.

Mateus Torres had had the right idea. He and his wife had left as soon as it became clear that there was to be no wedding. True, he'd had his driver standing by, so beating a hasty retreat hadn't been a problem, but the alacrity with which he'd made his smooth apologies and departed had been impressive. Teddy, however, was still hanging around. Colette found him down on the terrace, stinking up the atmosphere with his filthy cigar, his girlfriend sitting by his

327

side. Colette racked her memory. She did know the girl's name; they had been introduced. *Come on*, she encouraged her brain to retrieve it. It floated on the edge of her memory. Natalia! That was it. Colette wasn't going to be able to recall her surname, but at least the girl wasn't consigned to be forever 'Teddy's plus-one'. Tom and Charlie were on the terrace too, drinking champagne out of the bottle, lapping up Teddy's anecdotes. She wasn't surprised they were drawn to his flame – at least it was still flickering. Colette was pleased to see that Tom and Charlie seemed to have given up on pursuing Priya. Her quiet resistance had obviously finally convinced the pair of them that she was not on the market. Not for either of them, at any rate. Colette silently applauded her good taste.

Colette took a last look at the lake. She'd never swum in it, too worried about what lurked in the silt at the bottom. Colette liked her water clear and chlorinated. She turned her back on the inky expanse and headed back to the finca, glancing at the tower as she did so. It looked purple in the dying light. As she walked up the path a light came on in Maddie and Lou's room. The lemony glow shone out. Fancifully, it reminded Colette of a lighthouse – as she'd told her brother, the tower had originally been built as a lookout for spotting approaching attackers and to provide sanctuary. Well, one out of two was better than nothing.

Paul and Yvette were in the courtyard, at the heart of the finca, as close to the non-action as possible. The noxious Letty was in the staff quarters with Maria. She'd discovered the kittens and been obsessed with them ever since. Demands to take them home couldn't be too far behind. Priya and Lily were sitting with Paul and his wife. They fell silent as Colette approached. Paul beckoned her over. 'Col! Come and sit with us. Have a drink. You must be exhausted.'

She would have liked to have walked on by, but that would have been rude and she reckoned she had one last painfully polite conversation inside her. Paul slopped white wine into a glass for her. She lifted it and sipped, not because she wanted a drink, but because she didn't want to answer their inevitable questions.

But Lily didn't even give Colette a chance to swallow her Gavi. 'How is Alex holding up?'

The wine slipped down. It was good. Chilled, but not so cold that you couldn't still taste it. That was where so many places went wrong, too much aggressive refrigeration. White wine needed deft handling. 'He's okay.' Their disappointment with her response was palpable.

'Will Bobby be staying the night with him, do you think, given the situation?' Lily again.

'I wouldn't know.' Colette paused. Lily's expression was a picture, naked curiosity wrestling with manufactured sympathy alongside a huge dollop of self-pity. She was obviously not happy with her man choosing his friend's needs over hers. Colette couldn't imagine Bobby bothering to respond to Lily's texts. She was obviously not his priority, nor had she ever been, evidently. Colette added, just because she now could, 'But given how understandably upset my brother is, I would think that he'd stay, wouldn't you? He is Alex's best man, after all.' Lily blinked and subsided in her seat. What Lily didn't know about the current 'situation' and about her boyfriend in general could fill a book, but Colette had no intention of enlightening her, nor anyone else for that matter.

Paul opted for flattery as a way of trying to wangle some info out of her. 'You did a fantastic job today, by the way, sorting everything and everybody out with your usual calmness and efficiency. Bravo, my dear.' He raised his glass to her, forcing the others to follow suit. Colette acknowledged his patronising praise with a slight nod. He was so smug, so secure in his place at the trough, but he was going to need more than smooth talk to get out of the fix he was about to find himself in. He was her father's accountant, for Christ's sake, and he was about to get caught asleep at the wheel.

After fending off more oblique questions from Yvette, Colette rose to her feet.

'Stay. Have another glass.' Paul grabbed the bottle. There was a note of desperation in his voice.

But Colette was done with oiling the wheels for the guests. Let them sit in the loveliness of the courtyard, drinking the finca's fifty-quid bottles of wine, drowning their sorrows. 'No. I must get on. I've some last-minute travel plans to finalise.' She walked away with a rising feeling of relief. She was about to head back to her room in the staff quarters when she heard a loud thumping noise coming from the archway. She stepped into the shadows and waited. After a few more thumps, Ruby emerged. She was casually dressed in jeans, a perfectly white T-shirt, a fitted jacket and trainers. Her handbag was swinging awkwardly from her shoulder and she was dragging her suitcase.

'Can I help?' Colette's offer of assistance made Ruby jump.

'If you don't mind.'

Colette took charge of the suitcase, which allowed Ruby to untangle herself from her handbag. 'Where to?'

Ruby flushed. 'The car park, please. I've booked a taxi.'

Colette nodded and set off, taking care to minimise the noise of the suitcase wheels on the path. 'Not saying goodbye to everyone?'

'I wasn't planning to. Besides, I'm not in the mood for bitching and trying my best to exhaust your wine cellar.' She looked over at Paul and Yvette as she spoke.

Colette smiled. 'Good call. It has the atmosphere of a wake, and not an Irish one.' She parked the suitcase and turned to face Ruby. It was properly dark now, but Colette could still see Ruby's face under the car park lights. She looked as beautiful as ever, just a little less composed, which was no surprise. 'Sorry, it's been a bit shit!'

There was a fraction of a pause, then Ruby laughed. Her expression lightened. 'Well, put it this way: I shan't be leaving a five-star review.'

They stood in silence. Colette was very conscious that she was standing next to a pregnant woman with no partner, whose oldest friends were probably, at this very moment, cementing their very peculiar, insular brotherhood with tales of the treachery of women. No irony there. Yes, for all her glamour and poise, her impressive career, her international travel and her lovely flat in London, in that moment Ruby seemed very alone.

'Say goodbye to Alex for me, will you? Tell him ...' She was evidently struggling to think of what she wanted to say to Alex. 'Tell him that I had to leave early, work commitments. He'll believe that.' Colette lied with a nod of the head – she had no intention of speaking to her brother. Ruby didn't mention Bobby.

Colette spotted the taxi headlights in the trees. 'I

could have arranged for one of the lads to take you into Palma.'

'I know.'

'But you wanted to slip away unnoticed, in the dead of night.'

'Something like that.'

'Sorry I busted you.'

'That's okay. I think I'm safe with you.'

Colette didn't reply immediately. The taxi drew closer. 'You have my number.'

Ruby looked at her. 'Yes.'

'My personal one, not my work one. Should you ever want . . .'

'What . . . a wedding planner?' Ruby cut in.

It was Colette's turn to laugh. 'Fuck, no. I was going say . . . a catch-up.' The taxi pulled to a stop. Colette wheeled Ruby's case over and the driver hoisted it into the boot then climbed back into the driver's seat. 'Well, goodbye. And good luck with the baby.'

'Thank you.'

A hug seemed to be called for, but Colette didn't offer one. Instead she said, 'Contrary to what my idiot brother said, I think you'll make a pretty good mum.' Ruby smiled and climbed into the taxi. It pulled away and Colette watched the light on the top grow smaller and paler in amongst the trees until it finally disappeared.

Ruby was gone. Lou and Maddie were safely ensconced in the tower. The remaining guests were scattered through-out the finca trying, and failing, to entertain themselves. The staff were no doubt getting up to God knew what with all the leftover booze. And up at the villa her parents and

Bobby were attending to her brother. Colette's long shift was well and truly over. She unclipped her radio and lobbed it into the darkness. She pulled her hair free of its bun and raked her fingers through it. She reckoned she'd earned a proper drink.

The cellar door was, of course, open, but that wasn't her concern any more. She flicked on the lights. Much to her relief, there were no sounds of coitus as she descended. The last thing she wanted to see was Luther shagging yet another naive waitress. She made her way to the far vault, where the really good stuff was kept under lock and key. Here lay the bottles that had been bought as investments and were never meant to be drunk. Colette had the keys to this most exclusive and expensive collection, as she had to so many corners of her father's empire. She unlocked the metal gate and stepped inside, ducking her head to avoid hitting it on the arched roof. She knew exactly what she was looking for – the Macallan Lalique Fifty-Five-Year-Old Single Malt. She had memorised the reference number when her father got her to transfer the funds to purchase it – £161,419, plus packaging and shipping. Ray's malts were catalogued and stored like rare books; each had its own unique reference number and corresponding niche in the vault. The Lalique was resting alongside its cousins. Ray owned a lot of Macallans, but none as rare as the Fifty-Five-Year-Old Special Edition. It was one of only 420 ever distilled and bottled.

Having tracked the Lalique down, she wiped the dust off it with her sleeve and carried it back up to the kitchen.

Objectively, it was a thing of beauty. The bottle was shaped like a heavy-bottomed cocktail shaker and it was crowned with an extravagant gold stopper. The shape of the stopper reminded Colette of a pharaoh's headdress – totally impractical for opening and pouring, but exquisite nonetheless. Colette pondered how to get at the whisky inside. After a couple of seconds she picked up the bottle and struck it against the butcher's block. The headdress stopper flew off and hit the deck. Whisky splashed all over the floor. The smell was amazing: peaty, rich, with a hint of iodine, as promised. She'd read the description when she'd transferred the money, curious as to what a bottle of whisky that cost over one hundred and sixty thousand pounds might taste of. Pleased with her solution, Colette grabbed a tumbler from the shelf and made her way outside, walking through glass splinters and puddles of fifty-five-year-old malt as she exited the building.

For old times' sake, Colette took up her post against the wall in the alley. She poured herself a generous measure of the Macallan, then rested the bottle on the ground in amongst the rosemary, letting it breathe after its half-century of captivity. The thought made her smile. She would leave the bottle here, in the wild, to be found or not – either outcome was fine with her. It felt good to be irresponsible. She took a sip. The Macallan smelt soft and warm, but it tasted strong, astringent. She took another mouthful, swilled it around in her mouth, let it cleanse her teeth and palate. She swallowed. The heat came gradually, glowing then radiating inside her stomach. She relaxed into the sensation. She breathed along with the malt, looked at the stars, listened to the quiet, felt content. Until she heard the rustle. Surely, not fucking Luther again. The man was a bad penny. He had best be warned, she was off the clock and she had a broken bottle within easy reach. But as she listened, she realised that the noise was too delicate to be clumsy, Neanderthal Luther.

The weeds stirred. A waft of rosemary mingled with the fumes of whisky in Colette's nose. Then she heard a meow. The cat emerged from the long grass at a leisurely pace. Its bony haunches rippled beneath its black fur. It didn't check its pace when it clocked her; merely carried on by, indifferent to her presence. Colette raised the beaker of her father's ludicrously expensive whisky in a toast to her feline adversary and said, 'It's all yours.'

Alex finishes the bottle of Courvoisier, but makes barely a dent in the sandwiches that Marilyn 'rustles up' for us. As a result, he's drunk as a skunk by 9.00 p.m. I don't have to exactly carry him to bed, but I do need to drag and cajole him. I choose one of the downstairs guest rooms, not wanting him to slip and break his neck on the impressive marble staircase. Now that would be a tragedy. I dump him on the bed. I unlace his shoes and pull off his socks, unzip and yank down his suit trousers, all without his cooperation. I undo a couple of buttons on his shirt, but don't attempt to remove it. He's too much of a dead weight. Once he's debagged, I pull the sheet over him. He lies there muttering and miserable. I sit on the bed beside him. 'Try and get some sleep, mate.'

He raises his hand and waves it around like a blind man. I realise he's reaching out to me. I oblige. He crushes my fingers, pulls my hand onto his chest. I can feel his heart thudding away inside his ribcage. 'Bobby. Bob,' he slurs. 'What would I do without you?' He holds on, repeating my name at lengthening intervals. Eventually he slips under and starts to snore. Still he doesn't let go. When I'm sure he's out cold, I unpeel his fingers. I'm free to leave. But I made a promise to stay with him. Not to the ice queen, but to Alex himself, all those years ago, and I'm not a man who goes back on his word. I shove him over to create some space, strip down to my boxers and get into bed beside him.

It's good to be still and quiet, it gives me time to reflect on what's happened. There will be many versions told of Alex and Maddie's ill-fated wedding weekend – from Colette's no doubt smooth, bland rendition, to the nonsense made up by the short-changed guests, to the speculation of the staff – even big old Nige may add his account of the goings-on in the tower. I feel weary at the thought of having to manufacture my own heavily redacted version for Lily. Alex starts snoring. His chest rises and falls like an anaesthetised patient. I watch over him, as promised. The Archers will no doubt want to ensure that whatever tale gets told, and retold, reflects well on them and theirs. I confidently predict that Maddie will be assigned the key role of villain. She will be portrayed as the damaged, fragile, misguided soul who is to blame for the whole fiasco – which risks casting Alex as the victim. Ray and Marilyn will need to be careful with that. They can't have their son being seen as weak. A show of bravery will be needed, an appearance to reassure the departing guests – most importantly Teddy Largos and Mateus Torres – that, although heartbroken, Alex is determined to put these last few painful days behind him and heal quickly. I may have to convince him to participate in that charade. As with all storytelling, there will be many gaps and errors in the fable of Alex and Maddie's aborted wedding – timelines scrambled, facts mangled, characters mixed up. But the biggest omission will be any real understanding of the motivation of the key players.

Suddenly a wave of tiredness hits me. It has been a long, arduous few days for me as well as him. I tip my head back and close my eyes. Finally, I can take ownership and credit for my role

337

in all this. I am, after all, the *key character. Without me there would be no story.*

What is Alex to me?

My meal ticket? Well yes, obviously, he is that. He has – simply by virtue of his birth – what I have not: namely, wealth. In that, Maddie and I are not so different. We both believe we are entitled to our share and, given that people like the Archers aren't prone to sharing, we feel justified in taking what we want. But the fundamental difference is that I'm prepared to work for my percentage, whereas she was not. I've invested in the Archer family, and in Alex, for years.

But Alex is more than simply a cash machine for me.

He is my creation, my plaything, my friend, my mirror, my contrast, my past and, crucially, my future. I chose him and he chose me. It's a symbiotic relationship, not a parasitic one. I can't imagine life without him. And isn't that a version of love? Oh, not the romantic love they write about in fairy tales, where all it takes is a handsome prince, a dainty foot and a pumpkin. No, that sort of love is way too predictable and boring. Where's the reward in simply loving and being loved back? Any relationship worth having contains manipulation, trading, control. I have that relationship with Alex. It was deeply stupid of Maddie to think that I'd be prepared to step aside to let her lay claim to all my good work.

And yet for all the trouble she caused me, I have to acknowledge that Maddie has been good for me. Her tenacity forced me to fully explore what I'm capable of and her expulsion has cemented me in Alex's life. In a weird way, I think I'll miss her.

I watch Alex chew his bottom lip in his sleep, distress still haunting his dreams. I stroke his face. The gnawing stops.

338

But the path is clear now. Maddie is gone, Alex is weak and I'm strong, stronger than I've ever been. It's the perfect time for me to consolidate my position. If Marilyn wants my help in sticking her son back together then she will have to pay more. It's time for my fees for services rendered to the Archer empire to rise. I smile. We should renegotiate my contract on the terrace – that's where the important money deals are brokered, or so I've heard. Alex rolls onto his side and the snoring finally stops.

I really need to get some sleep. I have to be ready to go again in the morning. I lie down, match my breathing to Alex's. When the panic returns and his breathing catches, I put my arms around him and anchor him. Thus we make it through the night.

The Day After

Chapter 61

MADDIE

Lou woke Maddie early. She felt sluggish. Her eyes were swollen, but this time it was from crying rather than anything more sinister. She did as she was told. She got washed, dressed and collected everything that was hers into a pile on the bed. Lou began shoving her things into a bag. They were leaving. There was nothing to stay for.

Alex had not come banging on Maddie's door in the middle of the night begging forgiveness, professing his love for her, trying to explain away his decision as a moment of madness brought on by all the stress, or saying the police had been called, that Bobby was going to pay for what he had done and for what he'd tried to do. No, the only person who came to the door had been one of the waitresses – the pretty one with coal-black eyes – bearing a tray of food, some iced water and a bottle of lightly chilled white wine. It was thoughtful of someone, but feasting on what was obviously the remnants of her wedding breakfast had been hard for Maddie to face. No one wanted foie gras, courgette flowers filled with whipped ricotta or tiny, beautifully handmade almond tarts, with pastry so thin it looked like parchment, when they were heartbroken. No, Alex had not come to his senses. He had not come to make it right with her, or at least try. His silence was eloquent. He was telling her, loud and clear, that they were done.

'Have you got your passport?' Lou was being deliberately brisk.

'Yes.'

'Right. Come on then, shall we get going?' They picked up their bags and left the tower. It was a beautiful morning, perfect for the first day of your married life. The heat was only just beginning to stir and there was a lemony freshness in the air.

'Where are we going?' They were heading towards the lake.

'Just trust me, okay?'

'Okay,' Maddie said, but she added, 'whatever.' She knew she was behaving like an ungrateful cow, but she didn't feel full of the milk of human kindness, not even for her best, utterly steadfast mate. They trudged over the bridge through the soft early-morning light. The high wispy clouds were rippled with delicate shades of aqua, turquoise and rose. God knows why they'd had to get up so early. Avoidance of any further confrontations or drama, perhaps, but that hardly seemed a Lou-like approach. As they walked through the trees, flashbacks to her disfigured stumble along the same path under cover of darkness flickered across Maddie's brain. Poisoned flowers from a poisoned mind. Bobby really was quite mad. They reached the familiar door in the wall. Lou dropped her bags on the forest floor and shoved up her sleeve. The code was written on the pale skin on the underside of her arm. Lou never tanned – she simply burnt, went bright red then straight back to sliced-bread white. She punched in the numbers. Maddie was not in the mood for any more revelations, but when the door opened their crack-of-dawn escape route made sense. Colette was waiting for them on the other side of the empty road.

She looked different. It was her clothes. She was wearing cut-off jeans, a plain T-shirt and a zip-up hoodie. On her tanned, slender feet she wore flat, strappy sandals. Her hair was different as well. The excruciatingly neat bun was gone. She actually had pretty hair, thick, with a natural wave. 'Hi. Nice day for it.' She smiled, crossed over and took the bag from Maddie. 'You okay? Get any sleep?'

'A bit.'

Colette popped the boot of her Audi. So she was taking them to the airport. Her last act as the consummate wedding planner – the covert removal of the abandoned bride. They all stood at the rear of the car for a few seconds and listened to the birds, until Lou broke the silence. 'Thanks for sending over the food last night. It was appreciated.'

'No worries,' Colette shrugged. Even her posture was different: more relaxed, less tense.

'You won't be surprised to hear it was me who polished off the wine.'

There was something in the way Colette said, 'No', and how naturally Lou smiled in response that woke Maddie up. A penny the size of a full moon dropped. They turned towards her. Lou wrapped her arm around Colette's waist and hooked her fingers into her belt loop, joining them together at the hip and said, 'Yep', in answer to the question in Maddie's eyes.

'I'm an idiot.'

'Not an idiot . . . preoccupied.' Lou's smile broadened.

Colette laughed; it was a sound that Maddie had never heard before. But then, when had Maddie ever had a conversation with Colette that wasn't about the million and one things that needed doing for a wedding or about how to trap a madman?

Maddie sat in the back of the car and Lou rested her hand on the back of Colette's headrest as she drove. Every now and again her fingers reached out and touched Colette's neck. Colette and Lou. Right under her nose and Maddie hadn't seen it, hadn't even sensed anything. Christ, she'd been a bad friend, as well as a shit intended sister-in-law. For a while Maddie watched the scenery glide past outside the car. Colette was taking their trip down the mountain at a leisurely pace, no tyre spin or tempting-death cornering this morning. Everything about her was more relaxed, including her driving, so there was plenty of time to stare into the heart of the ancient silvery olive groves and glimpse the azure sea in the distance. Maddie lasted until they made it onto the main road before her curiosity got the better of her. 'So . . . can I ask?'

'Ask what?' Lou.

'Well, how long have you been . . .' she thought about the correct word to use, 'together?'

They glanced at each other. That small, simple demonstration of being courteous to each other's truth caused Maddie a pang. Love lived and breathed in the small stuff. Lou let Colette answer – that was interesting in itself. 'We met at the Valentine party. We were the only two hags in the room.' There it was again, further proof that Colette had a sense of humour.

Lou picked up their story. 'We got talking, kinda hit it off. Then we had to be in touch about the arrangements for the . . .' She paused.

Maddie helped her out. 'You're allowed to say "wedding". I won't shatter into a thousand pieces.'

'Yeah, well, like I said, there was a lot to organise, so we had an excuse to talk, and we discovered that we had things in common other than the obvious.' Maddie didn't say anything, but she was now awake enough to realise that Lou stumbling across her significant other at precisely the point that she was in the deepest throes of self-absorption made total sense. Lou went on, 'Then, when Colette came over to the UK on some family business in the spring' – this was news to Maddie – 'we met up. A few times.' There was a smile in Lou's voice.

'And you never said anything.' Maddie knew she had no right to feel jealous. She'd spent the past year with her head firmly shoved up her own bridal arse.

'No.' Pushback from Lou. It was fair enough.

Colette became the peacemaker. It was fascinating watching them switch and flex roles. 'This weekend has certainly cemented things between us – in all sorts of ways. You get to know what people are really made of in a crisis.'

Indeed you did. They all fell silent, obviously thinking of Bobby and Alex. But that way lay nothing but grief, and Maddie, the old version, who Lou had been trying so hard to hang on to, was slowly returning. Maddie had learnt things about herself as well as about her fiancé and his insane best friend over the past few days. The biggest lesson being that it wasn't all about her. Her brain began to fire up. She went back over events, the times when Lou had gone AWOL... her stomach churned at the thought that, in her fug of anxiety and panic, she'd suspected her best friend of somehow being involved in the campaign against her. She lowered her head. She didn't want Lou to see the shame that burnt on her face. 'So the night of the bouquet, when you came to my rescue so quickly, Colette?'

'I was in Lou's room.' Colette left a pause. 'When you started banging on the door, I hid in the bathroom like a character in a sitcom.'

So Maddie had been right to be suspicious, but she'd been wrong in imagining Lou's and Colette's behaviour had been motivated by spite – it had been driven by love, or at the very least lust. 'And the night by the lake, when I thought you were really pissed off with me and you arrived late...'

Lou interrupted her. 'I *was* pissed off with you, but that wasn't the reason I left you with the wolves. Colette and I had arranged to meet up. We thought no one would notice, given there was a party going on, but Colette kept getting calls. We grabbed a few minutes together, then she had to go off to find you a throw.'

There was another lull in the conversation. They were hitting the outskirts of Palma now. The countryside palette of sage green and burnished silver had been replaced by a patchwork of industrial greys. 'But why keep your relationship a secret?'

Another glance passed between the two of them. Lou nodded, passing the baton back to Colette. 'Lots of reasons.' Maddie waited for her to elaborate. She took her time. 'For a start, it was nobody's business but ours. Neither of us wanted the attention. Also, it was your and Alex's gig.' Maddie felt depressed that it was going to take a long time for the fiasco of her nearly-wedding not to be THE defining thing about her. For that fact, along with so much else, she hated Bobby. Colette carried on. They were passing airport signs now. 'And there was also the problem of my parents.' Marilyn's immaculate granite face reared up in Maddie's brain. Ray was harder to conjure. A generic, sociable bloke in his early sixties who also happened to be a hard-nosed crime boss floated by.

'They don't know you're gay...bi?' Maddie asked. Jesus, why couldn't she just wait and let Colette tell her own story?

'Oh, they know. Have done for years.' Maddie held her tongue this time. 'But they choose to ignore it. And up until now I've made that possible. I've kept my associations... well away from them. Since we moved to Mallorca it's been more difficult, although not impossible. I was allowed off the ranch occasionally.'

She heard the bitterness in Colette's voice. Maddie's inability to grasp, or more honestly, her lack of interest in, the huge disparity in the roles allotted to Alex and his sister within the Archer family was another of her epic failings. 'So are you going tell them? About you and Lou?'

Another glance. 'No.'

They entered the gloom of a high-rise car park and started their dizzying ascent of the levels looking for a space. It was physically disorientating, which matched Maddie's emotional confusion about Colette's intentions towards Lou, and about life in general.

Any further discussion was delayed by the practicalities of getting parked, unloading the bags and making their way to the departure hall.

I listen to Alex throwing up in the en suite and feel hungry. It's a long time since I've eaten a proper meal. Ray is old school when it comes to breakfast. Bacon, eggs, sausage, rounds of white toast thick with butter – I have high hopes. I'm not a big bloke, but I do have a healthy appetite. The vomiting stops. The toilet flushes. The shower is turned on. I sit up and glance at my phone. There are more messages from Lily. I'll send her back to the UK with Priya and some false reassurances. I can finish with her when I get back. She's not a priority at the moment. A little holiday is, for Alex and myself, somewhere cultural, interesting, busy. Rome, Paris, maybe Istanbul. It will be the perfect antidote to the honeymoon he would have been going on. The rebuild can begin while we are there, far away from the pressures of Alex's failed relationship and his family.

I get up. Pull on my suit trousers and my shirt. I have no option; all my other clothes are down at the finca. I decide to give Alex some space for the time being.

The shouting starts almost the minute I step out into the corridor. It's Ray, roaring full blast. 'I need you to get your fucking arse here, now!' There's a fraction of a pause, then he's off again. 'No, I'm not fucking mistaken. I'm telling you, it's cleaned out. Every last cent.' Nano-pause. 'I don't know.' Another pause. 'That's your territory.' His voice gets even louder. 'Don't start with that bollocks, Paul. Just get here and sort it out.'

So there's more drama in store for the Archers – this time not of my making.

I follow the sound and the fury, and the smell of breakfast. It will be nice to be a spectator for a change.

Chapter 62

MADDIE

Being in a busy public space felt good. It was proof that normal life had been jogging along as usual while they'd all been trapped in an eighteenth-century castle surrounded by dense forest, cut off from civilisation with a groom without a spine and his mild-mannered best man, who seemed lovely, but was, in fact, a complete psychopath. For the first time in a long while Maddie breathed normally. Colette had accompanied them into the departure hall. Maddie decided to give her and Lou some space to say their good-byes. 'I'll just go and buy a magazine.'

'Wait.' Colette put her hand on Maddie's arm. This time the look that passed between Lou and Colette was intense.

Lou said, 'Are you sure?'

Colette nodded. 'If you are.'

Lou grinned. 'I am.' There was a slight but very pregnant pause, then Lou said, 'We have a proposition to put to you.'

A woman hurrying past with a huge wheeled suitcase clipped the back of Colette's heel. Colette winced. 'Let's find somewhere less busy.' They moved over to a quiet spot near a set of escalators. Their only company was a fake plant in a massive pot and some abandoned trolleys. The plant pot appeared to have been repeatedly mistaken for a litter bin. Colette smiled. 'I'm not going back to the finca.'

'Oh.' Maddie wasn't wholly surprised. She looked at Lou for an explanation. She was bouncing on her toes, a ball of pent-up excitement.

'Lou and I have decided that life is too short not to go for it.' Colette reached out and took hold of Lou's hand. Another heavy penny dropped. Lou was not travelling back to London with Maddie. Having lost Alex, Maddie was now losing Lou too. She was really and truly on her own. The thought swamped her.

Lou took a deep breath and began, 'So the plan is . . .'

Chapter 63

COLETTE

Colette saw Lou's demeanour suddenly change mid-explanation of their plan. Lou stiffened and hissed, 'What's he doing here?' Colette followed the direction of her stare. And there, in the middle of the concourse, was Luther. He was scanning the crowd. They all froze, hoping their immobility would lend them invisibility. Luther's gaze swept up the escalators, back down and flitted over them. Perhaps they'd be lucky. No one breathed.

Of course, luck wasn't on their side. On his second sweep of the hall Luther spotted them. He didn't immediately react. Christ, how she hated his arrogance. He slid his sunglasses into his top pocket – and he wondered why people mistook him for a bellhop. Who wore shirts with pockets in this day and at his age? He smoothed back his hair, raised his hand in greeting and started making his way towards them. Colette set off to meet him. Lou and Maddie followed. Colette wanted this conversation to take place in plain sight, with as many witnesses as possible. She was damned if she was going to let Luther control how the next few minutes played out. She opened with a false smile and a mock-cheery 'Luther, what are you doing here?'

'I could ask the same of you.' He didn't smile, despite his pristine, regularly bleached teeth that he was so proud of. The hard man cometh.

She didn't waver. 'I'm dropping Maddie and Lou off.'

He looked past her. 'So I see.' He actually sneered. He was such a caricature.

'Did you want something, Luther?' Bright to the point of irritating.

'Ray sent me to fetch you.' Luther's right hand was hanging by the side of his leg, half hidden by his trousers. Colette saw his fingers curl into a fist. He was always on the lookout for an opportunity for violence, but surely even he wouldn't be stupid enough to throw a punch in such a public place. Although she wouldn't entirely put it past him – Luther liked an audience. He saw her looking and relaxed his fingers. Then he raised his hand and signalled her to 'come' with his index finger. Creepiness and threat in one small gesture. What a shit he was.

'Fetch me! What am I? A stick?'

He bristled. 'He wants you back at the finca. Now. There's a lot to sort out, what with the wedding being called off . . . and everything else.'

He said it as if she was unaware of what had happened and had played no role in it. He obviously knew something had gone down, but his default was to try to minimise her relevance. Well, that was about to change. It was a pity that she wasn't going to be around to see his face when he found out just how much agency she had, and what she was prepared to do with it. 'Does he, now?'

'Yes.'

She pulled a sad face. 'Well, I'm afraid he's going to be disappointed.'

Despite the noise and activity swirling around them they seemed suspended in their own personal bubble of pure, sharp, much-polished dislike. By this point even Lou and Maddie were irrelevant. This showdown was personal and had been a long time coming. All Colette could think was . . . *bring it on*.

He'd obviously had enough. 'Stop pissing about, Colette. Now's not the time for it.'

He was getting angry, and when he was angry he was both more dangerous and even less intelligent. Colette relaxed into her body, let her shoulders drop. She was enjoying their little chat now. It would be their last one. Best to make the most of it. 'That's where you're wrong, Luther. As you so often are. Now is precisely the time for "it".'

He stepped into her space. She didn't flinch. Let him come. The fury in his eyes was out of all proportion to her defiance, but that was why her father kept him around – his compulsion to squash any threat, perceived or real, had its uses. The fact that Luther allowed her sixty-three-year-old father to specify who and what those threats were was really quite pathetic. Luther was a grown man and he was still doing what he was told, like a child desperate for affection. They stood toe to toe, nose to nose, ego to ego. Her breathing was slow and steady, his fast and shallow. A few seconds passed. She toughed them out. She sensed Lou and Maddie at her back unsure of what to do for the best.

Then he made the error she knew he would, if she provoked him. He put his hands on her. On her slim, easily bruised bare arms, in full view of anyone who happened to be watching. And people were watching. Their tense conversation and their rigid stance had already marked them out as at odds with the general activity in the airport. By stepping over the line and touching her he'd drawn even more attention to them. A man should never lay his hands on a woman, certainly not in anger, and in public. To up the ante she put up some resistance, pulled away from his grasp, twisted and turned. The idiot held on. His fingers dug into her flesh. Now they were struggling in broad daylight in one of the most heavily monitored and policed environments on the planet. Lou's loud, uncompromising shout of 'Get your hands off her!' helped as well.

Colette saw a couple of rusty cogs click around in his brain. He looked from Lou back to her. 'Fucking hell! That explains a lot.' He shoved her away in disgust, and she made the most of it, falling to the floor with a dramatic flail of her arms and a loud cry. From their position over by the check-in desks two weapons-toting officers started towards them. It was time to bring the curtain down on their little show.

She got to her feet, leant into Luther and whispered, 'Unless you want to have a very uncomfortable conversation with the local boys in body armour, I suggest you piss off. And quickly. They don't look best pleased with you causing a disturbance on their patch.' He blinked, realisation slowly dawning. He twisted around and spotted the approaching officers. 'Oh, and one last thought, Luther. You'd better have a damn good excuse at the ready to explain to my father why you've come back without me. He's not going to be happy. Not one little bit.' She smiled.

With a hissed 'Bitch', Luther hurried away, zigzagging through the crowds, bumping and barging into people as he went.

One of the officers followed him, while the other came over to Colette. 'Are you all right, Miss?' he asked in English. Being naturally observant, as you'd hope, given his choice of career, the officer had obviously deduced that they weren't Spanish.

Colette dropped her armour and channelled girly. 'Yes. I am . . . now. Thank you.' Eyelash bat. 'We've been staying in the Hotel Universal in Es Trenc. He works there. A waiter.' It felt good to demote him. 'We got kinda friendly one night, like you do after too many sangrias. It was just the once, but he got the wrong end of the stick.' That was too colloquial. 'Sorry, I mean, he thought I liked him. You know, like, really liked him.' She shuddered. That part wasn't playacting. 'He wouldn't leave me alone after that.' She shrugged as if overzealous male suitors were a regular hazard. 'Thank you for getting rid of him.' The police officer lost interest, as she'd hoped. He radioed his buddy not to bother either. That was a relief. Luther being stopped by a police officer with a gun wasn't something that bore thinking about. Their officer walked away, cradling his high-powered automatic weapon like a baby.

Chapter 64

LUTHER

Luther checked behind him. The cop must have decided that he wasn't a person of interest after all, which was a good job, because if he'd been stopped and searched, he would have become far more interesting due to the piece tucked in the back of his waistband. Luther cursed as he dodged around the waves of passengers. He was mad at the world and at himself. He'd badly misjudged his choice of weapon – brought a gun to a fight that could have been won with a knife. Finally he got back to the minibus, stowed the gun under the seat and sat for a minute letting his rage run. 'What a total fucking bitch!'

But the bitch was right about one thing – if he went back to the finca without her, Ray would have his guts for whatever garment he fancied. Luther didn't know exactly what had gone down between Colette and her father, but whatever it was, it was a far bigger deal than Alex being left for a twat at the altar. And money was definitely involved, because Paul was involved, and Paul had, very obviously, been under the cosh. In fact, it had sounded like Ray was tearing him a new one when Luther had been summoned and given his instructions. Those instructions had been simple: 'Go after Colette and bring her back.'

Well, he'd failed to do that and, to add insult to injury, she'd known that his failure had created one fuck of a big problem for him. Luther watched more people arrive and enter the terminal. Every one of the fuckers was able to get on a plane and go wherever they liked because they had the one thing that Luther didn't – a passport. His was locked in Ray's safe back at the villa, where it had lain for nearly a year waiting for the big man's say-so. Well, that was never going to happen now.

But...

Luther had wheels and he had money in his current account. His side hustles might have been puny compared to Ray's vast and varied empire, but they did yield a return. He had enough to live on for a few months at least before he'd need to find alternative employment. His particular skills would be in demand somewhere on the Costa Del Sol. The risky part would be choosing an Archer enemy rather than an ally as his next employer. But that shouldn't be too difficult – Ray had fucked over a lot of people on his way to the top. The challenge was going to be getting off this sodding island. But there must be skippers in Palma who would take a man across the water to the mainland with no questions asked, if you paid them enough. Yes. It was a plan and it could work. The trick was to go now, while Ray had bigger fish to fry.

Luther started the engine, whacked up the air-con and banged on some tunes. Maybe the bitch had done him a favour after all. It was time for the great escape.

Chapter 65

MADDIE

Maddie was impressed. 'What the hell?'

Colette smiled. 'It's fine. He's gone and he won't be back. He wouldn't risk it. Let's get a drink and recoup.' In celebratory mood, they headed for the bar. When their drinks arrived they all took a slug without ceremony. 'So, our proposition.' Colette took a swallow of her gin. 'Do you still want to hear it?'

Maddie didn't hesitate. 'Hell, yes.'

'Okay. Like I said, I'm not going back to the finca. Ever. That means I have options in terms of what I do next, where I go, and who with.' Lou interlaced her fingers with Colette's and gave her hand a squeeze. 'I haven't had that sort of freedom for a very long time. The only slight problem is that London isn't one of those options. It's my dad's old stomping ground and he still has a lot of contacts there.'

Out of nowhere, the image of the tracksuit-wearing thug beating Alex up outside The Shed popped into Maddie's head. In hindsight, she should have pocketed the cash out of Alex's wallet and left it at that. Her life would certainly have been simpler. 'So what are you planning?'

Colette took another mouthful of her gin. 'Travelling. At least for a while.'

'With Lou?'

Lou leapt in. 'I'm sorry, Maddie. I know this is the worst possible time.'

Maddie smiled, but it was a 'brave face' kind of smile. 'It's okay. I get it. I can see that you two have something worth exploring. And what is there in London to go back for, other than a job you hate and a flat you can barely afford?' Maddie knew she was describing her own future as much as Lou's. Self-pity was an ugly emotion, but it didn't evaporate overnight, and in her situation surely it was justified.

'Well, that brings us on to you.' Lou said.

'What about me?'

'We wondered if you fancied coming with us?'

'What?'

Lou grinned. 'Come with us. Have an adventure.'

'No. I can't.' They were both looking at her as if it was a realistic possibility. 'You don't want me playing gooseberry.'

'We're not suggesting we spend every minute of every day together, but we could see a bit of the world, have some adventures before we have to face reality.'

'It's nice of you to ask, I really appreciate it. But even if I wanted to tag along for a bit, I couldn't afford it. I'm going to have pay my own way again from here on in. And before you ask, Lou, no, I'm not going to pawn my engagement ring. I left it on the sink in the suite.' Lou pulled a 'you fool' face. 'And, as you yourself pointed out so eloquently last night, the sooner I start standing on my own two feet again, the better.' The enormity of her precarious situation reared up and towered over Maddie. The necessary return to a life of monotonous, low-paid jobs with the odd side hustle would begin the minute she arrived back in the UK.

Colette's expression shifted and she smiled, a sly, curious smile that contained a definite touch of triumph. 'You don't need to worry about not being able to afford it.'

Maddie's old resentment of the Archers' deep pockets resurfaced. They were so blind to the fact that not everyone had access to a large, reliable pot of ready cash. 'I do.'

Lou joined in the grin fest. 'No, you don't. Show her, Colette.'

Colette reached for her phone. She tapped the screen for a few seconds, then handed it to Maddie. Maddie found herself looking a bank account in the name of Colette Archer. The balance was very healthy – to the tune of many thousands of pounds. Maddie didn't know what they expected her to say. So Colette was comfortably off, which meant that she and Lou could afford to go gadding around the globe downing margaritas for a few weeks, maybe a few months. Maddie didn't see how that changed her position one iota. 'So?'

Colette's smile didn't waver. 'That's just one of my six accounts. I also have a number of high-return investments – that were not arranged through my brother, obviously.'

Was Maddie supposed to be impressed? It was all the proceeds of dodgy dealings and worse. Not that she was in much of a position to judge, but at least her own initial attraction to Alex's wealth had been driven by necessity, not greed.

Colette's expression grew serious. 'I took what I was owed. I've worked for my father since I was fourteen. I had no choice. One of us had to, and I was the one they chose.

What I wanted was irrelevant. College, university, a life of my own, a career, even a home of my own. Not an option. The business was what mattered. And I've worked hard, very hard, for them without thanks or respect for seventeen years. I've run their errands, messages, drugs, cash, people, bookies, bars, restaurants, import/export ventures, their property portfolio and their fucking finca. I know the yields of each area of the business. I know when it's time to sit tight and when it's time to get out. I know when someone is trying to fleece us and when we're about to make a killing because the person we are dealing with hasn't a clue. I've made them thousands, more like hundreds of thousands of pounds over my lifetime and yet my father has never valued my opinions or my advice. Whereas Alex, the sun apparently shines out of his arse. He was the one who got the golden ticket the moment he came out a boy – the child they really wanted all along. Once they had him, they had their worthy heir. What I hadn't fully realised until recently was just how complete that transfer of power and funds was going to be.' The disgust on her face was clear. 'Archer Asset Management was their big, bold step towards legitimacy. And, once again, they never thought to ask for my opinion or even my involvement.'

'So how did you find out about their plans?' Maddie asked.

'Paul and his big mouth. Although he only confirmed what I already knew. It's amazing how useful people underestimating you can be. I listened in on conversations that they didn't think I'd understand. I got access to their laptops easily – you know what the older generation are like, they use the same password for everything. I've known what's going on inside the business since I turned eighteen, and I've been skimming for my retirement fund for years. Their decision to shovel all our capital into Alex's start-up simply galvanised me to make my move. That, and having Lou in my life, of course.'

'So it's their money?'

At that Colette flared. 'No, it's mine. I earned it.'

Maddie backed off. 'What are you going to do with it, longer term?'

'After I've had the holiday that I deserve, with the person I love, then I'm going to start looking for something to invest in myself. Something legit.'

'Not a wedding business!'

'Hell, no, I've had enough of bridezillas to last me a lifetime. Present company excepted.' Maddie accepted Colette's compliment, although it wasn't an accurate one. She had been troublesome, just not in the same way as most brides. 'Which is why I could do with somebody with your skills,' Colette added.

'Which are?' Maddie felt she had no skills whatsoever.

'Sussing out a wolf in sheep's clothing.'

Lou joined the conversation. 'Come on, Maddie, what have you got to lose? At worst you can have a couple of weeks in the sun, at best you could have a whole new happily-ever-after.'

Maddie finished her drink, thought about her options, looked from Colette, with her criminal credentials and her huge stash of cash, to Lou, her skint, loyal, 'up for anything' best friend, and made her decision.

They picked up their bags and headed back to the departure hall. Instinctively they searched the crowd for

Luther, or any other of Ray's other heavies. There was no sign of any immediate threat. Maddie looked up at the departure board. *Barcelona, Madrid, Valencia, Bilbao, Marseilles, Paris, Sofia, Ibiza, Sorrento, Rome.*

Colette broke into Maddie's daydreaming. 'So, ladies, where do you fancy?'

Alex is sitting in the window seat, I'm in the middle and there's a fat woman on the end. She's a talker, but she's already given up on me. She turns her attention to the elderly chap across the aisle. Poor sod. It's going to be a long two and a half hours for him. The drone of the engine as we take off doesn't quite drown out her prattle. The problem with short-haul flights is the absence of business class.

Our destination is Vienna. Some culture, at long last. I'm going to enjoy it even if Alex doesn't. We're staying at the Imperial. A broken heart will heal better surrounded by the finer things in life. Getting away from the finca was the priority. It was chaos up at the villa. Who would have guessed that Colette was capable of such criminality? Embezzlement, fraud, theft on a grand scale. From what I overheard she seems to have taken somewhere in the region of a quarter of their total wealth – which is classic Colette, if you think about it. She's effectively taken her share. Alex hasn't a clue about the depth and breadth of his sister's betrayal. All he knows is that she's run off with Lou and taken 'some money' with her. Marilyn and Ray thought it best not to burden him with the true extent of the havoc Colette has caused – which is code for, if Alex finds out he may very well totally spin out and that would put Archer Asset Management at even greater risk. Hence Marilyn's acquiescence to our rapid departure and her willingness to fund our little jaunt. She's going to come back to me on my retainer. She's hedging her bets until she sees how good a job I do on Operation Alex Reconstruction.

As the plane banks Alex turns and smiles weakly at me. 'Thanks for this, Bobby.'

'It's my pleasure,' I reply, with a gentle touch of his arm. It is going to be a pleasure. Five days together, on our own, all distractions and interferences dealt with. It's exactly what he needs. What we need. I've always known how to make Alex feel better about himself, how to mould his insecurities into something more coherent and comfortable to live with. And this time the clay will be even more malleable.

Alex returns his gaze to the painfully blue sky outside the window, but I know his thoughts are earthbound – still tethered to the dead weight that is Maddie Laughton. But elegant old Vienna will help to cure him of that disease. As we wander around the peerless architecture and stare at the old masters in the Kunsthistorisches Museum I'll show him true beauty and he'll remember what a genuine connection with another human being feels like. Our meaningful relationship will demonstrate to him what he and Maddie lacked and how perilously close he came to settling, not simply for second best, but for something – correction – for someone, far worse. I'll imperceptibly, but repeatedly, prove to him how flawed his judgement has been and how imperative it is that he listens to the voices of reason around him – namely, mine.

Yes, by the time we get back to London I will have rethreaded Alex's strings. Then the real fun can begin. One tug, one twitch, and he will dance to my tune.

Should he concentrate on his career? Heal his broken heart with hard work? Knuckle down to making some serious money? Or should he make hay while he can? Enjoy his freedom? Spend? Indulge? Party? Travel? With me as his willing companion. Perhaps he should move? Get away from the unhappy memories associated with his apartment. He could buy somewhere bigger, more fitting to his new status. Invest in property? Why not get into the buy-to-let market? He'll have the funds. He could let a property to me. Mate's rates, of course. Date? Not date? Pick this girl. Like that woman. Sleep with the brunette from Islington. Marry the blonde from Cheltenham. And the big one . . . should he embrace being an Archer or should he be his own man?

A lifetime of decisions lies ahead for Alex.

And for me.

Epilogue

Life began to change at the Finca Encantata from the moment the blonde woman with the fast walk and the phone perpetually clamped to her cheek disappeared.

Things normally done were left undone.

At first, the changes were small, but the cat noticed them nonetheless. Dust gathered in the corners of the courtyard and fallen leaves drifted behind benches and walls, where they collected in tinder-dry piles. When the sun struck the windows and doors it revealed patterns of smeary fingerprints and the cool metal work surfaces in the kitchen got so dull that the cat could no longer see her reflection in them, which was okay with the cat – she wasn't the slightest bit vain. The lights in the olive trees started to blink and go out, one by one, and whoever was supposed to water the plants in the courtyard either forgot or didn't bother. The cat did her bit. She chose a different pot to piss in every morning and every night, but it wasn't enough to stop everything wilting and withering away.

The people started to behave differently as well.

The fat man in the white outfit, who always smelt of fish, was to be found sitting in the sun outside the kitchen on an empty crate, taking deep, contented drags on his cigarette for longer periods. And the black-and-white-clad staff seemed to work more slowly, laugh more often and congregate more frequently. Sure, the loud, bright people still came in their droves. And the thin young women, dressed in white, still stood under the bower of flowers in the courtyard and repeated the sing-song words to the stiff-looking men, who came in a variety of ages and sizes. The guests still ate and drank and danced and fought and cried and occasionally fell in the lake. But it was not the same.

One day, having breakfasted at her leisure on an array of cold meats in the pantry, the cat took a stroll, seeking respite from the intense summer heat. Like the rest of the finca, the alley had become more overgrown in the past few months. As the cat slouched through the rosemary she disturbed the hundreds of biting and buzzing insects that lived in the undergrowth. They rose and whirled around her. She twitched her ears and picked up the pace in a bid to dissuade the bugs from hitching a ride in her fur. Midway down the alley was the pyre of broken tables, chairs and bedframes. It was as good a spot as any for a nap, and it would get her away from the mosquitoes. The cat crouched, leapt, landed perfectly on the top of the man-made mountain. But the tower of human crap was rickety and the slight weight of the cat was enough to destabilise it. The pyre rocked. Started to topple. Then collapsed – sending the cat and the broken furniture flying in all directions. As she tumbled through the air the cat heard a clink. She landed, softly and unharmed, amongst the weeds and debris.

The first thing the cat noticed was the smell. It was a scent she'd not come across before. She followed her nose and spotted a bottle lying in among the lengths of splintered wood. She approached it. There was a thin stream of brown liquid trickling out of the bottle. She lapped at it, expecting sweetness. The liquid burnt her tongue and throat. It tasted like poison. The cat's review of the fifty-five-year-old limited edition Macallan Lalique that Colette had left resting against the wall all those months ago was short, uncomplimentary and scatological. She took a dump beside the bottle, then slowly picked her way out of the alley in search of a palate cleanser.

The sun climbed up and across the sky. It was directly over the alley at 12.14 p.m. A shaft of sunlight struck the fancy glass bottle at 12.17 p.m. At 12.21 p.m. the first whisper of smoke rose on the hot air. It wasn't seen by anyone because no one came into the alley now, other than the cat. A chambermaid smelt smoke as she crossed the courtyard pushing a laundry trolley twenty minutes later, but she assumed it was coming from the kitchen. By the time one of the waiters went to investigate the column of smoke rising up between the buildings at 1.25 p.m., white-hot flames were already licking high up the walls and nibbling at the eaves of the buildings on either side of the narrow alley. By the time the fire engines arrived thirty minutes later the finca was ablaze.

Dawn brought peace. The firemen packed up their hoses and left, and the staff that had stayed behind to help with the futile efforts to fight the fire were ferried off site. There was nothing left to save.

When she was confident that they had all gone, the cat emerged from the forest and took a tour of her home. The stone bones of the finca were still standing, but they were smeared with rivers of tar. Huge filthy puddles had gathered inside and outside the buildings. The air was acrid and the ash furred the cat's tongue and stung her eyes, but still she prowled, adding the sooty blackness to her already dark pelt.

When she was satisfied that the destruction was complete, she headed for the terrace. Once there she sprang up onto one of the sunbeds. Some sort of garment had been left on it. The material was soft and slippery under the pads of her feet. She scratted at it with her claws. Three turns and a few seconds of ripping later her bed was ready. She settled down in the sunshine on the ruined Hermès scarf and was asleep within seconds.

The Finca Encantata might not be habitable for humans, but it was, once again, perfect for the cat.

Acknowledgements

My family and friends know that I love them.

The many talented individuals at Corvus and Greene and Heaton, who publish and promote my books, know that I value and respect them.

But there are two other teams who play a vital role in my writing and I want to take this opportunity to give them a mention.

Firstly, I want to thank the crew at Thornbury Costa – my second office. This is a place where I always feel welcome, warm and undisturbed – unless I want to be. It's a genuine community of staff, regulars and randomers. I appreciate the hard work, the long hours, the chit chat and the laughter as much, if not more than, the good coffee and the free WiFi. So, in no particular order – as they say on TV talent shows – thank you to: Amy, Katie, Joshua – gone but not forgotten – Marcin, Halima, Karolina, Habib, Beth, Romana, Ethan and Alesha.

Then there's The Leeds Library – a place of quiet, dusty beauty, eons of history, a very decent modern fiction section and a much-used tea station. It's the one place I can properly get away from the distractions of everyday life

375

and concentrate. A number of my books have been conceived in the seclusion of the much-in-demand corner of the inappropriately named New Room. My thanks go to the counter staff: Jane, Anna, Helen and Aidan for being the welcoming, unobtrusive face of such a venerable, but friendly institution. I also want to add a special mention to Molly, for always asking me how my writing is going.

The answer, I hope, is well.

Thank you.

Rachel x